the RIGHT WORDS

Meg Rosenthal

ISBN: 978-1-954614-97-0 (hard cover)
        978-1-954614-98-7 (soft cover)

Edited by: Karli Jackson

Published by WARREN Publishing
Charlotte, NC
www.warrenpublishing.net
Printed in the United States

For my sister Rylee, because she never failed to ask how Matt and Ember were doing during our lunch dates at Moe's. (Plot twist: now you can actually read their book to find out.)

"You've got to make the story true. Make it visceral. Make it real. Imagination is a beautiful supplement but in order for a story to be successful, it has to have some sort of human element of truth in your character's emotional response if it is to be received by a human audience. If you cannot write truthfully to your own experience and emotions, you are writing blind and lying to both yourself and your reader. Therefore, you cannot write it unless you live it."

–Oliver Van Dam, *To Write or to Dream About Writing*

"Keats would leave blank spaces in his drafts to holdon to his passion, spaces for the right words to come."

–Jack Gilbert

Chapter One

Fate's a fickle thing, but I never expected it to come from the inside of a top hat. Or for it to write me a literary death sentence of sorts. The top hat had been sitting on the corner of my professor's desk the entirety of night class. It was there when we sat down in our seats, myself a solid fifteen minutes early. It was there throughout the lecture on the assigned story we read. And it was there when the professor started handing back our first creative writing grades of the semester.

"Nicely done, Ember," Professor Pollard smiled as he gave me my folder, his long gray hair framing his face in bushy tufts.

I opened the folder and suppressed a grin when I saw the ninety-five marked on my short story. I quickly shut it to cover the grade and then casually glanced around.

"Overall, everyone did a good job with this story," Professor Pollard said. "I went through your final drafts and made a few notes for your portfolio at the end of the semester, but on the whole, excellent work with the revision process."

From my seat in the back-right corner of the classroom, I surveyed the other students' reactions to getting their stories back. Call it a competitive nature, but I was proud of the 4.0 grade point average I had managed to maintain throughout college so far.

A few of the students were still flipping through their pages, scanning the comments in the margins. My gaze stopped at one figure in particular who had his head hanging low between his hands, looking mildly distraught at whatever was on the rubric before him.

I shook my head. Matt Callahan. He was the only student in here not majoring in English so of course he would be the one to bomb the first story of the spring semester.

"Now that the first story is wrapped up," Pollard continued while resuming his spot at the podium, "we are naturally going to begin work on the second story."

"Duh," my friend Spencer whispered not so quietly from the seat in front of me. My roommate Brynn sat next to him and shushed him.

"Let me remind you," Pollard said, "that you all had complete freedom with the first assignment. No topic, no word count, really no other limitations besides the deadline." He tilted his head to survey all twelve of us in Advanced Prose. "I hope you used your freedom wisely and wrote the story you wished to write."

Pollard's short sleeve button-down of choice tonight was green, much like the color I imagined my own usually pale face was turning as I shifted in my seat and thought uneasily about the story I just tucked away. It was a science fiction piece, complete with lack-of-vaccination-induced-apocalypse and all. Although my story ended up being fun to write, my writer's block had been so bad that putting the first words on the page was excruciating. I was glad my first story earned an A, but I definitely wasn't in love with it.

By the looks of it, Matt wasn't so happy with his story either as he stuffed it into his bag at the foot of his desk.

"This next assignment is going to be structured quite differently than other projects you have tackled before," Pollard said. "It is a great honor that our school, Selwyn College, has been invited to participate in a writing contest for publication in one of the country's best literary magazines."

A small buzz started filling the room, but Pollard quelled the noise by saying, "*Noted and Quoted* is launching an annual competition, and its inaugural contest is specifically for undergraduate students. Several creative writing programs all over the country are competing, and the winning story from each college or university will be printed in a special edition of *Noted and Quoted* this fall. I have decided that it is in your best interest to start putting your work into the world. Therefore, I accepted the magazine's invitation and this next grade is dependent on entering the contest."

A contest? Putting our work into the world? It was like I was dreaming, grabbing the fragments of Pollard's speech from the air, clinging to them, almost scared to be hopeful. Being published was all I had ever wanted for myself. And here was the chance right in front of me.

Pollard walked to his desk. "As I mentioned, there are going to be certain constraints with this assignment, starting with the fact that you will be given a prompt directly from the magazine itself. Now, these prompts are intentionally vague. Hopefully they won't strip your creative intelligence, but they should at least give you a springboard and parameter to help you focus."

Pollard picked up the top hat and gave it a shake. "One by one, you will come up and pick a prompt. But here's the kicker," he said as he glanced around the room, eyeing each of us. "Per the contest rules, there are two of every prompt in this hat. When you draw your prompt, know that someone else in this room will draw its twin. This person will become your partner, and you will have to craft your story together, turning in one submission for both the contest and your grade."

And there went my dream.

The buzzing in the classroom turned into a heated vibration as voices rose. Some eyed one another from across the room, wishing that they could pick the other as their partner. Others cried lines akin to "How could you do this to us?"

On one hand, sure, writing with a partner sounded great. I would only be responsible for half the work. But leaving the other half up to a partner? That could be risky. Especially with a possible publication on the line. And I had learned a long time ago that when it came to counting on others, I preferred to rely on myself.

Brynn looked back at me, her narrow lips playfully pressed together. Though we had our differences, Brynn was one of my better friends on campus and working alongside her spunk and ambition could make this project a breeze. Her skills far surpassed most in the class, and the girl's creative well never seemed to run dry based on the multiple times she would bolt upright in bed in the middle of the night to run an idea by me, before slipping right back to sleep. If I was going to be able to pull off a partnership story with anyone, it would be her. I also figured that since the goal of a contest was winning, I would rather have her talent on my side than writing against me.

Beside Brynn, Spencer followed her gaze to look at me as well. He stuck out his bottom lip. "That's not fair. You two are the best in the class. You can't be partners."

Murmurs continued throughout the classroom until Pollard said, "Everyone quiet down." He tapped the hat against his desk to get our attention. "Listen. Aside from the workshop critiques you have been a part of, writing is and generally has been an individual practice for every one of you, correct?"

A chorus of yeses hissed through the room. Spencer's whole body sank dramatically, his shock of red hair skimming the back of the chair.

"Well, unfortunately, that's not always the case in the real world," Pollard continued, setting the hat down. "While the craft of writing can be a solitary environment, if you want your words to find their way out into the published world after they have been drafted, you are going to have to know how to communicate, collaborate, and cooperate with editors, proofreaders, publishers, marketers, designers, and the unsuspecting intern you might come across. Therefore, your grades will be dependent on your completion of drafting and revision, but most importantly, equal participation within your partnership."

The class had gone eerily still at his words.

"I'm sure you'll appreciate this in the long run," he added.

I sure hoped so.

"So, let's start at the front of the room and work backward, shall we?" Pollard gestured to the seat in front of him. "Gemma, would you like to start?"

I watched Gemma Fischer, a pretty girl with a slight figure and deep caramel skin, lean forward in her seat. Pollard gave the hat a shake, tossing its contents once more. Gemma's hand reached into its black abyss and plucked a small white slip of paper. Unfolding it, she read to the class in her delicate voice, "Write a story where the main character is hiding a secret."

Pollard nodded. "Sounds like an excellent start. Many ways you can go with that one. Charlie, you're up next."

Pollard continued along the rows of desks, offering encouraging words after each student's selection. Some prompts were quickly repeated. I knew that "write a story where the main character's past comes back to haunt them" and "write a story where the main character has to overcome a trauma" were out as options for me.

Brynn leaned back in her chair; the number two pencils holding her bun together at the back of her head threatened to poke my eye out. "By my count, there is still one more prompt that has two papers left in that awful hat. My money is on the literary fates conspiring for us to be partners."

"Let's hope your fates haven't lost their sense of humor by my turn back here."

"You're playing favorites again," Spencer groaned.

"Brynn, you're up," Pollard called from the front.

She smirked as she rose from her seat and whispered, "Wish me luck."

"Good luck."

"Break a leg," Spencer added.

My faint wish of good fortune did not appeal to any higher being of influence. Brynn withdrew a slip from the hat and read, "Write a story in which the main character is part of a crime."

"Excellent pick, Brynn. You and Holly will be partners. Like I said to her, it's open-ended enough so that your character could assume any role: perpetrator, victim, accomplice, investigator. Your possibilities are endless."

My gaze flicked over to where Holly sat in the far corner, her elbow on the table, chin in her hand while she blew a bubble with her chewing gum.

Brynn retreated to her seat, crestfallen.

"I don't think the townspeople I let get ruthlessly eaten by zombies in my last story were enough of a sacrifice to your literary fates," I deadpanned as she slumped in her chair.

"Shut up."

"Ember, you're next," Pollard said.

I made it to the front of the classroom and reached into the hat, grasping one of the few remaining papers. Unfolding it, I had to stifle a sigh.

"Well?" Pollard probed.

"Write a story in which the main character...falls in love."

Pollard nodded. "Again, loose structure. Plenty of room to expand and take the prompt in your own direction."

I forced my lips into a small smile before turning back toward my seat. Brynn glared at me and shook her head in dismay. I sat back down behind her and watched as the lavender tips of her dark hair started to unravel from her bun.

"Are you serious?" she hissed over her shoulder.

"What?"

"You get *love*? Really? Come on, you know I'm a hopeless romantic."

I couldn't agree more with her. "I'll probably end up killing one of them off. Nothing can quite top unrequited love like death. Just ask Romeo."

She rolled her eyes and resumed her slouch, arms crossed in front of her.

"Spencer?"

Spencer rose, catching the corner of his shared desk with his hip as he passed behind Brynn. "Sorry, sorry. Not sorry."

He pulled out a slip of paper. "Write a story where the main character is hiding a secret." He whirled around, index finger searching for his partner. "Gemma!"

She smiled, sheepishly.

"Good memory, Spencer. You can sit now," Pollard said. "Matt, would you like to conclude the activity?"

As Matt started to walk forward, vital information hit me like a brick to the gut, and I groaned. If Matt was the last one left and I was still without a partner—

"Write a story in which the main character falls in love."

No.

Chapter Two

If this advanced writing class was a fruit salad, Matt would be a tomato—technically a fruit, but he really didn't belong. He was the only person here not part of the English Department; the noncreative was actually enrolled in the Business School. He also played some sort of sport that made him habitually five minutes late to class every week. He would tote in the excuse, "Practice ran over," with a lazy half smile. And to top it all off, he always had his skateboard—his "green transportation" as he called it on the first day of class—tucked neatly under his arm.

Matt's gaze lifted from the piece of paper in his hand and his wide brown eyes met mine. A ghost of a smile played across his lips.

Great. Not only was I assigned to write about a topic that I could barely tolerate, I had to "communicate, collaborate, and cooperate" with someone like Matt, the oddball, non-English-majoring jock.

"Good pick," Pollard said. "That means you and Ember will be working together."

Matt's eyes were still locked on mine as the corner of his mouth pulled up into a deeper smirk. I slouched in my chair and averted my gaze. He stepped back to his seat.

"Well, that wraps up our class tonight," Pollard said, shuffling his papers and loading them into his briefcase. "If you have the time, please take a few moments to meet up with your partner. You are going to be spending quite a bit of time together in the near future, so it would be in both of your best interests to establish a working relationship early on. The entire story process from start to finish is going to take us right up until the Monday before Spring Break."

I quickly counted the weeks from now, the middle of February, until our stories were due. Five weeks. Five weeks writing and editing in partnership. I cringed.

"The winners from our college, chosen by a panel of judges from the magazine, will be announced at the annual Art Salon when you return from break. Your grades will also be posted the same day. A week from today, though, everyone should come prepared with a pitch for your prompt." Pollard tucked the hat underneath the crook of his arm and nodded in our direction before heading toward the door. "Have a good evening."

The noise returned to the classroom once Pollard strolled out the door. Spencer made a show of leaving his seat as he moved to embrace Gemma. Brynn rolled her dark eyes at his theatrics before she untucked her long legs from underneath her seat. She sucked in a breath as she headed over to Holly's isolated corner of the room.

I watched her cross the space between me and Matt's desk. He met my eye and I looked away, trying to stifle yet another sigh. Beyond the obscurity surrounding his enrollment in my class, I had a big problem with Matt's personality; he was like the poster child for the pretty boy who could get away with anything just because he was confident in his ability to do so. Like his habitual tardiness. Any other student would have been sent straight to Academic Affairs for showing up late to virtually every single class. But not Matt. He could just creak the door open, stopping Pollard mid-introduction with a wave, and sit down like it was nothing. Guess that was the benefit of being a student athlete.

And then there was his actual writing. I had read and workshopped his first story at the start of this semester, and while his content was innovative (historical fiction piece set during World

War II), his draft was more orange than black by the time I was done correcting his poor grammar with my signature editing gel pen. And based on his reaction to his grade, he must not have taken any of my advice.

Regardless, the smile returned to the tips of his mouth. He grinned as he rose from his chair and sauntered my way, left hand tucked casually into the pocket of his jeans.

"What's up, Owens?" Matt asked, taking a seat on top of Brynn's vacant desk. His blond hair was cropped close; the gold stubble along his jaw was sharp and even.

"Callahan." I met his smile with a thin-lipped expression of my own. As he crossed his legs at his ankles, swinging them back and forth from his seat on the desk, I couldn't help but notice his socks that stuck out from underneath the edge of his pants. Navy, with pink flamingos. I dragged my gaze back up to his face.

He was waiting for me to say more and when I didn't, he casually continued. "So, based on the dead body count from your last story, I think it's safe to say that you aren't exactly thrilled with having to write a love story."

I was surprised he remembered my story from workshop, but I scoffed anyway. "Just because romance isn't my preferred genre, doesn't mean I can't write it."

He lifted a brow. "I never said you couldn't, princess."

I narrowed my eyes. "Don't call me that."

Matt chuckled. "I'm afraid you are going to have to get used to terms of endearment, babe, if we are going to pull off a love story."

I bit the inside of my cheek. He had a point. "I don't recall any romance riddling your last story either, pal." Trenches, gunshots, death, sure.

He shook his head. "I don't think *pal* has quite the same effect, hon."

I rolled my eyes and crossed my arms in front of my chest, leaning back in my seat.

"But," Matt continued, "you're right. I can't say that I have ever tried to write a love story before. Seems like there is a first time for everything." He dropped a wink on "first time."

Oh my God. I think I hate him.

"Look," I said, drawing myself up a little taller in my seat. "I won't pretend to know why you are in this class, but for the rest of us, this whole writing thing is something we want to do with our lives. So, at the least, will you try to be the type of partner who doesn't get in the way of a good grade?"

Matt tilted his head. "Ember Owens, you don't know me in the slightest."

I sucked my bottom lip into my mouth.

Matt leaned closer to my desk. His mouth was easily parted and the corner of it pulled up, amused. Eyes glinting, he said in a low voice, "I don't do anything without giving a 110 percent. So don't worry, I will be doing my fair share of work on this project."

I fought to remain still, to not back away from him and his incessant eye contact.

"Well," I started, my voice much quieter than I would've liked, "I suppose that means we will be seeing a lot of one another in the near future."

Matt leaned back, swinging his legs to the side of the desk that faced away from me and pushed off, righting himself. His mouth widened into a full smile as he turned back to say, "I'll get your email address from the roster online."

He stopped at his desk to collect his skateboard and backpack before heading for the door. "See you later, partner!" He gave me a wave before disappearing.

I sank low into my chair and let out a breath I didn't know I'd been holding. "Shit."

***

I could say that my greatest blessing was that I was born a night owl and could tolerate the English night classes that seemed to be the only option for English majors here at Selwyn College. Although

I was also lucky to be attending a small liberal arts school in the heart of Charlotte, North Carolina, the best gift I could've lucked into was having friends that were as productive in the after-hours as I was—and shared a similar love of quirky coffee shops. More specifically, The Coffee House, or affectionately known to us locals as simply The House.

Located in the neighboring arts district, The House's walls were painted a pinstripe blue, and the length of the ceiling was adorned in chandeliers of all shapes, sizes, and colors: large blue and lime green chandeliers; small circular chandeliers decorated with silver spoons; black and white striped chandeliers that hung precariously on their sides; a huge red chandelier hanging on the opposite angle. Paintings were hung at odd and irregular angles across every wall. Most of them were reinvented masterpieces: Mona Lisa sporting sunglasses; Napoleon with a drawn-on mustache. To be fair, there were some re-creations of the originals, too, with their genius unaltered.

Even though there was a Starbucks around the corner from campus, The House's aesthetic was worth the drive.

I tipped the container of half-and-half into the mug of my black coffee, letting out a steady pour. "So, I know romance novels have populated the commercial market since the Victorian era," I said, twisting the cap back shut and plopping it down next to Brynn's mug of hot chocolate, "but who thinks it's a good idea for me to join this lovestruck cult? Like, does anyone really think writing an entire plot on falling in love is more than just a Hallmark special?"

Spencer snorted. "You're such a nerd."

Brynn tapped cinnamon onto the top of her drink, then picked up the creamer and twisted it open again. "Um, I don't know, maybe someone like Nicholas Sparks, Sarah Dessen, and definitely me would disagree with you. Cheesy romance novels are what get me through the constant disappointment that college boys are."

"You're telling me," Spencer said. His Russian tea—frothed orange juice with cinnamon—steamed between his hands as he waited for us to finish at the coffee station. "Boys are the worst. I've moved on to men."

I grumbled, my mind still reeling from tonight's class. I tried to ignore my irritation and went to find our usual table in the adjoining room, but my mug rattled a bit in the saucer I was holding. I steadied it with both hands before setting it down on the wooden table and sliding into my seat. Brynn followed close behind, mug in one hand and an assorted platter of macaroons, one of each flavor, in the other. Spencer sat down to complete our trio, both hands still cupping his drink.

"I wish I could trade," I said, pushing one of my stray strawberry curls behind my ear. "I wouldn't mind your prompt, Brynn. Main character part of a crime? I'd probably write it from a serial killer's perspective." I paused, imagining the story already in my head. "But you wouldn't know it was the killer at first. He would trick everyone in the story into thinking he's innocent, even the reader." And he'd probably do it with a smile that was charming and purposely lopsided—just like Matt Callahan's own personal weapon.

Brynn tilted her head, eyes slant and narrow. "That's not a bad idea, actually. I was kind of thinking something similar but making it easier to write as partners by doing split perspective; one of us writing from the victim's head and the other from the criminal."

I lifted my mug to my lips. "Serial killer. Run it by Holly."

"Yeah, I think she would be into that stuff," Spencer said, finally releasing his mug to the table. "She certainly looks dangerous enough with all of that eyeliner and leather."

"That's a stereotype," Brynn said. "Maybe she wants to write about something less dangerous. Like stealing."

"Like stealing someone's heart." Spencer looked pointedly at me as he said this.

Brynn looked up from her dissection of a purple macaroon. She grinned at me, mischievously. "So ..."

The coffee seared against my lips, and I blew across its surface, softly. "Yes?"

"Matt Callahan."

I rolled my eyes. "Like I said, I wish I could trade you." I went to sip from my drink again.

"Why? The man is hot. You're going to be writing about love with the elite love entity himself."

I coughed, spraying coffee across my hands. "Excuse me?" I squeaked, setting the mug down and plucking a napkin from the dispenser to wipe my hands. "What do you know about Matt Callahan?"

Brynn propped her elbows on the table, tearing apart another unfortunate macaroon without looking at me. "About as much as you would if you actually ventured out into the college universe with me."

I set my napkin down and risked another swig of coffee. The liquid left a slow burn in the back of my throat, but I swallowed. "I know that Matt thinks he's charming."

"And he's a senior, so he's graduating this year, like me and the rest of the Advanced Prose class," Spencer said. "Excluding you babies."

Brynn and I were still juniors. We were assigned as roommates freshman year, not because we were friends prior or because our lifestyles matched on the roommate survey, which we had both neglected to fill out, but because we shared the same major. *Opposites attract,* Brynn loved to say, and in a way, it was a balanced relationship because Brynn *did* things in college while I *thought* about doing things instead. But we shared all the same classes and notes so we continued to room together.

Spencer and I, on the other hand, had been friends forever. We grew up in the same town in Blowing Rock, North Carolina, and spent most of our free time in high school working for the school newspaper. He graduated ahead of me and loved Selwyn, so I followed him to the city the very next year.

"Matt is on the lacrosse team," Brynn said, continuing to list my future partner's accolades. "Which again, you would know if you went with me to any of the games. And he's in a fraternity, Alpha Tau Omega."

"You seem to be the walking Matt Callahan encyclopedia," I muttered and tugged at my sweater. I wondered if I was the only one who didn't know the top ten fun facts about one of the most popular boys on campus. It was a small school after all, and I chided myself silently.

Brynn paused, the top half of an orange macaroon halfway into her mouth. "It's mostly just because of Greek life. They were our brother fraternity for the last fundraiser."

"Mmmm," I mumbled and reached across the table to pluck a plain vanilla macaroon from the plate. I bit into it and asked with a mouth half full, "And you think I should be excited to write about love with, what did you call him, 'the elite love entity'?"

Brynn shrugged. "In terms of writing about experience, he's certainly been around the block. He's always dating someone, but it never lasts long. My sorority sisters say he's a player. So besides writing, I doubt he's your type of guy."

Spencer leaned forward at the table. "Sounds like my kind of guy."

"A player," I mused. "Well, you said he's on the lacrosse team." I meant it jokingly, but I couldn't help but feel a little defensive at Brynn's prompt analysis of Matt not being my type. I mean, she wasn't wrong, but it made me think of freshman year all over again when we had just moved in together.

Let it be known, on record, that I met Grant Morris first. We were partnered together during a welcome week activity our first year that had us chugging frozen ice pops and assembling letters into words. I made the words and he kept downing the popsicles in exchange for more letters.

It was a good partnership. So good, that we hung out afterward in my room, and I thought we were well on our way to becoming friends. I was stupid enough to think that, when he sat on my bed, maybe he would've wanted something more. But if he had that fleeting thought, it was quickly extinguished when Brynn walked into the room and introduced herself with her trademark coy smile.

Grant and I hung out a few more times after that, either studying in the library together or catching up for coffee between classes. I stopped seeing him after he asked if Brynn was single and then for her number.

"Very funny," Brynn said. "But for real, Ember. Matt's got a bit of a reputation for getting around. It wouldn't surprise me if he tried his magic on you too."

I rolled my eyes. "You don't need to worry. I prefer my men to have a bit more class and a higher IQ."

"Or for them to be fictional," Spencer snorted.

I shot him a death glare before turning back to Brynn's smug expression. "Besides, I don't find him nearly as attractive as you two seem to."

"Regardless," Brynn said. "Be a little careful, and try not to kill him in the process." She reached down to grab her bag. "Neither of us has the money to bail you out of jail, and we have stories to write and a contest to win."

Chapter Three

If I could have one superpower, I wish I had the ability to lie convincingly. A poker face has never been in my toolkit of tricks, but it's not been for my lack of trying. The first time I tried and miserably failed to lie myself out of a sticky situation was when I was six and my brother, Ethan, was nine. Growing up in Blowing Rock, we had a plethora of trees to choose from when we implored our father to build us a tree house. Ethan and I always had a love-hate relationship—as in, we loved to hate each other—so sharing was obviously out of the question. We compromised by having designated evenings in the summer when we would trade off who got to camp out in the tree house.

There was one particularly rainy week when I hadn't gotten to spend much time in the tree house, but Ethan would not budge on his Monday-Wednesday-Friday days. I remember climbing up to the fort the first clear afternoon, ready for battle. I thought I was slick when I rigged a trap that would trip when he opened the hatch door at the bottom of the tree house's floor, flinging leaves and pine needles in his face. I remember feeling pretty triumphant when I heard his high-pitched shriek and the thud of his boyish frame as he hit the ground.

Unfortunately, the snuffling sobs that followed told me I had gone too far in the prank and when I tried to tell my dad that it was an accident and he just slipped on the ladder, Ethan's broken arm provided enough evidence to out my lie and earn me a month of grounding. Literal grounding. No tree house, per Dad's punishment. My mom had always tried to be a bit more lenient with us, but that didn't matter after she left us four years later.

So, when I told Brynn that Matt Callahan wasn't remotely attractive, I felt my cheeks burn and I knew she could see right through the lie. She tried to let me think she had bought it by not calling bullshit, but the smirk that danced in her eyes told me otherwise.

I mean, she did have a point. Honestly, you would seriously have to be legally blind to not notice him when he walked into a room, and even if I wasn't wearing my plus one reading glasses, I had to admit that Matt was nice to look at. He was tall with broad shoulders and an obnoxious smile. That smile...he would let it slip from behind his laptop whenever someone in the class would note something profound, but he rarely looked up to let that smile slide past his own little world behind his computer. His freaking computer. He was the only student in the class to take notes and jot thoughts on a screen rather than traditional pen and paper. It was just another reason he didn't belong.

Even if Brynn could see right through the lie that Matt's appearance wasn't noteworthy, I had to admit that I was curious about him. To take the advanced writing classes, you had to have both poetry and prose prerequisites. I didn't remember seeing him in any of my fiction, nonfiction, or poetry classes. Come to think of it, I hadn't seen him much at all before Advanced Prose this semester. But that didn't mean much. I split the majority of my time between classes, the library, and my room, and he most certainly wasn't hiding in there.

Still, I couldn't help but wonder why he was even here in the first place. The creative writer in me had crafted all sorts of conspiracy theories since being paired with him: undercover reporter for the business faculty trying to gather intel on why funding should go toward the Business School rather than the small English Department; lost a bet with his frat buddies; stronger minds made stronger lacrosse players? I had no idea.

Regardless, even if Matt Callahan happened to be hot, which I could never admit to Brynn in a hundred thousand MILLION years, that didn't change the feeling of general loathing I harbored toward him. Winning this contest and getting my first story published could be the ticket to my future as a writer and, in my mind, Matt Callahan could only prohibit this success. In short, I was doomed.

* * *

Later that week, I walked out of American Literature and stopped cold. Matt was leaning casually against the faded yellow drywall. My stomach dropped, and I clutched my anthology close to my chest to keep my heart from plummeting with it.

He looked up from his phone as I stood, mouth agape. Although the semester had just begun, if the old language building was a frequent track for Matt at 3:40 p.m. on Tuesdays and/or Thursdays, I would have known that by now. But I never, *ever*, saw him outside of Prose.

"Owens," he said simply. A small smile played across his features as he pocketed the phone.

"Callahan," I replied warily. I moved to the wall opposite from him, letting the sea of students wash between us. When they cleared, I asked, "What brings you this way?"

He pushed himself off the wall and started walking toward the stairs leading down and outside. "I wanted to talk to you about our assignment."

I followed suit, stepping down the stairs behind him. "Oh?" I replied rather unintelligently, and I hated myself for it.

"Yeah," he said, opening the door for me to walk through.

The air held fast to its winter chill. I pulled the sleeves of my sweater over my wrists as I stopped before the fountain and turned to face him.

He tucked his hands into the pockets of his jeans. The collar of a blue polo peeked out from behind the quarter zip at his chest and the ever-present light smile danced across his face.

"I was wondering if you're free tomorrow," he said. "My afternoon practice just got canceled, and I'd love to get our pitch together before the weekend. I was thinking we could meet up at The House or something?"

My shoulders sagged on their own accord. My Friday afternoons were usually free, and I knew we needed to at least start brainstorming to have something ready for Monday night, but The House? That was basically sacred ground. I didn't need Matt tainting the creative juices I could usually get flowing alongside the café's strong coffee. And, honestly, I was surprised that Matt was part of the campus crowd that liked the drive to The House rather than just using the onsite coffee shop.

I reluctantly asked, "What time?"

He shrugged. "Noon? I could drive."

My stomach lurched. "I have a car. I'll meet you there."

Matt flicked an eyebrow. "You want to drive separately?"

I nodded. "I have an appointment at 11:00 a.m. so I can head there afterward."

His mouth drew into a thin line, and I prayed that he bought the lie. He nodded, so I guess it did the trick. "I'll see you there, then. Tomorrow."

Tomorrow. I mustered enough enthusiasm for a smile of my own. "That sounds great. See you tomorrow."

I couldn't move. His gaze was unnerving when settled on me. Plans were made, task done, checked the box, and I tried to tell my feet to move. *Leave.*

Matt was still looking at me. "You know," he said. "I get the feeling you're not looking forward to working with me, Ember. And

I wish I could lie and say I'm not excited to work with you, but to tell the truth, I think I just lucked into the best partner in the class."

I shifted on my feet, ignoring how strange it sounded to have my name, my first name anyway, on his lips. "And why is that?"

"Well, you're a great writer," he said. "And I think you're interesting. I'd like to know more about you."

My brow furrowed. He thought I was good? And ... interesting? I could put money on him using similar *you're not like other girls* crap on every other woman who had crossed his path.

I sucked a breath and summoned every last ounce of courage I contained. "Let me tell you something about how this is going to work, Matt. Yes, we are going to be seeing each other more than we usually do in the near future. No, that does not mean you get to practice your cheesy pickup lines, like the one you just tried, on me. I'm interested in writing this story, winning the contest, and putting this project behind us. Nothing else. So to do that, the working relationship we are going to share is going to remain just that—working. And platonic. And impersonal. Do you understand?"

There had never been anything more gratifying in my twenty years of life than the shock that colored Matt Callahan's expression at being put in his place by yours truly.

He coughed once, regaining his composure, amusement behind his eyes. "Noted."

I smiled. "Perfect."

My feet unfroze with my triumph, and I turned to head back to my room.

"I'll be at Bar Code tonight if you want to start to get to know each other," Matt said. I made the mistake of stopping to look back at him. "You know, for our working, platonic, and impersonal relationship." The grin on his face was impish.

I glowered. It was no surprise that Matt was a regular at Bar Code, the night club Charlotte undergrads were known to frequent on Thursday nights. "Goodbye, Matt."

He chuckled and turned, heading toward the Business School building at the front of the campus. "I'll see you tomorrow, Owens."

There was a skip in his stride as I watched him take the steps down to the lower quad. I scowled and turned, walking quickly away.

* * *

I sat on top of the orange and teal quilt on my bed, my back against the corner of the wall, hunched over the thick spiral-bound notebook I used for drafting and brainstorming various story ideas and poetry lines.

The lamplight from my desk illuminated the corners of my side of the dorm, casting a glow upon the otherwise shadowed room. I couldn't stand working under anything other than lamplight. Fluorescents only served to deplete any energy or motivation I had when it came to school work, let alone writing anything worth reading.

Regardless of the mood lighting I had set, I tapped my pen against my bottom lip feeling drained of any inspiration. I wished Brynn were here. She left a few hours ago to pregame with her sorority sisters before their ritual clubbing excursion. Almost every Thursday night tended to echo similar patterns of her asking me to tag along, knowing full well I would refuse. The persistent offer was kind nonetheless.

Write a story in which the main character falls in love. Gross. If Brynn were here, I'd at least have someone to bounce ideas off of.

I never usually felt lonely when Brynn left me on Thursday nights, but lonely was all I could attribute to the gnawing in my gut. The thought of Brynn dancing in the same club Matt said he'd be at tonight—and the offers from both to join them—ate at me. *If you want to start to get to know each other ...* I groaned and flopped lengthwise on my bed, flinging the notebook to the ground in exasperation.

My phone vibrated on my desk. I lifted my gaze from my face-plant to try to see the caller ID. It was my dad.

"Shit," I muttered. I tried to think of the last time I called him, but it had been a while. He tried to let me have my space at school, but he ended up calling me much more often than I called him. I tried not to begrudge his communication too much; Ethan never came back home after moving out to UNC, especially not after he married his girlfriend when they were both only sophomores.

With enormous effort, I righted myself and swung my legs off the edge of the bed, ignoring the wrinkled pages of the book that lay at my feet. I sat down at my desk and slid the bar on my phone to answer his call.

"What are you doing up so late, old man?" I asked by way of greeting.

There was a pause on his end of the line where I imagined my dad probably checking his watch. "Huh, 12:30 a.m. Would you look at that? Just about bedtime."

"How's that word count looking?"

I came by the trade of writing honestly. My dad was a consummate writer; anyone could see it in the words he spoke. There was always careful thought behind each sentence, and if he didn't have the next word on the tip of his tongue, he would pause and find the best choice before finishing his thought. Though he had studied psychology in college, he always tinkered with stories. Growing up, he wouldn't read books to Ethan and me. He would invent them instead, right on the spot.

My mom had grown tired of his endless daydreams about one day publishing a book, a fantasy that started to consume his every free hour, taking him further away from us and into his world of fiction. When my mom got her first real acting offer, aside from her volunteer hours at our local theater, she leaped at the opportunity—and the man who found it for her.

"I just clocked in two thousand words for the evening," my dad said, his voice tired and thick on the line.

"I'm jealous."

"Emmy," he started and the corner of my mouth flicked up at the nickname I rarely heard anymore. "No one can control how much or how little you write a day other than you. It's nothing but disciplining yourself. Lord knows I have never been able to discipline you."

"Comedy's not your strong suit, Dad. Stick to the best-seller life."

With nearly twenty best-selling novels on bookshelves across the country, my dad's dream had become reality. Despite his own wife's lack of faith, Sam Owens was a household name.

His murmur of agreement was audible on the other side of the line. "What's new on the quad?" he asked.

"Well, I got an A on our first short story for the advanced class."

"That's great, honey."

"And we got our prompts for the next one."

"Prompts?"

"Yeah. It's part of a contest. You've heard of *Noted and Quoted*?"

"Only one of the best literary magazines in the country."

"Just my random check on your sanity," I said. "But they are starting a contest geared for undergrads, and our school got invited to participate."

"Intriguing."

"But we have to write in partners."

He paused. "You? Working with someone else? Do they hate your partner or something?"

"Dad!"

"Sorry, kiddo," he chuckled.

"No," I said, exasperated. "I think it's me they hate. I got stuck with the bad apple."

"Bad apple, huh? I think you've got a better metaphor in you than that."

"See. He's already having a bad influence on my literary genius."

"I think it's going to present a good challenge, for sure," my dad said, "but one necessary for learning how to cooperate with other opinions on a plot line."

I groaned. "I know, but still." I tried to steer the conversation to something other than the project. "How's mountain life treating you?"

"About the same as it always does. I've been writing on the balcony when I can, but it's still so cold outside. The fireplace is almost always running."

Despite the weight of the unplanned story still sitting on my chest, I felt the start of a small smile when I thought about winter and the evenings by the fire we used to spend, Ethan, me, and Dad. The three of us. "I hate that you're seeing it alone."

"Well ..." my dad drawled.

"What?" The word came out accusatory instead of curious.

He was silent a beat too long. "Your brother is back home."

"Wait. What?"

My dad sighed. "I thought he would've told you. He said he was going to call."

"Like, is he visiting home again?" We had just been back for the holidays not that long ago.

"No." He blew out another breath. "I think he's planning on staying a little while."

"Why?"

"Emmy," he said. "It's really not my place."

"Dad," I whined.

The sigh that emanated from the phone was deeper and longer this time. "He went back to Raleigh for a few days after the New Year, but moved home right after."

So not just back, but *moved* back home. Ethan had been living at home a month and a half now, and I had no idea about it. Being three years older than me, he had already graduated from UNC and was living in the Raleigh area with his wife. He worked as a technical writer for a video gaming company, but I knew he had bigger goals of one day doing the writing on the screen for fantasy games instead of just the directions on how to format them. At least, that's what he had been doing. Up until now.

Ethan and I weren't exactly close, and we rarely felt the need to call one another just to chitchat, but still. It hurt that he hadn't called his own sister to say he was moving home. I was afraid to ask, but I had to. "Where is Hallie?"

My dad was quiet. "Not sure, currently. But from the mail I have been collecting for your brother she has been spending some quality time with a divorce attorney."

It was my turn to be silent. They had married quickly—after only dating for six months—and young, far too young in my father's opinion, but it seemed like they were actually in love. "So much for happy endings," I muttered, more to myself than anyone else.

"I think she cheated," my dad said. "Ethan quit his job; said he had to get away from Raleigh. He hasn't spoken much else about her. I've just been letting him try to get back on his feet."

Despite my own hurt feelings at just finding out, my heart ached for both my dad and brother. History was repeating itself. My mom up and left us a decade ago, and now Hallie was reopening the same wound on Ethan. And my dad ... he had barely known how to help himself out of the disaster my mom left in her wake, let alone try to cast a lifeline to Ethan now.

"Can you just," I said, my voice softening, "can you just ask him to call me at some point?"

"Will do, Emmy."

"I think I'm going to head to bed."

"Okay." My dad paused. "You good?"

"Yeah. I'll talk to you later. Get some rest."

"You do the same. Love you, kiddo."

"I love you too," I managed before ending the call. I swiveled the desk chair around to pick up my face-planted notebook. I laid it on the desk's wooden surface and flipped back to the list I had been making. Smoothing out the creases in the pages, I plucked a pen out of the mason jar I kept them stashed in. In bold black letters underneath the previous blue ink, I wrote out my last point for the night, NOT ALL LOVE STORIES END HAPPILY.

Chapter Four

You know how when you were a kid, you always had to have a thing that you did, something that defined you, something to tag along with your name in an introduction. For my brother, he always had the luxury of saying, *Hi, I'm Ethan, I play baseball.* Me? I never had that opportunity. I always loved to read—I did *that* thing—but rather than continuing to identify as a NARP (nonathletic regular person) for the rest of my college career, I started running.

I was lucky. I rigged my schedule to have no classes on Friday. Even though Brynn's previous night activities were usually far more exhilarating than mine, I usually got up when she did too. I never had to worry about being woken up by Brynn because her "recovery day" kept her sleeping five minutes until her class began. Though her previous night activities were usually far more exhilarating than mine, I usually got up when she did and would head to the student center. The handful of treadmills that were on display offered a constant reassurance of at least one availability around lunchtime on Fridays.

Today, however, I learned that at 9:30 on Friday mornings, the rush to run on a man-made machine in the dank gym was not in high demand. I had the room to myself as I pushed in my headphones and set the distance for three miles. The extra weight on my sleepy arms had me cursing Matt Callahan under my breath as the meter ticked down. It was his fault that I was here earlier than usual; his fault that I had to leave at 11:30 a.m. today to get to The House a good fifteen minutes before he said he would arrive; his fault that my palms were sweating more than I could ever admit to myself at the thought of being alone with him, baring my own ideas about love, or lack thereof—or that could be the extra half mile I tacked onto my usual set this morning to try to take the edge off. It was *definitely* the running that slicked my grip on the handlebars.

The beeping from the treadmill when I finished my set reminded me of something like a hospital, and I made a mental note to flesh out my lie to Matt about being busy before our meeting. A doctor's appointment, more specifically a gynecologist appointment if I didn't want him curiously asking any follow-up questions.

I turned the treadmill off and flicked open the top of my water bottle as I stepped off the belt. The water was cool against the back of my throat and I gulped, savoring the shock as sweat continued to bead around my forehead, making my already curly hair even more coiled.

I could barely feel the chill in the midmorning air when I left the gym. A few squirrels ran across the bricked walkway in front of me. I guess we were all immune to the cold today. The light workout hoodie I threw over my tank top did little to curb the breeze, but I felt like I was boiling inside of my own skin. I needed a shower.

The automatic sliding doors to the library welcomed me with a gust of air. The computers on the entrance level of the five-story building held only a handful of students. The tapping of fingers on keyboards was a dull clatter instead of the usual furor that accompanied the work week. I nodded in greeting to the few that lifted their gaze, and turned to my right toward the stairs that led to the top two floors.

If I had to pick one reason for loving my school, it would be for making my lifelong dream of living in a library come to fruition.

The added dormitories on the top of the existing three-story structure had only been built a few years ago, and I was grateful for the timing that had me starting my undergraduate studies at the same time construction was completed.

The hallways on the top floor were still eerily silent as I made my way up the staircase. I didn't bother knocking or muffling the creak of the gears as I pulled down the doorknob and pushed my way inside.

"Brynn," I said, flicking on the lamps on both of our desks. "You've got to get up. You have class in twenty minutes." I continued to make unnecessary noise as I kicked off my shoes and rummaged for my shower caddy from my closet.

Her groan was low and drawling in response as she rolled over and buried her face in her body pillow against the wall. "Can't."

I tugged my caddy out of the viselike grip my dirty clothes hamper had on it and sat down on the edge of my bed to untie my sneakers. Single knotted. I hated double knotting. "Shakespeare summons you," I said in a pretty terrible British accent.

"He already had me on Monday and Wednesday. He's a needy bastard."

"Imagine if he was actually alive."

She lifted her bedhead to peer at me through sleepy eyes. "I'd ask him why the hell he wrote 154 sonnets."

"And then ask him to introduce you to the Fair Youth he wrote about in the majority of them." I stood up and pulled my tank top over my head, adding it to the pile of laundry in my closet.

"I'm still jealous you took Shakespeare Studies over the summer. You're making me suffer alone right now."

I slipped my robe over my shoulders and shimmied out of the rest of my gym clothes. "What can I say. I'm an overachiever."

Brynn finally sat up in bed, tossing the covers off of her willowy frame. "You know what else I'm jealous about?"

I slipped on my flip-flops and picked up my caddy. "What's that?"

Her grin was sly. "Your date with Matt Callahan. That's today, isn't it?"

I never should have told her my afternoon plans. "Not a date," I corrected. "And I thought you didn't like him."

"I never said that. I don't mind him. He's just a scoundrel."

"Scoundrel, huh?"

"Yeah, but he's hot," Brynn said and shrugged. "So, it's allowed. It comes with the territory."

"Ugh," I groaned. "I'm going to shower."

My hand was on the metal of the knob when I heard Brynn's feet slap the ground as she jumped out of bed and chirped, "Make smart choices, Ems!"

I narrowed my eyes. "The only choice I have is to be or not to be visibly pissed off the whole time," I said, too proud of my Shakespeare puns not to slide them into conversation.

Brynn's smile looked almost wicked. "My my, Ember, what emotion Matt seems to elicit from you."

I ignored her and closed the door behind me with a thud, hating that she seemed to be right.

***

In short, Bugsy Malone was the love of my life. My old, beat up, Volkswagen Beetle served me well since the day I turned sixteen. Not only was he overflowing in antique character, but Bugsy also had a reputation for navigating me out of some serious trouble over the course of my driving career. Because teetering down winding mountain roads and then merging onto congested highways used to be my kryptonite, the little bug had been forced to maneuver me out of a multitude of near-death experiences.

My dad had published several books and had his first movie deal on the way by the time I got my license. He could have bought me a Porsche, but it was important to him that Ethan and I worked for our own money, like he had. I didn't mind. It felt even more gratifying getting behind the wheel every time I drove knowing that I had saved up my meager paychecks from the bookstore to get Bugsy secondhand.

While the back windshield had a large crack crawling across its glass frame, and the vinyl seats were faded and worn, nothing prohibited Bugsy Malone's radio from working in full force. That was my favorite part about him; Bugsy's tight and cozy interior was the perfect place for intense jam sessions. The practice had become common ritual for myself. Since rooming with Brynn, I had mustered the confidence to expand the lead singer role of my one-woman show to a duet between the two of us when I would drive her. Poor Spencer was well acquainted with the karaoke that accompanied the car.

With it being just me in the car on my way to meet Matt at The House, I turned the volume up to a healthy twenty-five, trying to use Bugsy's sound system to lift my spirits. My theme song of choice? None other than Survivor's *Eye of the Tiger*.

My windows were down, the wind whipping through the baby curls at my ears as I belted the chorus. It wasn't until I veered off the exit with my foot on the brake that I considered perhaps not all those at the approaching stoplight would appreciate the concert series brought to exit 3A by yours truly. I turned down the volume, cutting it in half and went to roll up the windows.

Apparently, I couldn't spare them all from the horror, for as I looked over at the car beside me in the left lane, I saw that the driver was staring straight at me. And it was a man. A gorgeous one. And unfortunately, none other than the one I was driving to meet. The lazy grin on his face told me he heard it all, including the last note I had held for dramatic effect.

Shit.

He took his hands off of his steering wheel and started clapping, slowly. "Bravo!" he called from the driver's side of the flashy black Lexus.

Shit. Shit. Shit.

Not only had someone just seen my highly personal way of venting any and all emotion, that someone had to be Matt Freaking Callahan of all people. His smirk was still on the corners of his lips, but if the amusement had met his brown eyes, I couldn't tell. They were hidden behind a pair of dark shades with thick rims.

My mortification had me seething, my teeth clenched tight in my jaw. "Thanks, but I wasn't really expecting an audience."

He leaned back in his seat and said, "I'm glad. Those are the best shows."

My cheeks burned and my eyes narrowed into thin slits.

The light must have turned green for the next thing I knew, Matt gave me a two-fingered wave and pulled away from the white line at the stoplight. I fumbled and threw my own car in gear to follow suit.

I ended up tailing him the remainder of the way to The House, and even though there was an open space right next to his car at the front entrance, I pulled into a spot on the far side of the parking lot. I shut my door with more enthusiasm than I would've wanted him to hear out of fear that he would think the slamming was on account of my monumental embarrassment.

He was leaning against the driver's side door of his car, arms crossed in front of his chest. His sunglasses were still on.

"I've got to say, Owens," he said, pulling himself off of the sleek exterior, "I didn't know you had that bellow in you."

I continued walking past him, imagining that my still wet hair was about to start sizzling in its messy bun at the top of my head due to the steam surely coming out of my ears. It was times like these I wished I was better with the blow dryer. Or the flat iron. At least I put on mascara in an effort to keep the illusion that I was somewhat put together. I didn't say anything as I opened the door and walked inside, not bothering to hold it for him as he trailed behind me.

"It's not that it's that horrible," he said, following me to the back of the long lunch rush line. "You'd certainly be the shining star out of a chorus of cats. I think you're the cat's meow, Ember Owens. Is that where they got that expression, do you think?"

I wheeled on him, and the halt of my step took his own by surprise as he pulled up sharply. "Just shut up, Matt."

"Hey, it's not a turnoff for me," he said with his hands up in a mock surrender. He stepped around me to join in line. "I'm totally a cat person."

"That makes so much sense," I said and stepped behind him. "I now understand why you're such an asshole, thank you."

"Possibly," he said. "But I happen to have immaculate taste in French desserts."

His back was to me as he leaned over the display cases, eyes raking the contents. I lifted my gaze to the ceiling and closed my eyes briefly. *Why did I get stuck with him?*

He looked back to me and chuckled. "Ember, you make it way too easy to mess with you. Now tell me what you want to get. My treat."

I glared at him and stepped around his tall frame. "Don't bother."

I proceeded to order my usual, just a dark roast coffee with room for cream, but then caught myself thinking that Brynn was always the one to order the macaroons we ate. It felt like some sort of betrayal to order those without her here, so I chose a crème brûlée instead, declining the second spoon they offered me. I wasn't in the sharing mood.

Matt paid for his own caramel latte and followed me into the second seating area. I picked a table opposite from the corner where Brynn, Spencer, and I usually sat.

"So," I said, plopping down on the red seat cushion, letting my crème brûlée tin rattle in its saucer. "Have you given this project any thought? Any ideas on what you want to write about?"

Matt surprised me by answering when he sat down opposite of me. "I have actually."

I stabbed the caramelized sugar seal with the edge of my spoon, causing spiderwebby cracks across the surface. "And?"

Matt leaned back in his seat, lifting his mug to his lips with one hand. "I think it depends on what kind of love you want to explore with this."

"Write a story in which the main character falls in love. The directions are pretty clear."

He sipped from his drink then shrugged, finally meeting my steely gaze again. "What kind of love is the character going to fall in? Romantic love, familial love, friendship love?"

"Self-love?" I added, lifting an eyebrow.

Matt set his drink down. "I feel a hint of judgment there."

"I just wish we could all have your self-confidence and adoration."

His eyes flickered ever so briefly. "You really don't like me, do you?"

"I'll be honest, you haven't made the best of impressions on me yet, Matt."

"You're breaking my heart, kitten."

I delivered a swift glare at the nickname, wishing it was sharp enough to cut through the embarrassment over my singing that he apparently was never going to let me live down. I took a deep drink from my mug and nearly spat, "I didn't think you had one to break."

"You seem to think you know a lot about my character."

I leaned back in my seat, crossing my arms. "Have you ever been in love, Matt?"

"Depends on your definition of it."

I glowered. "I think love is like cancer. They both grow and consume and swallow you whole."

He gave a dramatic shudder. "Sounds toxic."

"It depends on your definition of it," I said with a smirk. "And you didn't answer the question."

"Of course I've been in love," he said. "Several times."

"Several? How so?"

"In any relationship, there has to be some element of love," he reasoned. "It may be in varying degrees, but it's at the root of any partnership."

"And in exactly how many relationships have you had this experience of being in love?"

"Three."

"Three? In your lifetime?" I asked, thinking about how Brynn said he was always dating someone. "Or just since you've been in college?"

He grinned. "Just this past year."

I rolled my eyes. "There you go, proving my point."

Amusement plastered itself as a small smile across his face. "And what point is that?"

"That you seem to be callous when it comes to relationships because you apparently get bored and move on; therefore, you don't really know what love is." I picked up my spoon again. "You cannot write about it because it's impossible to write something unless you've lived it."

He didn't argue with me, but rather cocked his head, curious. "Who said that?"

"I did," I said, scooping another bite of dessert.

"No, you didn't," he said. "Oliver Van Dam did."

I paused, my spoon halfway to my mouth, still hanging open. "What did you just say?"

The half smile I was used to seeing on Matt's lips erupted and spread across his entire face, the corners of his eyes crinkling in victory. "You heard me. That's one of Oliver Van Dam's biggest philosophies. You didn't come up with that little line yourself."

If I was remotely religious, Oliver Van Dam would have been my god. My father had introduced me to his books when I was in middle school, and I had yet to read anyone who could match his ability to spin a science fiction tale. When I started delving into the world of creative writing more seriously in high school, I found my most prized possession: a nonfiction book written by none other than Van Dam himself titled *To Write or to Dream About Writing*. I followed this text as if it were my bible. The advice Van Dam stitched into each chapter was priceless; it carved the way for nearly every draft I wrote. And Matt seemed to know these words too.

"How ... how do you know that?" I asked, incredulous.

He crossed his arms, triumphant. "I have his writing book."

My mind simply would not accept that. "No, you don't."

"Yes, I actually do."

All possible replies had been wiped clean from my internal word bank. There was no way this jock had actually read anything from *To Write*. "Where did you get it? When did you get it?"

"A bookstore? I read it for class." He paused. My mouth was still agape when he added, "I took classes at the community college with an English focus during my senior year of high school."

I finally closed my mouth and tightened my jaw. So that was how he was in the advanced class and I never saw him in any prerequisite classes.

He chuckled. "Glad I could surprise you, kitten."

I had so many questions that I curbed my annoyance over the nickname. Like, why was he originally on an English track? Why did he switch to business? What brought him back to writing now for Advanced Prose? I wouldn't ask any of them, though. Couldn't. Because I was definitely not interested.

"The fact you know Van Dam ... yes, it's a bit of a shock. But what is not surprising is that he's right. Therefore, I'm right. Writing this project is going to be harder having never truly fallen in love."

His eyebrow flicked up. "There you go again, assuming things about me. And what about you? Do you think you have more firsthand love experience than I do?"

I stayed quiet. I wasn't about to let Matt in on anything about my personal life if I could help it. Truthfully, the extent of my experience with any sort of love went no further than a sloppy prom kiss and a half interested middle-school boyfriend. There had been one boy I really liked in high school, but that abruptly ended when I found out he had been leading me on while still hooking up with the head cheerleader. So that had been a failure, much like all of the relationships in my family too. Maybe we were all cursed.

"How about this," Matt said. "Let's do something fairly universal. Childhood best friends, bordering on something more. Almost everyone knows that story."

I considered it and thought about my notebook tucked away back in my room. "You know, not all love stories end happily," I mused. "I would be fine with whatever way you wanted to start this story if it told that truth."

Matt paused and looked up at me. His gaze looked hollow, but only for such a split second that I doubted what I saw. "No," he said simply. "Let's give this one the happy ending it needs."

I sighed and tried one more argument. "Childhood friends turned lovers might be too overdone. We would have to work hard to keep it from coming too cliché."

"It's not a cliché if it has happened to you."

I cocked my head. "You have experience in this field?"

Matt reached under the table for his laptop bag. "Wouldn't that just be grand if I did." He pulled out his sleek MacBook computer and opened it. "It would make both of our lives easier, wouldn't it?"

I sighed and took another deep slug of coffee. "Oliver Van Dam would approve, I suppose."

He looked up at me from under his lashes and grinned. "Our minds might be more alike than you think, kitten."

"Will you stop with the name?" I pleaded.

"Only when it stops bothering you." Matt's smile was cheeky, and I thought about kicking him in the shins beneath the table.

"Pick a number, one through twenty-six," he said.

"Why?" I snapped.

"Just do it." Matt punched at his laptop keys.

I sighed. "Twelve."

He hit one more button before turning the laptop to me. It was a list of baby girl names, all starting with the letter L, coincidentally the twelfth letter of the alphabet. "Pick one."

I had to admit, it was a pretty clever idea, although I didn't say that aloud to him. I scrolled through the list several times before finally deciding. "Lena."

He took his computer back. "I like it. My letter is W."

He scrolled, leaning back in his seat with his legs stretched in front of him. I had my feet shifted to the side of the table, giving him the extra space.

" 'Lena and Wesley' has a nice ring to it, don't you think?"

"It'll do."

He snorted and mimicked in a voice higher than my own. *"It'll do."*

I took the heel of my boot and accidentally stepped on the toe of his shoe.

"Ouch!" His feet slid only an inch or two away, but they didn't retreat.

Chapter Five

We didn't get any further than adding a setting and basic scenario for our story that afternoon. When I left The House, letting Matt get a healthy head start so I didn't have to converse in the parking deck when we returned to campus, I prayed that we had enough material to pitch the fragments of our idea to class on Monday night.

When pitch night rolled around after my weekend spent mostly in bed reading, Pollard had arranged the desks in a circle so we would all be facing one another. The inquisitive faces of the other students were a bit more intimidating than the backs of their heads from my usual seat in the rear of the classroom.

"You ready for your pitch?" Spencer asked as leaned toward me. To anyone looking at him across the circle, the swoop of his red hair hid most of his face.

I sank in my seat so I could lean into his hair curtain. "I sure hope so. We met up to work on it Friday."

"I'm jealous. All of that alone time with Matt Callahan." The comment suggested humor, but Spencer's tone was surprisingly dry.

"Don't worry. It was plenty awkward."

"How so?"

"He might have witnessed a good solo jam on the way."

"Shit."

I chewed my lip and crossed my arms. "He actually had some good ideas though." Together, we had taken a fair number of notes, his on his laptop and mine in an old leather notebook with my initials starting to fade on its cover. The tapping of his long fingers on his keyboard never ceased once they started bulleting out different ideas and plot points for the basic outline we came up with. My rhythm was slower as my pen struck against my bottom lip repeatedly; any of my own thoughts dried up like the cold dregs in the bottom of my coffee cup. My creativity had been at the mercy of his imagination, and I was almost embarrassed to admit that he had done the majority of innovation for our pitch tonight.

"I'm still not sure how this story is going to pan out," I said to Spencer. "But Matt seems to have a plan in his own head. I just hope it can transpire to the paper when it's all said and done."

"Good evening, everyone," Pollard said as he strode into the room. The door clicked shut behind him before reopening as a sheepish Matt appeared beneath the white frame.

"Mr. Callahan." Pollard blinked. "You were almost on time tonight."

"I couldn't leave Ember waiting for pitch night." He grinned as he moved to sit in the only open seat, across from me.

"Who said she would've been waiting on you?" Brynn piped up from her seat beside Holly. It occurred to me that everyone else in the room was sitting beside their partners; I hadn't thought to save a seat for mine. Whoops.

Matt winked at her but said nothing as he leaned his skateboard against the wall behind the open seat and sat down. The legs of his pants rode up underneath his desk to expose his socks: dark green with orange cats on them. I stifled a groan.

Pollard sat down at the head of the circle. "All right folks," he said as he pulled out a legal pad and green pen from his bag, "it's time to throw out your pitch."

Matt finished pulling out his laptop and adjusting himself in his seat then met my eyes from across the room. If we sank instead of swam on this project, I would blame his dead weight. Obviously.

"For next week's class, I expect you all to have the first few scenes roughly composed of these stories. But until then, Holly and Brynn are up first. What happens in the story where the main character ..." he trailed off, scanning his notes, "... is part of a crime?"

Holly was leaning back in her seat, smacking chewing gum between her teeth. She flipped open her notebook and read with zero inflection. "Following the perspectives of Officer Jacobson and Lil Jay May, this story explores what happens when a rising rapper star is accused of murder."

Pollard nodded his head. "And what is your plan for writing this story? How are you going to divide the work?"

My stomach clenched. Matt and I hadn't gotten that far in planning this project. I felt like we barely had a plot.

Brynn piped up. "Switching perspectives. I'm writing from the rapper, and Holly is writing from the officer."

Pollard jotted that down on his pad, nodding. "I'm looking forward to reading it. Let's just keep going around the circle. Emilio and Talia? What's your story?"

I leaned forward in my seat to look at the pair. They were quite the match, Emilio with his sharp Latino features and Talia with her spiky purple hair. I thought briefly how interesting the two would be to write as characters.

"We were given the prompt 'Write a story where the main character is given a gift,'" Emilio said.

Talia jumped in, crossing her arms on her desk and leaning forward on them. "And in this story, a young woman is reminiscing about time spent with her boyfriend as she looks through a photo album he gave her."

Pollard's pen scratched across his pad again. "And what is your plan for accomplishing this project?"

"As our main character is looking through the album, each photograph is going to trigger a different memory for her," Emilio explained. "We are hoping the result is a story that is almost episodic, a group of mini portraits in time."

"A vignette style," Pollard said.

"Exactly," Talia said. "We will divide the memories between each other and write those on our own before we finish the ending together."

Pollard tapped his pen against his notepad, waiting. Finally, he said. "What's the crisis of the story?"

"What do you mean?" Emilio asked.

"There doesn't seem to be any struggle or conflict so far. I like the premise and the format, but where is the twist?"

God, I was so not ready to answer any questions regarding our pitch.

"Well," Talia said, "we were playing around with the idea that the boyfriend could turn out to be no longer alive at the end of the story."

Pollard nodded. "Marinate on that thought. See if you can lead up to that reveal and still have time to let the reader down after that crisis is met."

Talia's pen skittered across her notebook.

"Next," Pollard said. "Gemma and Spencer. What happens in the story where the main character is hiding a secret?"

Spencer leaned back in his seat and put his arm around Gemma's chair on the other side of him. "This story follows a seemingly standard love triangle between three friends," he started, turning to look at his partner.

Gemma picked up. "The story will rotate all three perspectives, and the reader will be led to think that Rachel must choose between her two friends, Adam and Brent."

"But," Spencer drawled, "spoiler alert: Adam and Brent end up together. Because gay love shouldn't be a secret."

"Preach," Brynn said, clapping. The circle laughed and applauded alongside her.

"Great. How are you going to divide the workload?" Pollard asked.

"I will probably write Rachel," Gemma said. "Then I figured it would be good for Spencer to write one of the male characters and then us both write the remaining character together to tie up the ending."

I resisted the urge to stomp on Spencer's toes under his desk. Yes, their story seemed to be sticking true to a character hiding a secret, but he and Gemma ran with the love triangle, leaving whatever Matt and I pitched next seemingly like a secondhand love story.

Pollard wrote down their pitch. "All right. Best of luck to you both. Ember and Matt. What happens when your main character falls in love?"

I eyed Matt from across the circle, giving him the nod to start.

"In this story," he began as he scrolled through his laptop notes, "childhood friends Lena and Wesley learn the value of forgiveness and love as they are brought back together after a near fatal accident."

Pollard set his pen down. "What's the plan?"

Matt leaned back in his chair; his ankles crossed under his desk. "I think it would be really cool to play with time. We are going to use heavy flashbacks so that the reader is slowly fed information on their past friendship until they reconnect and that friendship turns into something more. I will write the flashbacks and Ember will write the present-day parts of the story."

That was news to me.

Pollard smiled. "I like that. It will give the past versus the present different and distinctive voices," he wrote a few more notes. "Ember, do you have any other thoughts on your story?"

I realized I hadn't contributed anything and immediately flushed. "It's going to be set in the mountains." I paused. "I grew up in the town of Blowing Rock, so that's where Lena and Wes are going to spend most of their time. The landscapes always seemed like they would be a good backdrop for romance."

It had pained me to admit that to Matt at The House. It was too personal of a thought, but I owed it to this contest to give this story the best landscape possible, and nothing had ever made me feel as nostalgic as the Blue Ridge Parkway. If the love of the mountains was one of the few things I could actually write about in reverie, I was going to have to use that to our advantage.

"I'm looking forward to reading it. Elle and Charlie, you're next."

I slumped in my seat and let out a breath. Matt met my eyes and flashed a smile. He continued to surprise me. I hadn't given the project much thought after we met up. Couldn't. This story wasn't mine. From his first suggestion, this story had always been his, and I hated to confess in my own head that I felt out of my league to try to attempt it on my own. There was something about the way he spoke in the pitch. He seemed ... interested? Like he actually cared about what we were going to be writing. He spoke with determination and a layer of pride, much unlike the cool, careless facade that usually dusted his features.

I tuned out the last of the pitches. Lena and Wesley needed to become my priority. Matt and I needed a storyboard. We needed another planning date.

***

Tuesdays were my mail days.

I guess you could say that I was a creature of habit. Once I found a schedule that worked for me, seldom did I venture from it. Like Monday night was The House post Advanced Prose. And Tuesdays after lunch, I went down to the mail room located below the cafeteria.

My sneakers scuffed along the squeaky linoleum flooring of the stairs as I made my way below. I passed a few other students. I knew some of their names from classes we had taken together and I gave them a wayward greeting, but many I did not.

I stopped at the very last cove of mailboxes and fished for the key from the cluster on my lanyard. I opened up box ninety-four to find my usual: bank statements, flyers, etcetera. I flipped through the stack absentmindedly, briefly pausing at the Poets and Writers monthly roster of literary magazines and submission dates, before I got to a pink envelope, addressed to myself in swirling cursive handwriting I knew, and abhorred, by heart.

"Mom," I whispered aloud.

I rarely heard from her anymore, aside from the mandatory holiday-themed cards that usually arrived a few days after said holiday had passed. I didn't care too much, honestly, and after a quick skim of the contents, her notes promptly ended up in the garbage. Aside from Christmas and New Year's, for which I received a joint card on January 5, nothing calendar (or card worthy) had happened. What was this about?

I placed the envelope neatly back into the stack under my arm as I locked the box back up. I turned from the cove to hurry back to my dorm so that I could read it in private and spare anyone who might be witness to my reaction. My head was ducked and shoulders tucked tight to keep the stack from coming loose. I didn't see the figure in front of me until their shoes were inches from my own and my nose collided with something hard.

"Oh my god!"

"Jesus!"

There was a clatter of my mail, shoes, bags, and a backside falling to the ground at the impact. As I rubbed my sore nose, I felt a flash of gratitude that I didn't completely wipe out myself. I squinted my blurring eyes through the pain in my face and groaned.

"Matt, what the hell?"

He was upright now, backpack sprawled and legs splayed out in front of him. The look on his face was incredulous as he sat in the fallen shower of my mail.

"You know," he said, "I'm pretty sure this scene is supposed to end with the pretty-but-doesn't-know-it girl on the ground and the hero picking her up, both literally and figuratively, after they crash into each other." He was laughing.

I was not. I stooped to collect my mail from around him. He picked up what was closest to him, the pink envelope resting between his fingers.

I narrowed my eyes from my squatting position in front of him. "Give it to me."

His eyebrow quirked up in playful amusement. "Make me."

I reached to snatch it from his grip, and he did the totally middle school move of stuffing it in his back pocket to sit on it. Out-of-bounds territory. The smile on his face read triumph.

The contents of that envelope knew no bounds, though. I feigned to snake my arm around the right side of him, and he shifted his weight closer to me, blocking me. In that moment when our faces nearly touched, I dodged left around him and snapped the envelope between two of my fingers.

"Challenge accepted," I said and swung my backpack to my front to pocket all of my mail.

I'd like to imagine that Matt's chuckle was of pure awe as he finally pulled himself into a sitting position. "You are truly something else."

I swung my bag back into place and threaded my arms through the straps, securing it. "You seem to bring out the worst in me."

He reached out an arm. "Help me up?"

My mouth wanted to say something like, *not a chance,* but honestly, he looked kind of pathetic sitting on the ground like that. I sighed and stuck out my arm.

He grasped my forearm, and I leaned back against his weight to pull him up. I marveled (unintentionally) at how much taller than me he was now that he stood right before me. I stepped back and placed my hands on the straps of my bag.

Matt hadn't moved yet. He was still grinning down at me.

I rocked on my heels. "So," I started, "we probably need to meet up again to start a storyboard ... or something."

"Something would probably be a good idea." He didn't go on.

I bit my lip. "When are you free?"

"Depends. When do you want to meet?"

My mouth thinned. "Tomorrow," I said stiffly. Why was this so hard?

"My place?"

"The House."

"I'm assuming I'll meet you there?"

"Absolutely."

He chuckled and stepped around me, presumably toward his own mailbox. "I can meet after night class. I get out at 8:30."

"Yes, I know the Business School hours are different than the College of Arts and Sciences."

He paused. "You sure do know a lot, don't you?"

I narrowed my eyes. "I know enough."

"Must be exhausting."

"What, knowing things?"

"No, being a know-it-all."

My jaw dropped at the sheer audacity this man had.

"It's a shame that you're going to have to let down that sharp-minded guard and tap into a softer side."

My heart stuttered. "What do you mean?"

"For the love story," Matt said, finally backing away. "Knowing things can only get you so far, kitten."

Every muscle in my face tightened, curdling my expression.

"Some things in life you can't just know." Matt put his hands in his pockets and turned. "Some things you actually have to feel."

***

It was a wedding invitation.

My mom actually sent me a wedding invitation.

To her wedding.

Well, her second wedding.

I barely made it through the door of my room, key still left hanging in the lock when I slung my backpack to the floor and tore open the perfectly sealed pink envelope. The opening I made with my thumb was jagged compared to the crispness of the printed parchment that read:

You are cordially invited
to the
Marriage Celebration
of
Ms. Ava Owens
and
Mr. Blake Carson

Below the names of my mother and the stranger who would be changing her name was the date, April 4, and an address somewhere in California.

"April?" I cried aloud. The paper vibrated between both of my trembling hands. That was less than two months away. In just a matter of weeks, over my spring break to be exact, my mom was going to get remarried, on the other side of the country.

The California part wasn't as much of a shock. Actress Ava Owens had made a name for herself in Hollywood beyond "mom" almost immediately after she moved there. I could thank her genes for the green eyes we both shared, but her hair favored a red more vibrant than mine, and her height and frame were in a modeling league of their own compared to my short, curvy stature. Ava's striking features coupled with her ability to dramatize any role had helped her on her way to the stardom she felt she was always born to.

A stardom that was short lived. She got one big acting break as a lead in one movie, but after that her name was usually attached to smaller projects, like commercials for razors. That was her big claim to fame now.

I liked to think my father always had the last laugh, though, when the first of his books got signed to be adapted into a major motion picture. From our small mountain town, my dad had also graced the worldly stage of fame. That was the truth I tried to hide from everyone who guessed at the relation between my last name and my parents. Although I was bred from storytelling royalty, I wanted—needed—to be able to develop my own name.

A name that my own mother seemed to be ready to disregard in her new love life adventure. A name that she had abandoned when she walked out the door. A name that I sometimes hid from, too, in an effort to disassociate with the heartbreak it came with.

I sat down on the edge of my bed, eyes scanning and rescanning the invitation.

"Mug-ger!" Brynn sang out as she crossed the doorway, stopping to wiggle my lanyard out of the lock. "It's not like you to leave our door open to strangers."

My keys landed beside me with a plop, and I jumped at the noise.

"Sorry," I mumbled, folding up the invitation and gently placing it back into the envelope.

"Hey," Brynn said. She stopped in front of my bed and tilted her head nearly sideways. The pencils stuffed in her bun threatened to fall. "Are you okay?"

I nodded, my thumb continuing to roam back and forth over the envelope. "I'm good."

I didn't look up at her, but the fact that she remained in front of me told me she didn't buy it. "Okay," she finally said.

That was one of the best things about living with Brynn: she rarely asked follow-up questions.

She set her backpack down on her desk and pulled out her laptop to start her homework. I got up and placed the invitation on the top shelf of my own desk, out of sight.

Matt was wrong, so wrong about me. For someone who apparently looked like she had no feelings, I wished in that moment that he was right and that I didn't feel a thing. Instead, I felt everything.

Chapter Six

"I've been thinking," Matt said as we sat at the same table in the back of The House the next night.

"That's a first," I said, sipping from my mug. The retort came out shorter than I meant for it to, and I'm sure he did do a lot of thinking in his spare time, but I couldn't help it. I was irritated. The invitation stashed on my desk had been eating at my every waking thought. Last night it even managed to seep into my dreams, feeling like something out of Harry Potter's nightmares. Dream Ember had been sitting in my dad's living room back home in Blowing Rock, curled up in the armchair with a book in my lap, when the windows and doors all burst and in came a flood of pink envelopes, slicing through the air and across my cheeks. When I woke this morning, it wasn't blood from the dream's paper cuts that dampened my face. It was tears.

"Rude," said Matt.

I said nothing, so he continued.

"I've been thinking about how Lena and Wesley should come back together throughout the story, but I think we need to spend some time figuring out their past and what scenes we want to highlight in flashback."

I nodded. Between pink envelopes and my Modernism class this morning, I had been dwelling on how to plot out this story from the snippets we strung together for pitch night. "I think that's the best way to start too."

Matt beamed. "Look at that. We finally agree on something."

I ignored him again and pulled out my notebook from the bag at my feet. "Lena and Wesley are childhood friends." I took notes as I spoke. "Where did they meet?"

"Summer camp," Matt said without hesitation.

I looked up at him. "Looks like all that thinking you've been doing is paying off."

"Funny," he said. "How old were they?"

I tapped my pen against my lip. "How old are they now?"

He contemplated for a moment. "Wesley is older than Lena. That adds dimension to their relationship. But I think they need to be in college."

"Lena is a freshman," I wrote. "And Wesley is a junior."

We sat at our table bouncing ideas and details off of one another for the time it took me to drink two cups of coffee and Matt to demolish eight, EIGHT, mini mousse cups.

"Why didn't you just get, like, two big ones?" I asked when he came back with his seventh and eighth.

"Because. The small ones are so cute."

By the time we had a rough sketch of where we were heading with our two characters that were becoming more real with each and every detail, it was well past eleven o'clock at night.

Matt let out a loud yawn and made a big show of closing his laptop. "I think we are done for the night. Do you want to work on the first scene when Wesley's mom calls Lena, and I'll start on the first flashback?"

"The call won't take me long," I said. I flipped the cover on my notebook and packed up my bag. "I can start on when she gets to the hospital for the first time too."

"Ah yes, well we can't all write with lightning speed like you," Matt said. "I probably won't be able to do much until the weekend.

We've got a game Friday." Matt was bent over his messenger bag, putting his laptop back in its place. He looked up, his grin looking more crooked from his sideways position. "It's a home game. Why don't you come and cheer me on?"

"Lacrosse, right?" I asked. The school had an outdoor complex at a different location for games like those. That much, I knew.

He nodded.

"You'll have cheerleaders rooting for you."

"Lacrosse doesn't have cheerleaders."

"Then you'll probably have loyal and adoring fans."

"All I'm hearing is excuses that will eventually subside."

"Not likely, but good try." I stood to leave, then paused. "So ... Matt."

He looked up again. "Yes?"

I bit my lip, contemplating if it was even worth asking the question. Curiosity won out. "How did you get into writing?"

He sat up and flicked an eyebrow at me that was playful and teasing. "You really want to know?"

I rolled my eyes and made to leave. "Not if it's going to be a tug-of-war game with you."

"Whoa, whoa, whoa," Matt said and gently put a hand on my wrist. "Sorry, I didn't mean to seem like I was playing games. Just surprised you actually asked."

I said nothing, but removed my hand from his touch and eased back into my seat, waiting for him to continue.

He sighed and ran a hand through his blond hair. "It's actually something I have always been into. I was really into stories as a kid. I read all the time. I even acted out stories with my younger brother when we were little. As I got older, I got into reading short fiction and anthologies. I liked to tinker with short stories, mostly because I knew I wouldn't have the attention span for longer works. I'm all about that instant gratification," he said and winked.

I rolled my eyes. "It would be more gratifying if you used spell-check every once in a while."

He laughed. "Regardless, I never really considered it a career path or anything. Just a hobby. But then I took a creative writing class my junior year of high school, and my teacher thought I was good at it and writing would be good for me, so she encouraged me to take extra classes at the community college before coming here."

"Wow," I breathed. "That was, um, very dedicated of you."

Matt harrumphed. "Thanks. Anyway, I stayed a business major because I figure it's more feasible to get a job with that degree, but I tacked on a few more classes this year to finish an English minor."

"I think you'd be surprised just how useful English can be in the job market," I said, defensive.

"Oh, I don't doubt that. My family, on the other hand, is a different story. But I don't mind. I genuinely like studying business and numbers. I just like words too." Matt smiled. "What about you? How did you get into it?"

My father is a best-selling author, and it has always been my dream to somehow amount to something in comparison. I squirmed in my seat and tried to sound nonchalant. "I liked to read, too, as a kid. Just kind of stuck, I guess."

Matt kept smiling. "That's cool. Glad you kept up with it and can carry this project for us. I'm definitely the weak link here."

A small voice wanted to tell him how much he was impressing me, but my pride quieted the noise in my head. "Don't sell yourself short," was all I managed instead.

"I can't," he said. "You're much shorter than me."

"And I'm going to head home now," I said, but I fought a smile as I stood up.

Matt rose as well, and I followed him out the door, which he held in a gentlemanly manner for me to pass.

"Thanks," I said and stuffed my hands in my pockets. The air was cold outside, and I wished I had thought to bring a jacket.

"Where are you parked?" Matt asked.

Leaving my hands in my pockets, I jutted my chin to point to the left of the door. "Back there."

"I'll walk you."

"No need," I said and started walking by myself. "See you later."

"See you, kitten," I heard Matt say from behind me with a teasing chuckle.

I ignored him. After I got to the driver side door and fumbled with the key in the lock, I pulled myself into the seat and cranked the heat as high as Bugsy's interior would allow. I looked up to see Matt still standing by the door, watching.

He didn't move from the cold to his own car until I started to pull away.

* * *

I changed into flannel pajama bottoms and a sweatshirt once I got back to my room and was sitting in bed, scrolling absently through my phone when it pinged. An email.

Brynn had long since passed out, and I had been careful not to wake her upon my return. I looked up to make sure that the alert hadn't disturbed her. It hadn't. I didn't think a fire alarm could wake her, though, honestly.

Regardless, as I clicked over to the school email tab on my phone, I was grateful for her slumber that hid the fact that there was one new unread message. From Matt. To me.

From: callahanm@sc.edu
To: owense@sc.edu
Date: Feb. 26, 2019 12:07 a.m.
Subject: SECRET PLAN FOR WORLD DOMINATION

Spoiler alert. Attached is not actually a plan for world domination, but the storyboard that I typed up for us.

You're welcome.
Matt

I eyed Brynn's sleeping form one more time, then suppressed a smirk as I turned my ringer to vibrate and hit reply.

From: owense@sc.edu
To: callahanm@sc.edu
Date: Feb. 26, 2019 12:09 a.m.
Subject: Re: SECRET PLAN FOR WORLD DOMINATION

I'm disappointed. I've been known to overthrow governments in my spare time.

Ember Owens
Creative Writing, Selwyn College
(828) 454-4962

My phone vibrated just a few seconds after hitting send with a text from an unknown number.

ember owens are you flirting with me?

My chest gave a little jolt. It had to be Matt.

Absolutely not.

God, I was definitely *not* flirting with Matt Callahan. I typed back immediately.

Goodnight, Matt. And stop texting me.

He wrote back moments later.

you should've deleted your # from your email

* * *

I didn't mean to go to the game Friday night. I really didn't. It was Brynn's fault, actually. It had taken her long enough, but I guess she finally got fed up with my reclusive nature. She had invited me out again Thursday, which I, as usual, politely declined. On Friday, however, her own formalities had evaporated when she stormed into the room, kicking open the door around 5:00 p.m.

Brynn: Get up.

Me: Why?

Brynn: It's dinner time.

Me: You know, I never understood the college tradition of early bird specials. We aren't really old enough to be eating at five o'clock in the afternoon.

Brynn: That's because college kid mealtimes run on an alternate universe. Lunch at 11:00 a.m., dinner at 5:00 p.m., and Cookout milkshakes close to midnight to fight the hangovers.

Me: Fascinating.

Brynn: Come on. Dinner. Then we are going to the lacrosse game.

And so, we went.

I'll be honest, I had been at Selwyn College for two and a half years, and this was the first time I had made it to the outdoor complex. It was surprisingly crowded.

Brynn found a few of her sorority sisters and waved at them when we made our way toward the bleachers, moving to find seats close to them. I managed a tight-lipped smile and trailed her path as she weaved between the cluster of legs and feet.

"Hey!" Brynn said as she climbed a chair to sit one row higher in the empty pair of seats.

"Hi, Brynn. And Ember! Good to see you," Brynn's sister Katie said to me as I followed her. I had freshman English class with Katie our first semester, so I was closest with her out of the trio we had joined. I only ever saw Mia or Skylar in rare encounters, like this one, where I was the tagalong friend.

"Hey, guys," I said.

"How much did Brynn bully you to come here tonight?" Mia asked with a laugh that sounded fake.

"Terribly."

"Did not," Brynn whined.

"You'll be glad you came, Ember," Skylar said. "We should have this game in the bag. Callahan has been on fire recently, and this team never beats us."

My stomach flipped at hearing his name, then immediately sank as I cataloged my reaction. I chalked it up to surprise at hearing of him outside of our class and assignment. I could almost pretend I had forgotten that he had another persona, the *lacrosse player.*

But I hadn't forgotten. I knew I would see him tonight, but I felt a bit more at ease when I took in our seats, at the back of the riser, away from the grass field. He wouldn't see me and wouldn't know I had come after he asked me to. He couldn't, because that would mean he had some sort of power, which he didn't.

I mentally groaned. I was going to kill Brynn.

"Hey, ladies," a voice behind us crooned. A loud stomping of feet making their way down the bleachers followed closely behind.

I looked up to see a guy in an overly large hoodie clambering toward us.

"Hi, Kyle!" Mia said in a voice that rang an octave higher than when she last spoke.

"How's it going?" the guy, Kyle, asked as he sat down right beside Brynn. Mia turned away from the two of them.

"Better now," Brynn said and nudged his side with her elbow. Envy flared for a brief second inside me at how smooth she could be.

"Have you ever met my roommate?" Brynn asked. "Kyle, this is Ember."

He stuck his arm around her back, holding out his hand for me to shake it. "I don't think so. It's nice to meet you."

"Likewise," I said with a thin smile and shook his hand briefly before folding my arms around my center and looking intently at the field.

Music blasted and each team welcomed on their starters, Matt being the last player to run out on the grass for our school. The crowd was already roaring, and if it were possible, the noise grew for him. I guess this meant he was good. Brynn nudged me hard in the side with her elbow and I clapped too.

I didn't know much about the ins and outs of the game, but it was hard to deny: Matt *was* good. Really good. Several of the players on the grass rotated on and off the sidelines; however, Matt stayed on for the majority of the game. He scored half of the points for Selwyn himself.

The buzzer sounded to signal halftime, and I looked up at the scoreboard. We already had a four-point lead. Our team cheered as the announcer called out the current scores. Several of the players jogged along the student section where we sat, waving their arms and encouraging the crowd. Brynn cupped her hands around her mouth to holler her approval. I surprised myself and raised my arms above my head to clap.

Matt was the last player in the line of athletes to rile the crowd. Even from my seat in the sky, I saw him scanning the rows and I immediately dropped my arms. He found me though, and a smile consumed his face.

He wiped the sweat from his brow and clapped twice before pointing directly at me. I kept my arms locked firmly by my side. He held his smile as he took his seat beside his teammates.

Skylar, Mia, Katie, and even Kyle looked at one another, then over at me. I shrugged at their bewildered expressions.

"You're friends with Matt?" Katie asked, a note of awe laced in her words.

"'Friends' is a strong word," I said and briefly wondered what constituted the label of *friendship*. We certainly spent time together, and had conversations about things, like ... words. "We are writing partners for class."

"Matt is a writer?" Skylar asked, incredulous. "I thought he was a business major."

I didn't bother to explain to her because the truth was, I was just as lost as she looked when it came to Matt Callahan. Watching him play tonight—seeing his fierce skill and drive, his uncanny ability to focus on nothing but the ball and net in front of him—showed me yet another side to him. The image I had in my head of the person I thought him to be was dissolving the more time I spent around him.

It almost pained me to admit to myself, but I realized that I didn't know Matt at all.

Chapter Seven

The next morning was Saturday, and I didn't wake up until well past ten o'clock in the morning. Brynn was already gone when I finally let the sunrays pry my lids open. She had a retreat, I remembered, with her sorority, which meant I could raid her stash of toaster pastries and not have to leave the sanctuary of our room until at least late afternoon.

I got up, got dressed, brushed my teeth, and pulled my hair into a high bun. Pulling out my reading glasses from my desk drawer, I sat down at the wooden desk and fired up my laptop, determined to finish the hospital scene I started late last night after the lacrosse game … that blasted game.

I shook my head and flexed my fingers before setting them against the keyboard. My rhythm was slow and staggering as I started, but I didn't let myself stop until I filled at least a page of text, even knowing half would be deleted later. I was finding it easier to spill words onto the page the more time I spent thinking about Lena and Wesley and, coincidentally, the more times I met with Matt.

I wrote and rewrote my opening scenes until around noon when my phone chirped from its charger at the head of my bed. I pushed away from my desk to grab it.

seems like you're a lucky charm. now you have to come to all
the games

The text still had no name attached to the number. Attaching
Matt's contact to the message stream we had growing made the
whole thing seem permanent in a way I didn't think necessary.

I typed back quickly.

Word on the street is you don't need any luck.

My phone pinged again.

so you've been talking about me

I rolled my eyes for no one to see.

Listening to the gossip.

i will take it. wanna meet up tonight and go over what we
have so far?

His next message came a heartbeat later.

since im assuming you are probably almost done with
your section

I glanced over at my laptop, black text blurring on the white
backdrop. I was close to being finished. For a first draft, anyway.

I wrote back:

Sure.

I swiveled my chair and pushed myself back across the room to
anchor in front of the desk once again. I just started scanning my
pages from the top when my phone rang. I tilted my head toward
the ceiling and closed my eyes. Matt refused to stay out of my head.

I got out of my chair to answer his call and stopped, my hand
hovering inches from the screen. The caller ID read Ethan Owens.

It rang once more, and I bit my lip. Had my dad finally convinced
my brother to call and break the news to me about his divorce? I'll
admit, I hadn't given his whole situation much thought over the last
few days, and I felt a little guilty just now recalling it. But it's not
like he had been giving me much to work with.

The phone rang again and my stomach flipped. What if
something happened to Dad? Again ...

I snatched the phone, jerking it from the charger to answer it
before it went to voicemail.

"What's wrong?" I asked, almost in a panic.

There was a pause on the other end of the line. "Nothing," my brother said slowly. "Are you expecting something to be?"

I let out a breath. "I thought maybe something was up with Dad." I had been there the last time something terrible had happened, in the midst of the sleep-deprived, delusional stupor he had sunk into right after Mom left. It hadn't happened again since, but every time the phone rang, that memory still haunted the back of my mind.

"You haven't called since you've been home," I said to Ethan. It came out more accusatory than I intended.

"Good to hear from you, too, sis." He sighed deeply on the line. "You have a phone, too, you know. You could've always called me if you wanted to talk."

"I didn't need to. I'm fine," I lied.

"Okay," he said and nothing else.

I started pacing the length of my room. "So ... how are you?"

I imagined him raking a hand through his hair, the way he usually did whenever he got tense. "To tell you the truth, I've been better, Ember."

I stopped walking. "I can only imagine," I said in a voice that had lost its edge.

Silence congealed between us, the heavy emptiness speaking volumes.

"Did you ..." Ethan started, then cleared his voice. "Did you get something from Mom?"

I clenched my teeth. "Yeah. You?"

"Yeah," he said. "Are you going?"

"It's in California," I said. Why did he even need to ask? Unless ... "Wait, are you?"

He was quiet before saying, "She said she would pay for the flight."

"You talked to her?" My voice climbed.

It was weird. It didn't take long for my father to forgive her after everything, and he had always encouraged us to reach back out to her. *After all, she is your mother,* he would say. My brother and I were on the same side, firm in our belief that no, she wasn't. She had given up that right. Perhaps my grudge was stronger than Ethan's, because here he was, ready to go out and celebrate her marriage to another man. Something someone whole and healed might do. I couldn't believe it.

"Ember ..." he said in an awful condescending tone I immediately cringed at.

"No," I said.

"You don't understand."

"Don't even talk to me about this. I'm not going."

"Why not?"

I deviated. "Why haven't you called me?" I asked, hating that I couldn't hide the hurt echoing in my voice.

He paused. "I couldn't."

You could have, I thought. *You just didn't.*

"So, you obviously weren't planning on telling me about Hallie," I started. "And you didn't tell me that you have been talking to *her*—"

"I'm calling you now, aren't I?" Ethan asked, but I could hear his usual calm demeanor crackling.

It's too late.

At the very least, Ethan and I always had each other's backs. We fought, and we could throw a cold shoulder like no one else, but he was my brother. We were a team, of sorts.

But when I realized just how firmly rooted Ethan and I were on opposing sides, the loneliness that came with that clarity stripped my insides raw in what felt like a wave of fresh abandonment. Ethan had jumped ship—or, in this case, was planning on taking a plane without me—leaving me desolate.

I snapped, feeling a small, wet weight against the back of my eyes. "You're right. Maybe I don't understand. I don't understand how you could choose to support a woman who walked out of our lives years ago, let alone walking away from your marriage—"

"It's not your life!" Ethan's voice flared. "Dammit, it's mine, and this is another reason why I didn't call you. Because I knew you would find a way to make it all about you, just like you always do!"

Hot anger roared in my chest, but it was quickly overtaken by pain. His words drew tiny cuts with their icy edges. I clamped my mouth shut, fearful of saying anything more that I would regret.

Ethan cursed under his breath and then regained a forced calmness in his tone. "I just called to ask if you were thinking about going to the wedding. I did not call you to talk about Hallie." His voice broke on her name.

My voice was low when it finally crawled back out of my tightened throat. "I'm not going."

A dull hum droned between us before he said, "Fine. That's all I needed to know."

"Okay."

I kept my phone by my ear a few seconds longer, even after I heard the telltale click from his side. When I drew my phone away from my face, eyes stinging, there was a message on the lock screen.

> the house?

I slumped to the floor and typed back.

> Your place.

I didn't wait for the response from Matt before hurling my phone across the room and letting the tears escape from behind my pressed eyelids.

*＊＊

Stupid, stupid, stupid, stupid. I had been so stupid to suggest that we meet up at Matt's apartment tonight. APARTMENT. Of course he lived in an apartment and not in the dorms because of course his living space had to be just another reminder of how different we were. Living in an apartment meant he was beating me at adulting, and that pissed me off.

I was so angry after Ethan's call, and I needed out. I didn't want to take that negative energy to The House to taint my oasis. And knowing Matt's normal quip, his place was the first thing that came to mind.

"You're an idiot," I mumbled to myself as I idled on the curb outside of his complex.

I picked up my phone from the cupholder and slid the bar to unlock it. My lock screen of the Blowing Rock mountains was replaced by the text that Matt had sent with his address and the meetup time.

I glanced at the clock on Bugsy's dash. 7:58 p.m. I could sit and twiddle my thumbs for the next two minutes, calculating a single-minute walk to locate his door so that I could casually arrive at 8:01, but I thought better of it because if I sat any longer, I'm pretty sure I would just speed away from the curb and claim some sort of stomach bug.

I groaned and pulled the key out of the ignition.

Much to my disappointment, it didn't take long to find his door. It had a bumper sticker that read *Selwyn Dad* just above the handle. I confirmed the number and took a breath before knocking.

"One sec," a muffled voice called from behind the door.

I tugged the sleeves of my loose, tan sweater over my hands.

The door swung wide open, and I took a step back. "You're not Matt." The words slipped out of my mouth before I could stop them.

The stranger chuckled. "Quite right. I'm far more dashing."

His accent was almost as strong as the muscles cording his forearms. He had them crossed in front of his impressive chest as he leaned against the doorframe. He had dark hair and dark eyes to match. Much darker than Matt's. Matt's were more of a deep honey color.

"You're from the United Kingdom?"

He nodded. "London, to be exact."

"And somehow you ended up in Charlotte."

"Swimming," he grinned.

That explained the shoulders.

I rocked on the balls of my feet once before sticking out my hand. "I'm Ember Owens."

His grip was sure as he shook my hand. "Bastian Taylor, but everyone calls me Bash. The man said he was expecting an Owens to come by." He stepped aside and motioned for me to enter the apartment. "He should be just about out of the shower. Practice ran late."

I nodded and stepped through the doorway into the living room. I was immediately floored. Not only was the space spotless and orderly, but the far wall that held the television was lined with shelves filled to the brim with books upon books upon books.

"Can I get you anything to drink?" Bash asked from the kitchen beyond the library threshold.

"I wouldn't mind a water," I said, my tongue suddenly dry.

"Are you sure you don't want anything stronger?" Bash's tone was light. "After all, this is Matthew Callahan."

I let out a laugh and my shoulders eased. "I'm pretty sure the saying goes, 'write drunk, edit sober.'" I tapped the strap of my backpack at my shoulder. "Edits tonight."

"Suit yourself," Bash said from the fridge. He placed a cold water bottle on the counter for me and popped the metal top on a beer for himself.

I took the water and sat down at the small table adjoining the kitchen, twisting the top.

A door slammed shut, and Matt came padding into the kitchen with his laptop tucked under his arm. He had on gray sweatpants that hung low on his hips and a plain white T-shirt. His hair was wet.

"What's up, kitten?" he asked as if it were the most normal thing in the world for me to be perched awkwardly on his kitchen seat.

And because of said awkwardness, I couldn't even come up with a fast enough retort to the nickname that was apparently not going to disappear anytime soon. "Why the 'Dad' sticker on your door?" I asked and took a sip of water.

"I collect them," Matt said with zero other explanation as he fumbled in the fridge a few seconds more. Long enough for Bash to dramatically sigh.

"Well, the night is young, friends, and I have some *Call of Duty* to catch up on. Have fun with your ... edits." Bash dropped a wink at me as he moved through the kitchen back, presumably, to his room.

I resisted the urge to roll my eyes. It's almost like they were the same person. The same arrogant, cocky—

"Did you bring your laptop?" Matt asked. He sat at the opposite end of the table and fired his up.

"Um, yeah." I tugged the zipper of my bag open and wiggled mine free from the clutch of my notebooks.

"How much did you get through?" Matt's voice was unusually short. I looked up from the top of my screen. His eyebrows were drawn close, eyes narrowed.

I ignored his question. "Is everything okay?"

He looked up at me. The hardness in his expression melted slightly, only to be replaced with amusement. "Did you just ask me about my feelings?"

My own face soured. "Forget it."

Matt's laugh was clipped as he shook his damp hair from his forehead. "I'm fine. Just a few things on my mind. Don't you worry your pretty little head about it."

"Wasn't going to." I didn't lift my gaze from my screen as I spoke. "I got through Lena getting to the hospital, right before she sees Wesley for the first time again."

"Guess you win. All I got through was the first flashback at camp." He paused and reached across the table to pluck my laptop away from me.

"Hey!"

"Is for horses," he said and replaced the empty space he created with his own computer. The first part of his story was pulled up on a Word document.

I glowered. "You could've just emailed it to me."

He waved me off with one hand and adjusted the screen on my laptop in front of him with the other. "Tell me what you think, then we can work on blending them together."

I gave in and scanned the brief scene over and over and over again, biding time until Matt's eyes quit flitting back and forth over my words. What did I think?

Matt Callahan wasn't a bad writer. In just a few short paragraphs I caught glimpses of preteen Lena and Wesley; their conversations were every bit as honest as they were awkward, from Wesley's charismatic introduction to Lena's interior monologue, worried about how she had just used the word *wiener* in front of a boy. It was playful and innocent, and I was left feeling nostalgic for this past encounter that wasn't even mine.

"Thoughts?" Matt interrupted.

How could this dude, this frat boy, this jock, be capable of writing something so ... sweet?

"It's good."

He snorted. "Good? That's all I get?"

I glanced back at his scene. "You need to work on formatting your dialogue correctly."

He nodded, taking in the critique better than I had meant for him to. "Noted."

I was quiet as he scanned my pages once more. "Well?" I finally probed.

"It's good."

I felt a surge of annoyance, one that he had likely felt as well at my own lack of effusive praise.

"Hell, Ember it's nearly perfect. I didn't know you could write with such ... emotion."

My annoyance flared. "Why would you think I couldn't?"

Matt opened his mouth to answer.

"You know what, don't answer that." After Ethan's phone call, I really wasn't in the mood for any other critiques on my personal character. "Just remember that we don't really know each other, so you're not really in the position to be making any judgments."

He tilted his head at me. "You're right." He closed my laptop and pushed it back toward me. "Do you want to get to know each other?"

"What is that supposed to mean?"

Matt sighed. "Would you like to get to know each other? For what it's worth, I would like to get to know you, but you've got this wall stacked a mile high around you. I can see it there now, in your eyes."

I slid my gaze away from his. For a girl who claimed to be good with words, I was, yet again around Matt, dumbstruck. "I don't know," I finally whispered, shocked at the honesty of that admission.

Matt leaned back in his seat and crossed his arms. "Well, that's not a no ... Mind if I try something?"

I looked up and wished I had an intelligent, or funny, or flirty, or witty—or any!—retort, then looked away again when nothing materialized but frustration.

"How about you tell me your favorite books?"

I stared at him, fairly impressed by both his effortless discourse and the intuitive question that had just fallen so seamlessly from his lips. He held my gaze while I perched nervously on the edge of my chair.

I finally broke the silence. "Classic or contemporary?"

He didn't miss a beat. "Both, but contemporary first. Please don't bore me to death."

"Well, *Harry Potter* for sure then." My lips curled into a smile on their own account.

"Of course, they're a staple. What else?"

"Um," I said, sliding back in my seat. "*Looking for Alaska* by John Green. *The Perks of Being a Wallflower* by Stephen Chbosky. *Thirteen Reasons Why* by Jay Asher."

"Also excellent choices."

I was surprised that he seemed to recognize all of those titles. "I pretty much read anything young adult," I said.

"I'm gathering that."

"What about you?"

"You didn't tell me your favorite classics."

I paused, tugging at the sleeves of my sweater. "Honestly?"

"No. Lie to me."

I bit my lip. "I really enjoyed *The Great Gatsby*."

He cocked his head. "That's a love story."

"A failed love story. With very flawed characters."

"But still a love story."

"I suppose so." I opened my water bottle. "What about you? What are your favorite books?"

"Well …" Matt started, "I have to say that I'm pretty loyal to the *Game of Thrones* series."

I raised an eyebrow and capped my drink, thinking of the numerous pages that comprised those books. "That's quite the reading commitment."

"I can be incredibly committed … in all aspects of life." Matt dropped a sly wink.

"Reading a book is a short-term commitment," I countered, then considered, "which you know, might just be your specialty … in all aspects of life."

Matt chuckled. "A commitment is a commitment, no matter the duration. The level of devotion is the same."

Was he still talking about books, or had we both gotten on the same page of his back-to-back relationships he tended to find himself in? "So … do you currently have a girlfriend?"

If he was at all shocked at the personal question, he didn't let it show on his carefree facade. "Not at the moment. Why, want the job?"

"When was your last relationship?"

He chuckled. "What are you, a journalist? Spy?"

"Curious intellectual that thinks it's only fair that if you are going to be soul searching me, I should know a little about you."

He paused. "Fair enough." He rapped his knuckles against the table before responding. "I broke up with my last girlfriend right after school started this year. We dated for the summer, but I didn't see the relationship going any further than that."

"I bet she also went back to school in the fall; easy reason to close that chapter."

Matt grinned. "Guilty as charged. She did move back to school, but if I thought we were actually compatible longer term, I would've tried to make it work. She's only in South Carolina."

I rolled my eyes. "I'm sure she's nursing her broken heart, wondering how she might never find another man like you."

"Don't worry. Snapchat tells me she moved on rather quickly to someone with better hair. Bruised the ego a bit ... I'm still recovering from the blow." Matt winked.

He was quiet a moment before continuing, his tone suddenly somber. "You know, a lot of where we are going with this story is hitting pretty close to home. Not from that last relationship, though. It was a ... different one. It hasn't been as easy as I thought it would be reliving some of those memories."

He looked up at me then, the small smile on his face sad.

"I'm sorry," I said. I wasn't expecting that sort of confession.

Matt seemed to be deliberating something. He slowly stretched his neck from side to side, but then his expression shifted, reverting back to his casual mask. "But what would our dear friend Oliver Van Dam say? At the least, I fit the cliché of being a tortured artist."

"And you're therapeutically writing about it."

"Yeah," Matt nodded. "You can't change it, so what else can you do?"

**

I left shortly after that conversation, despite Matt's offer to binge-watch all eight *Harry Potter* movies. It took three rounds of polite declination and acute justification. Marathons like that took planning, including time management, scheduled bathroom breaks, and snacks. Lots of snacks. And no, his half empty bag of spicy hot cheese crunches did not count as sufficient snacks. He asked.

I got home just after ten o'clock. My phone buzzed in my pocket as I stepped into my darkened room. I flicked on the lamp and tucked my bag under my desk before pulling out my phone.

> in my quest of searching for your soul, i shouldve asked. do you have a boyfriend?

I flopped down on my bed.

> Yes. His name is Jem.

Fake boyfriend? Check. I just hoped Cassandra Clare wouldn't mind me borrowing one of her characters for my fake relationship.

> jem carstairs? i know him. nice guy but very fictional

Fake boyfriend? Busted. How had Matt read *Clockwork Angel*?

> You got me.

> if there is not a real guy, you should go out on a date with me

My stomach clenched.

> Not happening.

I couldn't go on a date with Matt. I didn't mingle with his crowd, sporty or frat. I wouldn't even know how to do it.

> why not

> I'm very busy.

> busy working on a project that happens to involve seeing me on the regular

This man was impossible. I kicked off my shoes before sending my text.

> I'm going to sleep. Goodnight.

I shimmied out of my clothes and into pajamas as his next message came through.

> do you know why I like the word goodnight so much

I clicked off my desk lamp and tucked myself under my covers, the blue light from my phone casting shadows on my wall.

> There is absolutely no telling.

His next message came through after a minute longer.

> i like knowing that im the last thing you are thinking about before you go to bed

I didn't respond, but I would be damned if he wasn't exactly right.

Chapter Eight

Brynn came home from her retreat Sunday evening, slung her bag onto her bed, and announced, "My partner is useless."

I was reading in my bed, buried underneath a cavern of pillows from both my bed and hers. I peered through my reading glasses at Brynn as she rummaged in her backpack. My favorite hoodie was pulled over my chin, so I wiggled around it to say, "Good to see you too."

She pulled out her laptop and plopped down on her bed. (She didn't say anything about her missing pillows.) "I told her that I was going to be out of town for the weekend and to email me her first scene so that I could put the two together. And what do I have?" She flipped her laptop around to show me her inbox and seethed. "Nothing."

"I'm sorry," I said and tucked my chin back into my cove.

"Ugh. This contest will be the death of me."

"A slow, painful death," I agreed as I turned the page of my book.

"Your story isn't going much better?" Brynn asked. She leaned back against the wall and shimmied the laptop into place across her legs.

"Hmm?" I mumbled absentmindedly.

Brynn groaned. "Your story, Ember. Your story with Matt. How is that coming along?"

"Oh," I said and turned another page. "It's going."

"That's it?"

"What's it?"

"That's all I get? 'It's going'?"

"Well, our first few scenes seem okay."

"Yeah, I'm sure they are. But what is Matt like to work with? As bad as Holly?"

I turned another page to finish the chapter I was on. "He's all right."

"I thought you didn't like him."

"He's useful."

"More so than Holly?"

"Apparently."

"Damn. I should've traded you partners."

I looked up at Brynn again over my glasses but said nothing. She was hunched over her laptop, punching the keys rapid fire. Come to think of it, my partner owed me an email. After I had fired another page over to him this morning, he said he would compile everything we had written so far and get the whole thing back to me tonight.

I fished my phone out from underneath my pillow to refresh my email inbox. Nothing new.

I tabbed over to shoot him a text, asking about the story. His response came a heartbeat later.

just finishing it up, kitten

"What are you smiling at?" Brynn asked.

I startled, dropping my phone square on my chin. "Shit!"

"Who are you texting?" she pressed.

"No one." I didn't want to think about why that was my immediate response and what that might mean.

Brynn looked up at me over the rim of her laptop and smirked. "Liar."

**

I got to class my usual fifteen minutes early and sat in my usual seat in the back of the empty room. I just started pulling out my notebook and pens when the door creaked open again. Literally creaked. This building was ancient.

Matt poked his head around the off-white door. "Owens."

I did a double take. "What are you doing here?"

He stepped inside and gently shut the door behind him, skateboard tucked firmly under his armpit. "I happen to be in this class."

I rolled my eyes and wondered if it was possible to develop some sort of eyeball dysfunction from the chronic eye-rolling I seemed to do around Matt. "I *know* you're in this class, but you're never here on time."

He grinned and strode across the room, his long legs quickly eating up the space between us. "Practice ended early tonight." He leaned his skateboard on the wall behind me before sitting down next to me.

"What are you doing?" I asked, suddenly tense.

He leaned down to his bag to pull out his laptop. "Um. Sitting?"

"You don't usually sit over here." No one usually sat back here.

He snorted. "Am I not allowed to sit here or something?"

"I mean, you can." Except for the fact that he was breaking the code of unassigned assigned seating.

"Hey, Ember?"

"Yes?"

His expression around his mouth was playful, but his brown eyes were serious when he said, "Go out with me."

My whole body froze. He wasn't being sincere, was he? I tried to blow it off. "Yeah, that would be a negative. Good one, though."

"Why not?"

"Why would you even want to?"

"Because."

"That's not an answer."

"Because, I meant what I said."

"You say a lot of things."

He shifted in his seat, turning his whole body toward me. "I want to know more about you."

His relentless eye contact was unnerving. I tucked my legs underneath my seat. "I'm sure you say that to all the girls."

His lips tightened, and his expression wavered just a fraction, enough to make me think that his question wasn't entirely a joke to him. The moment flitted away, and he nodded to himself before smiling again. "Damn. I was hoping the rejection would hurt less in person."

I opened my mouth to stutter something unintelligent I'm sure, but I was granted a reprieve by the arrival of Professor Pollard.

"Good evening, Ember. Matt," Pollard said and set his bag on the desk at the front of the room. "You're early."

"Seems like I've got an influential partner." Matt grinned and nudged my heel with his toe. I scooted my feet away, but not before glancing down at our legs underneath the desk. Tonight, Matt's socks were black with red hearts on them.

The clock ticked closer to 6:00 p.m. and more students came into the classroom. I tried to focus on the whiteboard at the front of the classroom, but I couldn't shake the hurt I had seen in Matt's dark eyes. For argument's sake, I'll pretend he wasn't joking when he asked me out. But what was he getting at? He said he wanted to go on a date, but if I said yes, what happened after that?

He didn't honestly think I could *date* him, right? He was a player, like he had all but claimed to be, and I didn't want to be played. Above all, I didn't want to be the next one he got close to … then left. Like it was a challenge or something.

Brynn came in next with Spencer trailing behind her. She paused when she saw Matt sitting beside me in the usually vacant seat and threw the back of her hand against Spencer's chest to stop him too.

Matt looked up at them and waved, big and goofy. Spencer's smile thinned. I suddenly got very interested in the empty pages of my notebook.

"Hi, *friends*," Brynn said, emphasizing the plurality.

"Brynn Song. You look beautiful this evening. How have you been?" Matt asked with a charisma I could almost see oozing from his words.

"Great!" Brynn said. Her smile was radiant, and I don't know why, but I kind of wanted to punch her for it. "How is your story coming along with Ember?"

Matt swung his arm over the back of my chair. "So far so good. What about yours?"

Brynn and Matt fell into easy conversation, leaving Spencer to turn to the front of the room and me to look away. It was hard to place the feeling, but I think the churning in my stomach could have been something close to jealousy.

My phone vibrated from my pocket, and I leaned over to check it, shielding it from Matt's vision with my body. It was a text from Spencer.

> Since when does Matt Callahan sit in our corner?? What's
> going on with you and lover boy??

I peeked at the back of Spencer's red hair and tapped my phone nervously after I replied:

> Nothing.

The clock tower outside of our classroom chimed, and Pollard called the class to order, thankfully.

"Good evening, folks. Just a bit of housekeeping to start things off. The first drafts of your stories will be due a week from today. If the endings aren't completely coherent by then, just give us an outline of how you will wrap it up. The following week will be workshop, where you will give and receive feedback to revise for the second draft. But for tonight, I figured that a good way to check in and touch base on all of your stories would be to stand up and read them in front of the class."

I sank in my seat, and my shoulder brushed the edge of Matt's hand that was still lounging on the back of my chair. He shifted beside me and dropped his arm. I flicked my eyes toward his and found an alarming amount of concern instead of his usual playful gaze. I presumed it was due to the beginning of our story, which was rough at best and not ready for a public reading whatsoever.

"Any objections?" Pollard asked.

Tons. Several scenes full, to be exact.

If anyone else in the class shared a similar sentiment, no one piped up aside from the voice in my head.

"Great," Pollard said. "Talk amongst yourselves for a minute and figure out how you would like to present your reading. This is very informal. No pressure from anyone here, least of all myself. I am very aware that your opening scenes are in early drafts, but we will follow your reading with a quick, informal critique on character and premise that will hopefully help you all shape your stories as you continue to move forward."

He stepped away from the podium and walked to sit at the back of the room, leaving the front of the class vacant. "Whoever is ready first, go ahead and take the lead. Just jump up when you are set."

Matt knocked his knee against mine from under the table. "Do you mind if I read this one?"

"Uh, yeah, I guess. That's fine." I paused. "Why?"

He grinned. "Because the prof just said he's going easy on us. If I read now, I am exempt from a later reading where he might not be so lenient." He tapped his finger to his temple. "Always thinking."

I was mildly impressed, but I tried not to let it show. He really was kind of smart. "Go right ahead, slacker."

Matt dropped a wink at me before standing, lugging his laptop with him.

"Matt, wonderful," Pollard said and jotted a note on his paper in front of him.

Matt set his laptop down against the podium. His eyebrows scrunched together, and his shoulders leaned toward the screen as he clicked at the mouse pad. "All right guys, this is the beginning of the story that Ember," he gestured toward me without looking up, "and I have been working on. It's still in its early stages, so go easy on it. And if you don't like it, well, she wrote most of it so far."

The class chuckled unanimously while I glared at the top of his head.

"And it has no title, so we are really batting a thousand," he added as an afterthought, which was met with more laughter. His eyes trained on the screen as he read aloud. *"When I got the call that Wesley had been in an accident, it felt as if a fuse had been relit inside of me and something heavy detonated, sinking to the bottom of my gut ..."*

I don't know what it was. I mean, partly it was weird I guess because I had never heard Matt read out loud. And it was strange to hear my opening words falling off of his tongue as he spoke. No, falling wasn't the right word. It was like the sentences were dancing, with a musical lilt as they swayed, and Matt was reading with a gentle voice that I never knew he had. The way he spoke, the way he perfectly paced each breath and line, it wasn't like any story I had ever heard be read. It was like he was reading poetry.

I didn't know my words could sound like that.

I didn't know *Matt* could sound like that.

I didn't realize until after the scenes were finished and the class erupted in applause that I was leaning forward in my seat, my palms red from having gripped the edge of the desk so hard, trying to get closer to the story. His story. Our story.

Matt lifted his eyes from his computer screen and closed it, a small smile on his face. His gaze met mine, and his eyes crinkled to echo the upward tug on his lips as he came to sit back down. He pulled out the chair beside me and stowed his laptop neatly away, resuming his laid-back position in his seat. Charlie was the next student to make his way to the podium, and when he reached the front of the room, I felt the heel of Matt's shoe come to rest against the toe of mine. I listened as Charlie started to read, but I didn't move away from Matt.

***

I was quiet on the drive to The Coffee House after class that night. It was Spencer's turn to drive and Brynn had yelled "Shotgun!" as soon as Pollard dismissed our class, so I was left sitting in the back of Spencer's minivan alone.

Brynn ordered the macaroons with her hot chocolate. Spencer changed up his order again, and what did he happen to try this week? Caramel latte. The same thing Matt ordered when we came here.

I mumbled a black coffee and a thanks to the guy at the register before following my friends to embellish my cup with cream.

"Seems like your new partnership is off to a good start," Spencer said while he waited beside me. The words were neutral, but it sounded like gravel between them, making conversation forced.

My hand twitched on the handle of the half-and-half dispenser, causing a little splash. I had already gone through a similar conversation with Brynn. I didn't want to relive an interrogation with Spencer, no matter how mild it may or may not be.

"Seems to be," I said casually. I picked up my doctored mug of coffee and led our group to the adjoining room.

"Hey, earth to Ember." Brynn's singsong tease carried from farther behind me. "Where are you going?"

Dammit. I walked right past the corner booth where Spencer, Brynn, and I usually sat. I was on autopilot to the discreet table in the back that Matt had picked both times we were here. "I'm sorry," I muttered. "I wasn't even thinking. Just walking."

"Daydreaming?" Spencer asked.

"Zoning out," I clipped and sat down. "Matt and I have, uh, met here before, to work."

"Wait," Spencer said and stopped walking. "This was where you two came to work?" Spencer's voice sank a volume level. "But this is where we always come."

"As does almost half the school," I said, but guilt nipped a nice little hole in my stomach. Spencer was right. Even though The House was public domain, it had become a ritual among our trio. I don't think Brynn or Spencer had ever come here unless it was the three of us together.

Spencer pressed past me and plopped in the booth. "How often have you come here with him?"

Why is he asking so many questions?

I bit my lip. "I don't know, twice?" I didn't mention anything about the night we worked in his apartment. Or the fact that Matt asked me out.

I wasn't ready to tell either of my friends about that exchange yet. Probably because they would both blow it up and make it mean something more than it did. Regardless, I had a feeling that information might have worsened Spencer's strange mood.

It was quiet among us, and I wish I had something to say that could ease the tension thickening the air.

"So ... both of your stories are really good so far," Brynn said, trying to lighten the mood.

"Why thanks, bud," Spencer drawled. "I was impressed with yours too. Your characters seem to fit both you and Holly."

Brynn ended up writing from the perspective of the detective, and Holly wrote from the accused killer.

"I'm glad you liked it," Brynn said. "It just started to come together last night if I'm being honest."

Spencer looked shocked. "Just last night? That's so unlike you."

"Yeah well, we can't all be like Ember and Matt. The dream team had theirs done before the weekend was even up."

"Color me impressed," Spencer said with zero inflection.

Spencer was the guy who was always the life of the party. There was rarely anything that could get him down, and I have only ever seen him angry exactly twice in the forever that I've known him. The first time was when the Mexican restaurant forgot his side of *queso* in his to-go order after he had just broken up with his boyfriend, whom he dated since middle school, when he was a sophomore. The second time was when the college changed the library closing time from two in the morning to midnight.

He wasn't anywhere close to those levels of upset, but the clip in his tone meant he was definitely peeved about something. And the gnawing in my gut and his intentional diversion of eye contact from mine told me that *something* probably had to do with me.

Chapter Nine

There was nothing exciting in my mailbox the next day, which was good. The arrival of last week's pink envelope had been enough to quench any remaining thirst for surprises.

I still hadn't RSVP'd.

Even though I doubted my mom really thought I would come, I knew I should still let her know that I wouldn't be at her wedding. However, the invitation remained on top of my desk, untouched.

After dropping my bag in my room and changing quickly into leggings and a T-shirt, I made my way to the gym to hopefully run off the funk I had been in since leaving The House last night.

I couldn't stop thinking about Spencer's strange mood and wondered what his problem was. He didn't like that I'd been at The House with Matt—that was clear—but I felt like there was more to it.

I opened the door to the gym. Brynn was already in there running, earbuds in. She waved to me from the treadmills.

"Hey," I said and pulled out my own earbuds. They were a tangled mess.

She jumped to the side of her treadmill to lean against the armrest, letting the belt continue to run without her. She took one earbud out and wrapped it around the back of her neck. "What's up?"

"Have you talked to Spencer?"

"Not since last night, no."

"After The House then? Did he text you or something?"

"Why?"

"I feel like he's mad at me."

Brynn jumped back on the treadmill, her feet slapping the belt in a slow, even rhythm. "Have you talked to him about it?"

My earbuds refused to unwind, so I gave up and dropped them beside my machine. "No."

"Well, wouldn't that be the most direct way to find out if he's mad at you? To ask him if he's mad at you?"

I set my time and pushed start. "You know, I really hate it when you battle with logic."

"Hmm," was her reply as she pushed her other earbud back in and kept running.

I clicked the speed on my treadmill up a notch.

A short time later, the door to the gym opened again, and laughter erupted from the open archway. I looked up to see a familiar face pull into a wide smile. It was Bash.

"Ember Owens!" he called and waved. "Long time no see."

I offered him a tight smile and a tilt of my chin in acknowledgment and prayed that Brynn hadn't heard him. Since Brynn didn't know I had been to Matt's apartment, I really didn't want to explain how I knew his roommate.

He dropped his gym bag next to my treadmill and leaned on the armrest. "How's it going?"

"Good," I said and copied Brynn's move and sidestepped to the ledge of the treadmill to let it keep going without me. "I don't think I've seen you in here before." I know I had never seen him in here before. I would have recognized those shoulders and accent when I had first run into him at Matt's place.

"Usually, I'm below in the pool or on the bikes." He shrugged. "Your man wanted me to come with him here today, though."

"He's not my man."

Bash grinned. "Funny that you knew exactly who I was talking about."

I flushed and felt a jolt on my treadmill as Brynn landed on the edge next to me.

"Who's your friend, Ember?" she asked as she pulled out her earbud again.

Bash didn't wait for my introduction. He held out his hand for her to shake it. "Bastian Taylor. It's a pleasure. You are?"

I'll admit it. Bash's smile was dazzling underneath his dark hair. Almost as gorgeous as the one Brynn threw back at him. "Brynn Song. You and Ember know each other?" she asked without looking at me.

Bash opened his mouth, but I quickly cut him off. "You're Matt's roommate, right?"

Bash looked back at me with curious eyes. My eyes silently pleaded with him to say no more.

"I am, indeed," he said slowly. The question of why I was denying knowing him remained locked behind his perfect smile.

Brynn shook his hand. "Well, it's nice to meet you, Bastian."

"Call me Bash." His smile was wide again and focused directly on her. I wished I could've started running again, but unfortunately Bash was still leaning on my machine.

The door opened again and in came the man himself.

"Matthew!" Bash turned and called him over. "It's about time you showed up!"

As an artist, I could appreciate beauty. Bash was the definition of tall, dark, and handsome with the body and accent to boot. I was caught off guard at my realization, though, that Matt seemed to be in a league of his own in comparison. Like, godlike gorgeous. I felt flushed. Even in his loose-fitting basketball shorts and a tank top, my bodily reaction to his entrance was embarrassing.

"I'm not late," Matt said and dropped his bag beside Bash's. "You're just early."

They did that secret guy handshake hug thing that all guys seem to innately know. Brynn used that time to elbow my ribs, dropping a not-so-discreet wink in my direction. I sighed and cut off my treadmill in case either one of us happened to accidentally step back on it and get swept off of our feet.

"Hey, Ember," Matt said, then paused. "I had no idea you were into running."

"Wow, thanks. Good to see you too."

He grinned at me before turning to Brynn. "Brynn, we meet again. Good work on your story so far."

"Thanks, I appreciate it. Yours seems to be coming along pretty well too."

"Thanks. Speaking of, we need to meet up again," he said, looking at me.

"Yeah, I guess so." God, I prayed he wouldn't suggest his apartment again. Not in front of Brynn. And after last night, I couldn't suggest The House either. "Um, what day are you thinking?"

"Thursday night? I think I'm going to stay in this week."

No clubbing this Thursday? The question "why" almost erupted from my mouth, but I bit my tongue. *I don't really care what he does*, I told myself. As I happen to always be free Thursday nights, I told him that I could make that work.

"Where do you want—"

"I'll text you." Then I mentally slapped myself because now Brynn knew that I had his number.

Matt didn't seem to be bothered by my abrupt interruption. "Sounds good, kitten. See you later, Brynn." He clapped Bash on the shoulder and picked up his bag, heading toward the weights.

"Kitten, eh?" Bash asked with a smug cross of his arms.

I rolled my eyes. "It won't go away."

"I like it," Brynn said.

I glared at her, but she seemed too enamored with the Brit in front of her to notice.

Said Brit was still smiling at Brynn. "Are you going out this week?" he asked.

Brynn shrugged, nonchalant. "Maybe. I haven't decided yet."

Bash cocked his head, ever so slightly. "Well, maybe I'll see you later then."

Did Brynn just blush? Was that an actual blush on her cheek? "Yeah. See you around, Bash."

He backed away from the both of us, waving, before turning to set up beside Matt.

With his back to us, Brynn groaned soft enough for just us to hear.

I stole the rare opportunity and teased her. "'See you around'? That's all the game you've got?"

"I know! I know. That was pathetic. But did you see that boy's biceps?"

She sighed, leaped across my treadmill, and fell right back into an easy rhythm running on hers. I looked forlornly at mine, wondering if it was really worth turning it back on with Matt in here now. It would be my luck to embarrass myself and wipe out or something stupendous of the like. I started to gather my things instead.

"Done already?" Brynn asked, still going strong.

"Yup."

"Okay. I'll see you back in the room then."

I started toward the door, but Brynn called me back.

"Ember ..."

"Yes?"

She smirked. "Now I know why you've been smiling at your texts."

***

I took Brynn's advice and resolved to talk to Spencer myself. I got back to the room and sent him a text instead of calling, though. At least I was trying ...

> Hey. You seemed a little off last night. Are you mad
> at me?

I sat down on my bed, still in my gym clothes, and all but twiddled my thumbs while I waited for Spencer to respond. I was about ready to give up staring at my phone and start staring at the walls instead when it pinged.

I was. I'm getting over it.

Uh-oh.

Do we need to talk about it?

His next text came in before I had even set my phone back down.

Probably. Come to my room.

Crap. I grabbed my keys on my way out the door.

Spencer lived on the floor above us. He moved into the library dorm for his senior year instead of staying in his previous dorm across the quad for the third year in a row. It worked great last semester. Spencer didn't have a roommate, so I crashed whenever I wanted, and we would huddle under a pile of fuzzy blankets to have a horror movie marathon. I hadn't had time yet to repeat the endeavor this semester. Or at least, I hadn't made the time. Especially not with this contest looming.

I climbed the stairs slowly and walked to his room at the end of the hallway. I knocked twice. After a few beats, he opened the door. It was dark inside, and he was wearing sweatpants.

"Were you sleeping?" I asked.

"Napping."

"Oh," I said. "Sorry."

"S'okay. Come in." He turned and crawled back into bed without checking to make sure I had followed him.

I shut the door behind us and flicked the desk lamp on before shimmying to sit at his feet, my back against the wall.

Spencer hugged a pillow to his chest and stared at me.

I stared back, not wanting, or really knowing how, to start this conversation.

Spencer finally broke the silence. "It honestly was really dumb."

"Your feelings are never dumb," I said automatically.

"No," he said. "But it was a pretty dumb reason to be mad."

"I'm sorry that Matt and I went to The House. I obviously wasn't thinking. You were right, that's our place."

Spencer shook his head and sat up in his bed. "It's not that you went *with* Matt." He paused. "I feel like an idiot for even saying this, but I was madder that you went *without* us. Without me, I guess."

I let the weight of his words sink in a bit longer. The unspoken truth between them hit me right between the eyes. I was with Brynn a lot. We lived together. But when was the last time I had made my friendship with Spencer a priority?

I realized I hadn't.

Spencer shook his head. "Like I said, that part was stupid, but I feel like we should talk about something else too."

I braced myself. "Okay."

He chewed his lip for a second, then sighed deeply. "I blame it on this stupid dream I had."

"Wait. What?"

He grumbled. "I had it at the beginning of the semester. About Matt Callahan."

I stifled my laugh. "What kind of dream?"

He glared at me. "The good kind."

"Oh."

"Yep. In this dream, Matt could not keep a girlfriend for long."

"That's not a dream. That's reality."

"Shush, I'm confessing."

"Sorry." I drew my knees up to my chin. "Continue."

"As I was saying," Spencer drawled, "in my dream, he was never able to stay in a relationship for long because he was never happy in one … because he's actually gay. He professed his undying love for me, and we rode off into the metaphorical sunset of my fantasies."

I waited a beat to make sure Spencer wasn't going to add any more details before saying carefully, "I don't want to be the dark cloud on your metaphorical sunset, but I really don't think Matt is gay."

He harrumphed. "I know that, Ember." He nudged my foot from under his blanket. "Especially after I saw the way he was looking at you in class."

Everything inside me silently screamed. "What are you talking about?"

"Oh, come on." Spencer looked exasperated. "The man is infatuated with you. I don't know what kind of witchcraft you worked on him at our innocent little café, but there's a reason Matt was sitting at your seat. And it's not just because you two are writing partners."

"Of course that's why he was sitting there!"

"Ember. Listen very closely to me, right now. I am a guy. I might play for a different team, but I still speak the rules of the game. And from what I witnessed yesterday, you've got a tough player on your hands."

"Well, we already knew that," I muttered. "But that doesn't mean he's interested in me."

"Sure it does. He knows you're single. He's moving in."

My gut twisted, and I thought back to our texts when he was asking me about my fictional boyfriend. "How do *you* know that *he* knows I'm single?"

Spencer chewed his lip again. "He might have asked me after partners were assigned."

"He did what now?" Matt had known that I wasn't seeing anyone? Why did he bother to ask me then? Was he just using that question as an excuse to text me? "Spencer, why didn't you tell me?"

"Because," Spencer sighed. "That's why I've been a little upset. I'm watching my crush fall for one of my best friends. And I know it sounds childish, but it kind of feels like I'm being replaced." His jovial smile was forced and didn't reach his eyes.

"Spence. We've been friends since we first learned to read. That's never changing." I put my arm around him and gave his shoulder a squeeze. "I'm sorry, though, for letting you feel that way."

He shrugged out of my touch. "I'll get over it."

"And I'll do better." I cleared my throat and added quietly, "I think you're wrong about Matt and me, though. We couldn't be any

more different if we tried. I'm nothing like his type. He should have a cheerleader for a girlfriend, not ... me."

Spencer shuddered theatrically. "Good lord, please don't try to be a cheerleader! You'd be awful."

I gave a half laugh. "Got it."

"But seriously, Ember. You need to stop selling yourself short ... you're really kind of okay."

I leaned back against the wall. "Thank you, Spencer. I think you're kind of okay too."

"I'm not mad anymore," Spencer said. "But I'm going to go ahead and apologize in advance if I am unnecessarily sad around you two. It's just something I will have to get over, I guess."

"I'm really sorry."

He tucked himself back under the blankets. "Just get over here and snuggle me. I need human comfort in the form of a big spoon."

"Yes, boss." I wiggled to the other side of the twin bed and laid down on top of the covers. Maybe someone else would think it was weird, but Spencer and I had been napping together forever, or at least since preschool when we were an acceptable age to take naps.

"Ember," Spencer muttered into his pillows.

"Spencer."

"I think Matt knows you're kind of okay too."

***

Wednesday night, Brynn, Spencer, and I all sat on the second floor of the library on one of the couches in the corner. Brynn and I had our stories out, and Spencer was doodling on the back of his right hand, consumed by Rita Ora's new album blasting through his headphones.

It was nearing 10:00 p.m. when my phone buzzed beside my laptop. It was Matt, still without a name on his text that read:

hey can you send me brynns number

Brynn looked up from behind her laptop. "Who is it?"

I tried hard not to let any emotion slip past the iron mask I locked on my facial features. I checked to make sure that Spencer hadn't heard her question before I answered. I didn't want to hurt his feelings anymore by continuing to talk about Matt. But he was nodding his head in rhythm to whatever song hammered his eardrums, oblivious.

"Um, Matt," I told her. My heart was thudding down the steps of my rib cage into my gut, but I forced out the next words in what I hoped was a nonchalant manner. "He wants your number. Do you want me to send it?"

Brynn raised a delicate eyebrow. "Interesting. Go ahead and give it to him." She paused. "Thanks for asking."

If she was thinking about the Grant Morris incident from freshman year, or any of the other times that my roommate had been sought after via a not-so-subtle interaction through me, she didn't say. Maybe she was used to her superiority when it came to dating.

My fingers felt like rusted gears as they mechanically jerked against my phone's screen to hit *send*.

thanks

Spencer had been wrong. Matt wasn't interested in me at all. And, obviously, being writing partners did not omit my roommate from Matt's pool of prospective girls. Part of me thought that I should be worried about Brynn and his reputation, but she could handle herself. I bet she could handle him too.

I didn't want to think about that.

Spencer stopped drawing on his hand and pulled his earbuds out. "Tomorrow is Thursday," he said matter-of-factly.

"You're not wrong," I muttered. His music was audible through his now ear-less buds splayed on the table in front of us.

"Are you going out?" His question was directed more toward Brynn, which was fair, but it kind of stung knowing he wasn't asking me.

"I am," Brynn said. "Ember's not."

Spencer rolled his eyes. "Shocker."

Again, I knew it was good humor, and I probably deserved the subtle jab, so I clenched my jaw and said nothing.

"You're writing with Matt tomorrow night, right?" Brynn asked me.

"Yeah," I muttered. "Good memory."

"Matt's not going out?" Spencer asked, incredulous.

I shrugged. "Guess not. He suggested Thursday to get together last time I saw him."

"Huh," Spencer said as he grabbed his earbuds. "Weird."

"Do you think Bash is going out?" Brynn asked. Her fingers had stopped flying across her laptop.

"I don't know," I said. "If he thinks you're going out, then maybe." I realized the truth of that statement as I spoke it. She had that kind of power.

She looked pleased as she struck up her typing rhythm again.

I set my fingers against my keyboard. They rested there while I scanned the last few sentences I had written, my right pinkie finger tapping against the shift key, impatiently.

My phone buzzed again.

also where do you want to meet tomorrow? my place?

I opened his message to reply, glancing over the rim of my reading glasses at Brynn's intent gaze, locked on her screen.

I typed back:

Yes.

Chapter Ten

Brynn had her makeup bag packed and several outfits slung across her arm before eight o'clock Thursday night.

"Are you good if I head over to Skylar's to get ready?" she asked, but she was already at our door.

I looked up at her from my desk. "No."

She gave me a sort of sideways smile. "Funny."

I let half of my mouth turn up in response. "Have fun. Make smart choices."

She opened the door with her elbow. "You too. Don't do anything I wouldn't."

My face fell as she let the door close with a thud. As if I could even dream of doing anything like her. There was a time last year when I almost caved and asked her for help in trying to talk to someone, but before I could hit the download button on a dating app, I backed out of the idea. It was embarrassing for me to admit how inferior I sometimes felt around her.

I turned back to my desk to pack up my things before heading over to Matt's. I had my car parked and was walking to his front door not even twenty minutes later.

I was about to knock on the Selwyn Dad door when it burst open. I stumbled back from the threshold at the sight of a smaller, skinnier version of Matt standing in the doorway with his backpack slung casually over one shoulder.

"Oh, sorry!" mini-Matt said and sidestepped.

"No worries ..."

Matt, the full-sized version, slipped into view behind the fun-sized one and put a hand on his shoulder. "Owens. I see you met my little brother, Critter."

"Critter," I repeated.

Smaller Callahan grumbled. "I told you, high school means no more Critter." He turned his attention back to me. "I'm Christopher."

I hid my smile at the crack in his voice. Besides their obvious age difference, the two could have been twins—and it was strange to think that I was looking at the younger version of Matt. They had the same sharp features, brown eyes, and blond hair, though Matt's was trimmed much shorter than his brother's current Bieber-pre-adolescence style. "It's nice to meet you, Christopher. I'm Ember."

"I know who you are," Christopher said. "Matt just got done telling me all about you. About how you two are writing a story for a contest, and how pretty he thinks you are, and—"

"It's time for you to go," Matt interrupted, taking both of Christopher's shoulders and pushing him past me, out the door.

My flush had to be deep crimson, but Christopher's smile was sly at having gotten even with his brother.

"It was nice to meet you, Ember!" Christopher called.

Matt promptly shushed him, Christopher chuckled, and I stood dumbfounded by the door.

Christopher's car started up, and Matt jogged back to me. "Sixteen years old and he thinks he can pull a fast one on me," he said, shaking his head. "We weren't really talking about you, for what it's worth."

"Of course not."

Matt gestured for me to go inside and closed the door behind me. "He's not wrong, though."

I set my bag down on his table. "What do you mean?"

He looked me in the eyes and grinned. "I do think you're pretty."

I coughed. "Um." I coughed again.

"You know," Matt said as he set a water bottle down in front of me, "most people just say 'thank you' instead of choking when they get a compliment."

"I'll remember that." I took a sip of water. "Thanks."

"No problem."

"I still don't understand why you have a Selwyn Dad sticker on your front door."

"Neither did the last girl."

I stiffened, and Matt obviously saw the change in my posture. Laughing, he said, "Relax, you're my only kitten."

My face pinched together. "Fantastic."

"My dad used to collect them," Matt continued. "I grew up with those kinds of stickers all over the house. I thought it was funny so I've found a few of my own over the years. Let me grab my computer, and we can get to work."

I nodded, thankful to be pulled back into business. I set my laptop and papers on the kitchen table. Matt came back out from his bedroom as I was powering up.

"So, I, uh, guess I never thought about where you grew up," I said, not a little awkwardly. "You lived close, I'm guessing, since your brother was presumably driving home?"

"Grew up here in Charlotte," Matt said and sat down across from me. "Didn't fly far from the nest, did I?"

"You continue to surprise me."

The corner of his eyebrow edged up. "Do I?"

"Something like that ... So, what was your brother doing here?"

"Critter?" Matt asked and looked up at me. "He needed help with math this week. Kind of a 9-1-1 situation. The kid just wasn't getting it, and he's got a big test tomorrow so he came here right after school."

"So that's why you weren't going out this week." It all made sense now.

Matt shifted his gaze to his screen and squinted as he started to hit the keys. "Bingo."

He continued to type while I watched him, unable to look away.

"All right. So for tonight, we've got to work on—" He stopped and looked at me, inquisitive.

Shit. Got caught staring.

"What's up?" he asked.

"Nothing," I said quickly. What was it about seeing guys care for their younger siblings that seemed to universally make girls drop their guard? "You were saying?"

The corner of his mouth pulled up a little higher. "I was saying that for tonight, we need to figure out the next flashback. You're at the part where Lena sees Wesley for the first time after the crash, right?"

I nodded.

"Right, so something in the hospital has to trigger her flashback where they held hands for the first time." He clicked a few more buttons.

"That's correct."

"Yeah, but we never figured out what actually happens in that scene. I literally just have written here in our notes, *they hold hands first time.*"

"Isn't that scene in the past? So shouldn't that have been on your list of things to do?"

Matt groaned. "I was a little busy playing tutor."

Right. The cute, nice thing he did for his younger brother.

"Well," I started, "for what it's worth, I don't think it should be a love scene."

Matt looked confused. "Why's that?"

"Because, presumably, we are going to keep a happy ending with this story, so there needs to be some unhappy parts too. You know, to have, like, tension." I swore I was more educated about craft than I was sounding in that moment.

If Matt noticed my inarticulacy, he didn't mention it. He just nodded. "That makes sense. So, if it isn't a love scene, why else do they hold hands?"

"Comfort," I said immediately.

"Right. Because only the broken get their story told."

"That sounds like another Van Dam quote."

"That's because it is," he said. "And you call yourself a fan."

I rolled my eyes and continued. "So if Lena is visiting Wesley present day and holds his hand, then let's switch it in the flashback to Wesley reaches for her hand."

"Sounds good," Matt said. "Family trouble? That way the reader gets some interiority on Lena's life outside of Wesley." His fingers were already striking the keys as he spoke.

"That works," I said, impressed with his literary vocabulary.

"Good. I've got an idea for it. If you don't mind, can you go ahead and do a round of line edits while I knock this out? You're so much better than me at that kind of stuff."

My cheeks puffed with a pinch of pride. "Sure," I said, then paused. "So, where is Bash tonight?"

Matt's rhythm didn't falter from his typing. "With some of his swimming buddies going to Bar Code tonight." He looked up. "That reminds me. I was supposed to thank you for him."

"What for?"

"Sending Brynn's number."

My mind reeled. "I sent her number to you." Matt asked for her number. Matt wanted Brynn's number.

He sighed. "Yes, and then I sent it to Bash. He didn't have your number to ask you himself."

Bash asked for Brynn's number. BASH wanted Brynn's number. Not Matt.

"Why didn't you just give Bash my number for him to ask me?"

"Because." The grin on Matt's face was cheeky. "I like having your number all to myself."

***

It was only 9:30 p.m. when Matt dramatically closed his laptop and sighed. "I think I'm done for tonight. I need fresh eyes to look at it in the morning."

"Do you want me to read it now?" I closed my laptop as well.

He shook his head and stood up. "No, that's okay. It's not quite ready for you to see."

I raised an eyebrow but said nothing as he walked into the kitchen.

"So," he said. His voice was muffled from having his head stuffed in the pantry. "I would just like you to know that I am prepared this time." He came back to the table with an armful of snacks: pretzels, popcorn, candy bars, and, of course, spicy hot cheese crunches.

"Prepared for what? The apocalypse?" I asked.

He grinned. "Movie time."

I opened my mouth to protest, but he cut me off.

"I know you like planning, and I'm not suggesting all of Harry's journey. Just the first movie tonight." He tilted his chin. "C'mon, watch it with me?"

I was speechless as I surveyed the snacks he dropped on the table.

"I thought it would be a little weird of me to do some reconnaissance and try to find out all of your favorite snacks, so these are some of mine. I'm watching my main man Potter, even if you don't want to." He paused. "But I would prefer you stay."

At that last part, my lungs contracted. I took in a deep breath. "Just the first movie?"

He nodded, his puppy dog eyes silently guilting me into staying.

I sighed and nodded back, against all of my better judgment and sense of time management.

"Yes!" He scooped up all of the snacks again and carried them into the living room. "Come along, dear."

I rolled my eyes at the back of his head.

"I've got blankets in that chest back there." Matt set down his stash and fiddled with the remotes. "Make yourself comfortable while I get this set up."

I couldn't believe I was doing this. If someone had asked me even a month ago if I ever thought I would be watching *Harry Potter* curled up on Matt Callahan's couch—

Shit.

SHIT.

The couch.

Where was I supposed to sit on it? I glanced back at the sofa directly across from the television where I assumed we would be sitting. Three seats.

Not that a love seat was ideal, for all the reasons you could think of (i.e., two seat proximity, the NAME), but a couch with three seats? Too many options.

Was I supposed to sit on the side? Which side? Would that be awkward then because we were too far apart? Did I sit in the middle? No, that would look desperate, and I was *not* desperate.

"You ready yet?"

"Uh, yeah." I grabbed the top two blankets and went back over to him, all but thrusting the quilts into his chest. "Here."

"Thanks," he said and took them gently from me.

Matt grabbed the popcorn bag and carried it with the remote and blanket back to the couch.

I let him sit down first.

Plot twist. He all but laid down on the couch as he sat on the side closest to the front door and swung his legs across almost the entire thing.

"Well come on. You're going to miss the Dursleys." His mouth was upturned and impish as he opened the bag and threw a few kernels into his mouth.

I groaned and basically had to *climb over him* to sit on the opposite side and sandwich my legs between his and the back of the couch.

From the heat flushing my cheeks and spreading to other parts of my body, I doubted that we were going to need both blankets.

Oblivious, Matt tossed his over the two of us to share.

"Popcorn?" He wiggled his socked toes against my side as he asked.

I leaned forward, away from his touch that was unnaturally ticklish, and took a small handful.

I leaned back against the couch armrest. Matt's foot rested at my side again, his calf against my thigh.

Matt hit play.

***

By the time Hagrid told Harry that he was a wizard, Matt's hand came to rest against my ankle.

I jumped at the touch through my sock and jeans, jerking my leg back.

He looked over at me. He didn't say anything, but the question in his eyes was all I could hear.

Slowly, I slid my leg back to its position on the couch.

I turned my attention back to the Dursleys, currently chasing their son Dudley around the shack, screaming about his newly acquired pig's tail.

Matt gently replaced his hand on my leg. His palm was on my ankle, his long fingers delicately touching the base of my calf. His touch was light, but it felt as if he was burning a hole through the denim between us.

***

It started with his thumb. I don't know when it was exactly, but sometime during the trip to Hogwarts, Matt slid his thumb under the hem of my jeans and began brushing the knob of my ankle bone in slow circles.

I turned my gaze a fraction his way, and he met my eye again. There was the same questioning gaze in his expression.

Is this okay? It wasn't a challenge; it was a concern.

I gave the smallest of nods, and his focus turned back to the screen. I tried to pretend that his touch wasn't currently electrocuting every nerve I didn't know my ankle could have. That it wasn't a big deal that his bare skin was currently against mine, no matter how small the connection.

I looked back at the movie and relaxed deeper into the couch. His hand shifted, and his thumb started repeating the same, lazy pattern, this time against the tendon on the back of my leg.

***

I was tired. My eyes felt like leaden discs I had to pry apart with every slow blink I made. The rhythm in which my chest rose and fell grew slower. Deeper.

***

Harry Potter defeated Lord Voldemort (spoiler: for not the last time) and won the House Cup. My head had slid to the armrest of the couch, using it as a pillow.

As the credits rolled in, Matt got up and went over to the TV.

"It's only midnight." His voice was husky as he tinkered with the console.

Only midnight? I was usually still wide awake at this time of night. My usual bedtime was closer to 2:00 a.m.

He looked over at me. "Do you want to watch the second one?"

My eyelashes had been busy trying to thread my eyes shut, and my mouth felt like paste. I swallowed twice and opened my eyes. "I should really get going."

Matt looked worried. "You sound exhausted. You can sleep a little here on the couch if you want and then go, but I don't want you to drive half awake."

He had a point.

And I appreciated him not offering his bed, like me crashing on his couch wasn't a big deal. None of this was a big deal, right? And Brynn was probably just now entering the club and wouldn't be home for several more hours.

"Put on the second movie." My voice was quiet and scratchy.

He continued to look at me a beat longer, the concern still in his eyes. "Are you sure?"

"Yes."

He worked on loading the second disc, and I forced myself to sit up.

"Where is your restroom?" I asked.

"Oh yes, the necessary bathroom break." Matt pointed with his chin. "Down the hall on the left. Right across from my room."

I stood up and went to go pee quickly, without looking into his bedroom, although the door was open.

When I returned, Matt was back on the couch, this time sitting upright, though his legs were still stretched across the back of all three seats.

I rubbed at the sleep crusting my eyes, trying to decide how to sit this time. My neck was a little stiff from the armrest.

"You ready?" His voice was gentle, soft.

I nodded and sat down opposite Matt again, mimicking his upright seat.

The second movie started.

***

Not long after Dobby showed up, Matt's whisper carried itself across the couch.

"Hey."

I looked over to him.

He held out his hand. "Come here."

I don't know what in God's name possessed me to take it.

I blamed the sleepy stupor I was in.

I blamed Brynn, because she would have obliged without a second thought.

I blamed Matt, because he kept my phone number for himself.

His hand was warm against mine. He tugged my arm gently, guiding me to lay down in front of him.

I was living in a parallel universe, and I wasn't sure what was stranger: me, being a little spoon to Matt Callahan, or the fact that we both managed to be laying down on no more space than just the couch, my head resting against his arm.

But his chest was solid against my back.

And I was so tired.

***

Students were still getting petrified at Hogwarts, but Matt's hand dipped from my shoulder to wrap around my waist.

His breaths were slow, deep. He might have already been asleep. My own breathing was slowing, and my eyes grew heavy.

I could feel Matt's heartbeat against my shoulder.

And his grip was strong around my core.

And he was so warm.

Sleep eventually overtook everything else.

Chapter Eleven

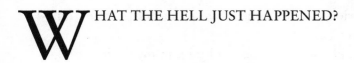

WHAT THE HELL JUST HAPPENED?

Chapter Twelve

Like, seriously, did I just spend the *entire night* on Matt Callahan's couch?

I blinked several times and took in my surroundings.

The digital clock on the television console was blurry. I squinted, trying to make out the numbers.

5:32 a.m.

The TV was humming a dull static song, long since having finished the second *Harry Potter* movie.

Matt's heavy arm was still wound tight around my waist, and he was still sound asleep based on the slow rhythm of his breathing.

I had to get out of here.

I started to slide out from under Matt's grip, trying not to wake him in the process. It took a good five minutes of subtle movements, but by the time my legs were free from his, he had already shifted to consume all the space the couch had to offer, still sleeping.

I let out a quiet breath and went to gather my things from the kitchen. My keys made a little jingle sound as I picked them up, and I quickly muffled them with my fist. I checked back on his sleeping form.

Scratch that.

Matt was sitting up, leaning on his forearms, looking at me through sleepy eyes.

"Hey," he croaked. "Where are you going?"

"Back to my place," I whispered hoarsely.

He looked distant, his focus far away beyond me. "Don't leave."

My breath hitched in my chest. "I have to," I said.

Do I?

He lay back down, nestling deeper into the cushions of the couch. He didn't respond other than a light snore. He was asleep again.

***

I couldn't get over how dark and empty the streets were on my way back to campus. It was like all the characters that usually bustled through life had been sucked out of the scene, leaving only the lampposts with their orange balls of light and the trees.

And I had just slept with Matt.

In the most innocent sense of the phrase, but still.

I pulled into the parking deck on campus, and by some stroke of luck, there was a spot open on the first floor. I parked Bugsy and made my way back to my dorm.

The steps were endless, and my feet felt heavy. I finally made it to my door and looked up, thankfully, before I slid my key into the lock. There, drawn on our whiteboard on our door in thick, purple marker, was a giant smiley face.

"You've got to be kidding me," I muttered. I had only ever seen the purple smiley face twice before. Once after freshman year Casino Night and the second time after Brynn's sorority formal last year. It was the agreed upon sign that Brynn made us use to let the other roommate know that it was probably not a good time to be entering the room. As in, ALERT: BOY INSIDE. The only time I had ever drawn it before was on April Fool's Day.

I checked my watch. 6:05 a.m. Spencer was going to hate me for this, but I started heading up to his room to hopefully catch a few more hours of sleep.

I knocked softly, once. Twice. Harder, two more times. I waited a beat then just started banging on it, praying that no one else would be woken up at the commotion.

"What, what, what?" Spencer mumbled as he rubbed his eyes. He was wearing nothing other than his boxers. He opened one eye and saw it was me. "Seriously?"

"I'm sorry!" I whisper-snapped and stepped around him.

He shut the door. "What are you doing here?"

I started sliding off my shoes. "Purple smiley. And I'm exhausted."

Spencer grumbled. "Why do I put up with you?"

I jumped onto his bed and shimmied under the covers, against the wall. "I'm really sorry. I just need another hour or two. Tops."

Spencer hauled himself up onto the mattress. "You're not waking me up again. You are going to stay right there until my alarm goes off. That's the condition."

"That's fair," I whispered. "Thank you."

He grumbled and turned his back to me, pulling the covers up to his chin. "Snuggle me, woman."

I complied, curling close to his shoulders like a human jetpack.

"Ember." His voice was muffled into his pillow.

"Mhmm?"

"If you weren't in the room when Brynn got back, where were you?"

My stomach lurched. "Don't worry about it."

If Spencer had a guess for my whereabouts, he didn't say. I mean, he knew I was meeting with Matt so the dots weren't that hard to connect.

He shifted once more. "Your jeans are uncomfortable," was all he said before falling back asleep.

***

Spencer's alarm went off at ten o'clock in the morning, right in time with the clock tower that tolled outside. I hoped Brynn was already in class, and that whoever had been breathing my air in our room was long gone.

Groggily, Spencer reached out an arm from under his pillow to fumble for his phone. He turned off the incessant alarm with a string of curse words.

I had already been up for at least an hour, replaying my night over and over and over again in my head while I lay on my back. Me, dozing on Matt's couch. Matt, his arm casually wrapped around me. Me, running away just when things got comfortable.

Spencer rolled over onto his back, running a hand through his hair and across his face. "Morning," he muttered.

"Thanks for letting me crash," I said as I sat up and scrambled over his limbs.

He groaned as my knee knocked into his thigh. "Yep. No problem."

My feet hit the floor, and I slipped on my shoes and picked up my backpack. "I'll see you later."

"Ember," Spencer said. His voice was still groggy, but he was at least propped on one elbow. His red hair was stark against his pale chest in the filtered sunlight that tried to seep through the cheap dorm blinds.

"Yeah?"

"Why did you come into my room in the middle of the night?" Spencer asked.

I looked at him blankly. I didn't have a response prepared. Instead of answering, I countered, "Technically, it was just really early in the morning."

He laid back down. "Whatever. I just didn't know story writing could take that many hours."

Busted. The clip in Spencer's voice said he wasn't too happy about me spending quality time with his crush.

"I will deny my whereabouts to anyone you tell," I said.

He turned his head to me and flicked up an eyebrow. "Especially Brynn?"

I felt my face melt into a pool of desperation. "Please don't tell her I was with him," I pleaded.

"Why not?"

"I just ... don't want her to know right now." It felt too weirdly personal, and I was still trying to process it all myself.

"What is there to know?"

"Nothing," I said and pulled open the door.

"If you say so," Spencer said as I let the door fall shut.

I made the trek back to my room. The truth about the secret keeping? As much as I wanted to be more like Brynn, I still wasn't ready to share with her this new friendship I had with Matt, if friends were what we were actually growing to be. Part of me was hopeful, or stupid, enough to entertain the idea that whatever this was might be more than friendship. Maybe telling Brynn would break the in-between tightrope that we currently sat on? But the most selfish truth was that, for once, it felt surreal that this time, it was me. Not Brynn. And I didn't want that illusion to shatter just yet.

Not talking about it was definitely safer.

***

Brynn busted through the door to our room. "I'm *really* sorry I didn't give you a heads-up last night."

I was sitting at my desk, scrolling absently through the internet. I looked over my shoulder. "It's okay."

"We got to Bar Code kind of late, and the line was really long already, but when we got there we ran into Bash and some of the swimmers," Brynn retold her adventure in a breathless rush as she moved about the room. "So instead of waiting in the cold for at least another half hour, one of the guys suggested we just go hit up a bar down the street."

"You don't have a fake," I said, ignoring Bash's presence in her story. I didn't trust myself to lie around the fact that I knew he would be there.

"I know. I told him that, but he said the bouncers were really chill and, sure enough, they let us in." She sat down on the edge of her bed to take off her boots. "So we get a few drinks, and Bash and I started talking, and he's like, amazing, and well, long story short, everyone is buzzed, and the place starts shutting down, so we are all calling cabs, and I swear to God, Ember, he was just going to walk me to our room, but then you weren't here, so I said he could come in, and we could hang out, and I know I should've texted you, but this man, Ember." She sighed, finally breathing through her soliloquy. "I could listen to that accent for hours. I mean I did, but he's just so—"

"Amazing?" I supplied the same adjective.

She looked dreamy and far off. "Yeah."

I waited for her to continue. When she didn't, I asked, "So you just talked?"

Her grin grew sly. "I mean, we kissed a little."

"Mhmm."

"That's it, I swear!"

"Sure," I said.

"I promise!" she cried, then paused. "Where were you last night after working on your project? I didn't get back until three something."

My fingers twitched. "With Spencer. We were watching *Harry Potter*." Only half of that statement was a lie. I would have to text him as soon as possible so he would back my story. I hoped he would.

"Of course you were," she said as she sat back against the wall.

Heat rose to the tips of my ears, and my eyebrows scrunched together. "What is that supposed to mean?"

She laughed. "Just that I don't know why I asked. I didn't really expect you to be anywhere else."

I knew the burning anger that was rising in my gut wasn't justified, but the truth of her words was ringing in my ears and to be honest, it hurt.

After my time with Matt last night, it didn't feel fair for her to just assume that I couldn't date or do anything like she did. "Are you the only one allowed to have a social life, Brynn? I know I may not be as good at it as you ..."

Brynn's playful expression faltered. "Ember, you know that is not what I meant."

My mouth narrowed, and I looked back at my computer, trying to find words.

"I'm sorry." Brynn's voice was uncharacteristically soft.

I shook my head. "It's okay."

Brynn was quiet as she pulled out her books from her bag and started setting them out on her quilt. My phone buzzed next to my laptop. It was a text from my dad.

> Hey Emmy, Ethan got a call from the attorney and they need him in Raleigh to sign some papers. He was going to head out first thing tomorrow so he could pack a few more things from the apartment. I think I need to go with him. Any chance you want to come home this weekend and watch Jaws?

Jaws. My brother's five-and-a-half-pound rescue dog. He looked mostly Pomeranian, but I always thought there was part velociraptor in there. If you let him be, he mostly left you alone unless he was hungry or needed to pee. Then he would yip incessantly. But he adored my brother and my dad. And he tolerated Hallie for the few years he had to share my brother with her. He didn't, however, particularly care for me.

But a weekend getaway back home? That was doing something other than sitting in my room, like I was apparently known for doing. And even with the fight over the phone my brother and I had yet to reconcile, I still felt bad for what he was going through.

I sent my dad a quick reply.

> Sure thing.

There were exactly three days until we had to have a rough draft turned in for workshop in class. I could definitely use the space at home to get some writing done, and it would help actually being in the mountains to write about the mountains.

I got a pretty terrible idea at that thought.

It would be good inspiration to be up there.

And there just so happened to be two of us sharing the mountain setting.

I sent Matt a text.

> What are you doing this weekend?

His response was almost immediate.

> depends

I took a deep breath, trying to play it cool. Like I still wasn't flustered about what happened last night. And that what I was about to ask was totally normal. Totally ordinary, something Brynn would have no problem asking.

> I need to go home to Blowing Rock to watch my brother's
> dog this weekend. Want to come and finish up the story?

I reread the message. It sounded kind of lame, even to me. I sent a follow-up:

> Mountains are inspiring.

The three dots appeared briefly at the bottom of our message chain (still no name attached to his number) before disappearing. My head started to hurt.

The dots appeared again. I stared at my screen until they were replaced with a gray block of text that read:

> not sure let me check lax schedule

Shouldn't he know the schedule? That had to be an excuse. Matt didn't want to spend any extra time with me than he absolutely needed to. I typed back quickly:

> No worries. I'm heading out early tomorrow.

Then I shut off my phone.

Chapter Thirteen

I was careful not to wake Brynn the next morning when I got up to head home.

After I shut off my alarm, I did a quick scroll through my messages to double-check that I hadn't missed anything from Matt.

Nothing. He hadn't sent a word.

I should have never texted him. I'll admit it: when I asked him to come with me, I was pissed at Brynn. And jealous. I was tired of always being the sidekick that everyone knew me to be.

But offering to take Matt home with me probably wasn't the best way to go about breaking that title. Rejection only added to the inferiority.

I groaned as I shut the door behind me.

Bugsy's cozy interior was a welcome comfort as I cranked the engine. I was plugging in my phone to pull up my music playlist when a new message came through.

> have you left yet

Matt. Seeing our message thread on my phone made my insides drop, like how it felt to fall from the top of a roller-coaster. I typed:

> Just pulling out.

His next message was quick to come through.

> i can be ready in five if you pick me up

I read it again and narrowed my eyes:

our place is going the other direction.

Part of me wanted to tell him off that he missed his chance. The other part ... the other part wanted him with me.

only by like five minutes ill see you soon

I rolled my eyes. He sure was presumptuous.

But as I pulled out of the parking deck, I turned toward his apartment.

***

I checked the clock on Bugsy's dashboard as I entered the parking lot at Matt's complex. 6:56 a.m. Then my eyes flicked up to the rearview mirror. My small duffel bag rested in the back seat.

There was one significant detail I thought of as soon as I pulled away from campus. Sleeping arrangements.

When I originally texted Matt, full of spite for Brynn, I hadn't thought of how weird figuring out sleeping would be. Matt wasn't expecting more nights like the couch, right?

I wasn't.

I definitely wasn't.

Right?

But then would it be really awkward to say, *hey so you're cool sleeping in my brother's room?*

He would probably take the couch after all.

I slid Bugsy into park. 6:59 a.m.

I thought about sending Matt a text to let him know I was here, but in all fairness he still had one more minute before his promised five were up.

I did open up a new message to send to Brynn, though:

Going home for the weekend. Room is all yours.

The clock ticked to 7:00 a.m. right in time with the sound of a door closing. I was impressed. Right on time, Matt was walking toward my car, his bag slung casually over his shoulder.

I gave a weird sort of half wave through the window.

He opened the back seat and tossed his bag next to mine.

"I meant to tell you last time I saw you in this thing," he said by way of greeting, "I like your car." He shut the door.

When he reopened the passenger door to slide in, I said proudly, "Matt Callahan, meet Bugsy Malone."

Matt looked at the car's dash and chuckled. "It's a pleasure."

I watched as Matt reached beside him to tug the seatbelt and click it shut. He shifted several times in his seat, stretching his feet toward the edge of Bugsy's footboard, but his legs never quite straightened out.

He noticed me watching him and paused his wiggling. "I thought we were on a strict time frame?" He was teasing me.

"No lacrosse this weekend?" I asked.

"There's a practice."

"You're skipping?"

He shrugged. "You said mountains were inspiring. I decided I needed to see if you were right."

"They aren't exactly far away," I said. How can you live in North Carolina and not visit mountains?

"I know," Matt said as he fussed with his seatbelt some more. "My parents like exotic getaways. I've seen a lot of the Caribbean."

"Wow."

"Also," Matt flashed a smile at me, "I couldn't possibly stand to be away from you that long."

"It's two days."

"Two days too long, kitten. Two days too long."

***

I got off interstate 85 as quickly as I could, taking the Blue Ridge Parkway for the majority of the trek.

"I wish it was fall," I said. "The leaves are really pretty in October." The word *pretty* didn't really do them justice. When the emerald leaves faded in autumn, replacing them were freckles of ruby and gold, save for the tall, green pines that regally watched over the others.

"It's okay," Matt said, looking out of the window at the long, spindly limbs. "I think the trees are pretty without their clothes on too."

I laughed.

About thirty minutes into the iconic winding parkway, Matt complained, "You're making me carsick."

"Really?" I eased my foot off the gas as I hit another turn. "I'm sorry."

"You should be. I think it's your poor driving skills."

"I highly doubt that," I said and expertly navigated another hill. "I could drive this with my eyes closed."

"Let me drive."

I looked over at him, suspicious. His face split into a wide grin. The cheeky bastard did not appear at all nauseated. "Not happening."

Bugsy's sound system continued to buzz some obscure indie band that my music playlist had suggested. It should have felt awkward having Matt in my passenger seat. Bugsy's other seats were rarely occupied by anyone other than Brynn or Spencer. Matt should have looked out of place with his long legs taking up too much space in the small interior.

But the strangest part was, it didn't feel strange at all. Here we were, driving in near silence, not needing to fill it with any extraneous small talk that meant little anyway. Just us, the music, and the colors of late winter.

Until Matt opened his mouth again. He cleared his throat. "So, about Thursday night …"

Goddamn. I gripped the steering wheel a little tighter. I could've gone this entire drive without bringing up this conversation. Probably a lifetime, actually.

The tightrope that held our friendship at each fragile end wavered as I said, "Yeah, I guess we need to talk about that." Good deflection. Ball back in his court.

He sat up a little straighter. "I just wanted to say that I'm sorry if I made you uncomfortable. I was definitely not planning on you staying the night."

That was not what I was expecting. At all.

"Um—"

"I mean, don't get me wrong. I'm glad you did. I just ... I don't know. I didn't want you to think that it was something I had planned ..."

What a role reversal. I never thought I would see the day that Matt Callahan got flustered.

"It's okay," I assured him. "It wasn't a big deal, right?"

He looked relieved. "Good." He didn't answer the question though. He probably wasn't having to endlessly convince himself that spooning on the couch was, indeed, not a big deal. I couldn't decide how I felt about that.

"So," I started, figuring I might as well get this out of the way. "Keeping on the topic of all things fun to talk about. My brother, um, has a room you can have."

Matt laughed, the tension in his shoulders falling away. "I will take you up on that." He poked my shoulder. "But part of me is going to miss the couch."

***

By the time we got off the exit for my house, Matt had taken over the music and pulled up what he called *the greatest jam playlist of all time,* otherwise known to his three followers as "Millennial Mix."

Not that I was going to tell him and make his big head any larger, but it was a pretty good jam, complete with all sorts of good throwback songs.

It would be fitting to say that Matt sang like an angel to add to the mystery unraveling about him, but alas, his voice was close to a tone-deaf lemur.

That didn't stop him from rapping every word to Soulja Boy and T-Pain, though. It had taken a solid five songs of his soloing for me to finally cave and join him. He grabbed my hand in excitement, shaking it like I was his co-reigning car singing champion.

My hand was still hot, even after he let it go.

We rounded a turn and downtown Blowing Rock opened up before us.

And by downtown, I mean Main Street, because pretty much the heart of the small town was laid out quite neatly on just one street.

"Wow," Matt said as he finally turned down the music. "This looks like something out of a storybook. I didn't know places like this existed." He turned to me. "You're basically like Hansel and Gretel, living in a cottage in the woods. Do you have lots of candy?"

I laughed. "I'm afraid I'm not that big of a sweet tooth. Your candy options here go about as far as Kilwins here on your right."

Matt pressed his face against the window to watch as we passed the chocolate and ice cream shop. "No way! I haven't been to one of those in forever. Can we go?"

His enthusiasm was just a little bit adorable.

I checked the clock on the dash as it neared 9:00 a.m. "Not yet, it's too early for dessert."

"Not breakfast though," he said and sat back up.

I eased my foot on the brake to stop at the red light. "You hungry?"

"Always."

The light turned green, and I kept going straight instead of turning left to take the hill up to my neighborhood. Rounding the next curve, I pulled into the parking lot of the cute southern diner that Ethan, Dad, and I ate at more often than we cared to admit. "This work?"

Matt laughed. "That was easy."

"Perks of a small town," I said, turning off Bugsy's ignition.

We got out and walked side by side to the front door, close enough for our fingertips to casually brush.

Matt jumped ahead of me to grab the door. "After you."

"Thank you," I said quietly.

The wind chime attached to the door announced our arrival. The restaurant was about half full, the booths occupied by mostly the senior citizen age bracket, with the occasional grandchild.

"Emmy Owens!" a deep voice called as the man attached to it burst from the kitchen, arms outstretched. "Long time no see!"

The restaurant's owner, Jack Gardner, enveloped me in a bear hug that lifted my toes off the ground.

"Jack!" I squirmed in his grasp. "I'm not as small as I used to be!"

He set me down, keeping his hands on my shoulders. "Pretty close to it though."

Matt chuckled behind me, not so discreetly turning his laughter into a cough.

Jack's attention shifted behind me. "You picked up a straggler on your way back into town."

Matt raised his eyebrows, and I joined Jack in teasing him. "I know, he looked pretty sad and hungry. I had to do something."

"She's right, I'm starving." Matt played along, smiling.

"Well, you came to the right place," Jack said. "Sit anywhere you like, sweetheart. I'll be right over to get your orders."

We thanked him and simultaneously picked a booth in the corner. Matt sat across from me, facing the door.

"Small town charisma," Matt marveled. "I like it. I didn't get to see much of that growing up. My parent's country club membership isn't quite ... the same."

I smiled, looking back toward the closed kitchen door. "Jack's pretty great. He and my dad grew up together around here. He's like an uncle to me."

I turned back to Matt to find him watching me peculiarly. "What?"

"Nothing." He shook his head. "It's nice to see you so happy."

I didn't know how to respond.

He didn't let the silence linger for long. "Tell me about your family. Why are we going to watch your brother's dog?"

Supposed happiness evaporated, but it was a fair question. I just didn't know how to best answer it.

I squirmed. "The short version is that history seems to be repeating itself. My mom left my dad years ago, and now my brother's wife is leaving him. Ethan moved back home recently, but he and my dad are heading to his apartment in Raleigh to get his things and then meet with a divorce attorney early Monday morning."

I didn't elaborate on the terms of the original divorce. It was hard for me to think about, much less discuss.

Matt was looking absently at the table, nodding, listening. Some waiter, a teenage boy, dropped off two cups of coffee in front of us, unsolicited but much needed.

Matt finally asked, "What's the dog's name?"

He bypassed the news of my parents being divorced, and I was surprisingly thankful he didn't say anything along the lines of *I'm so sorry. That's terrible.* I had heard the pity several times over the years.

"Jaws," I said, reaching for the little containers of cream at the edge of the table.

"Jaws?"

"Yeah. I kind of, uh, called him that once and it stuck."

Matt chuckled. "How scary is this dog?"

I paused, mid-pour. "Terrifying."

Jack knocked back the kitchen doors and made his way toward our table, small notepad in his large hands. "What's it going to be, friends?"

I didn't even glance at the menu. "Do you remember my usual?" Two pancakes, two scrambled eggs, bacon, and toast. It never changed.

"It would be damn near impossible to forget. It's been the same order as long as you've been able to use a fork," Jack said as his pen scratched across the page. "Speaking of, isn't your birthday coming up soon?"

I grabbed both of our menus and tapped them into a neat stack. "Next week. Good memory."

"Your twenty-first, right? You better make fun plans."

I narrowed my eyes. I was accustomed to Jack chiding me for my hermit-like behavior. Even as a kid I was never the most social of butterflies.

"I didn't know your twenty-first was so soon," Matt said and leaned forward on his elbows.

"Well, as Jack just outed me for, I don't do birthdays."

"That'll be different this year," Matt promised.

"I like this boyfriend, Emmy." Jack clapped Matt's shoulder firmly.

"Not boyfriend," I said a little too quickly, resulting in a smirk from Matt and a blush across my cheekbones.

"I'll have whatever the *usual* is," Matt said with a grin that was too charming for his own good.

Jack laughed, a deep bellowing reverberation. "Two Emmy specials, coming right up."

He headed back toward the kitchen.

Matt was smiling at me again. "Emmy," he said simply.

I rolled my eyes and smiled. "Childhood nicknames refuse to die."

"Can I call you that?"

"Nope." I laughed out loud.

"What do Spencer and Brynn call you?"

I leaned back against the cushion of the booth, cradling my coffee with both hands. "Crazy enough, usually just Ember."

"I'll stick with kitten, then," he said, picking up the container of sugar to pour into his own mug. "I like having that name to myself too."

Chapter Fourteen

"This is no simple cottage in the woods." Matt's voice was quiet and laced with awe.

We were still in the car, but now we were parked at the house my dad bought after the divorce was finalized, around the same time he officially became a *New York Times* best-selling author. It was on the opposite side of Main Street than the house I grew up in, back when my parents were still together.

I liked this house more, and on the surface it was easy to see why. It was certainly bigger, where the original one could only be described as "quaint." But the truth was, I liked the memories better here. It lacked my least favorite one, at least. That one was still in the old house, concealed to the new owners by time.

"Wait until you see the view," I said to Matt and opened my car door.

He followed my lead, still looking at the grandeur of the front entrance. Though the flowers were trying to escape their winter hibernation, it was fully landscaped, complete with rows of rose bushes and ivy that climbed the timber walls in the warmer months. The archway we stepped through to reach the front door was taller than the both of us combined.

Matt was several steps behind me, head still tilted all the way back, looking at the gas lantern glowing above him. His mouth was slightly open. "You really live here?"

I fumbled with my keys, trying to find the house one that I rarely needed to use. "No, I just figured I'd pick up the habit of breaking and entering."

"You might need to get a little quicker at that if you wanted to make it a career."

I shot him a swift glare as he stepped closer, watching me struggle to get the key in the lock. It finally gave, and the wooden door swung open to reveal a tiny ball of chestnut fluff. He was rocked back on his haunches, prepared to launch with his lip curled back into a snarl. The growl emanating from his throat was low.

"That's Jaws?" Matt asked, incredulous. "He's so tiny!"

"But ferocious," I said and stepped around him through the door. He remained frozen, still growling at Matt.

"Aw, just look at him," Matt said, crouching down onto his knees. "He's so cute. Come here, buddy!"

Jaws immediately quit his growling and began yipping as he trotted the remaining distance into Matt's outstretched arms.

"Seriously?" I cried. "He likes you too?"

The monster in discussion was currently flopped on his back, tongue lolling to the side as he panted at Matt's hand rubbing his belly. "Everyone likes me," Matt said simply.

I snorted, but didn't say anything as I went to get the leash from the kitchen. He didn't seem to be wrong.

"Come on. You can lead Satan's spawn on a walk."

"No tour yet?"

"No tour." I clipped the retractable leash to the squirming fluff's studded collar and handed it to Matt. "You haven't seen the mountains yet."

He stood up, mumbling nonsensical squeaky words of affection to the dog.

I rolled my eyes as we went back out the front door.

"So, I really don't know how to say this without sounding rude," Matt said. "But I didn't know you were rich."

I locked the door behind us. "What makes you say that?"

"Um, this house is amazing."

I looked back at it, and I couldn't argue with him. My dad was sort of good at the whole design thing. Not only was the house beautiful, but it felt like a home.

"I'm not rich," I corrected him and stuffed my hands into my pockets as we started walking. "My parents are." *Individually* was what I didn't add.

"What do they do?"

Here it was. The moment where my identity ceased to become my own. I walked a little ahead of Matt and Jaws, simultaneously leading the way and concealing my facial features. "Well, my dad writes."

"Oh yeah? That's cool. What does he write?"

"Crime fiction."

"Like, books?"

"Novels, yes."

We walked a few more paces in silence before Matt interrupted the peace with a loud realization. "Ember Owens. Are you telling me your father is Sam Owens? Like *The* Sam Owens?"

"So you've heard of him?"

"Nineteen books later, yes, I'd say the name rings a bell. But I also read him for class in high school too. My junior year teacher was really into all the North Carolina authors."

I tried to stifle my sigh. "It'll be twenty books next year. The newest one is under contract."

Matt let out a low whistle, and Jaws looked up at him expectantly. "That's something else, Ember," he said.

I thanked every God listening in that moment that he didn't call me Owens.

"What about your mom?" he asked. "What does she do?"

"Well," I fumbled to come up with an answer. "She hasn't been around for several years. She's been busy trying to be an actress in the meantime."

"Woah," he said. "I wasn't expecting that."

"Not many people do." Not that I broadcasted that fact often.

"Like a real one? In movies?"

"Well, sort of," I said, looking at my tennis shoes as we walked. "She got lucky and had one really big break as soon as she got to Hollywood. Since then, it's been mostly advertisements and commercials."

"What was the movie?" Matt asked.

The cracked cement turned uphill. Jaws's trot picked up a notch to keep up with the both of us as we made the climb.

"She was the lead in *Let's Say You Love Me*. It was a rom-com that came out almost a decade ago." Ironic, since she caused anything but comedy in her own love life around that time.

Matt stopped walking. "Lillian?"

"She played her, yes." I kept up my pace.

"My mom loved that movie." Matt jogged a few steps to catch back up with me, tugging Jaws along with him. "So, your dad is best-selling novelist Sam Owens, and your mom is actress Ava Owens?"

"Yep."

"Huh," he puffed beside me. "I didn't know they were married."

"Divorced."

Matt looked sheepish. "Right. I'm sorry."

I was expecting some sort of continuation of marvel that usually accompanied those realizations. From those that made the connection between our shared last names, I was used to getting compliments about both of my parents' talents. I would thank them for the ones about my dad.

"You and your mom have similar eyes," was what Matt said instead.

I didn't have a response prepared for that.

"I can't believe your dad is Sam Owens, and I didn't figure it out."

"Not many people do," I said, pushing the curls that escaped my bun away from my face. "Ethan and I have tried to stay out of the spotlight. Too much drama."

I felt Matt looking at me. I couldn't bear it if he started to look at me differently now that he knew the truth of my family name. That was why I tried so hard to avoid it. It was amazing to me how fake people could be if they thought they had something to gain. After my mom had her breakout role, her name and face continued to float around for several years that followed. In both middle and high school, I found myself with tons of people that were suddenly interested in being friends with me when they had never been before.

I really didn't want the same ending with Matt.

I turned to him, meeting his curious gaze. "What?" I asked, a little sharper than I probably needed to.

"Nothing," he said, still looking at me. "I'm just wondering who Ember Owens is underneath all of that." He gave me a little smile.

I didn't know what to say. There was a weird sort of lightness I didn't expect to feel in confessing part of my familial history to Matt. For some reason, I felt like I could trust him. Maybe it was because he was removed from my past, and time had scabbed over the wound in my chest. Although I had only confided a fraction of the story, it almost felt like I could breathe.

"But that is a whole lot of life experience to add to your writing toolbox." Matt winked, then let his gaze drift to Jaws. "Thank you for sharing. Van Dam might even be proud."

My step hitched. He wasn't wrong. It was a lot of life experience, but I really had only been witness to the stories my family experienced. And for so long, while I chose to suffocate under that heartbroken relationship, all I had really been doing was walling up my ability to experience … more of life.

You cannot write it unless you live it.

I was caught off guard by the dawning realization of how stupid I had been. By not having my own experiences to draw from, the self-protection I practiced all these years as a defense mechanism had turned me ... stagnant. I needed to find my own limelight, rather than shying away from the one my mother had chosen to embrace. I needed to *live*.

I never found my tongue to voice this epiphany to Matt. In that moment, we rounded the corner and the row of mansion houses stopped to reveal a viewing platform on what looked to be the edge of the world.

Beside me, Matt stopped and audibly lost his breath, his focus suddenly beyond me. "Oh my god," he whispered.

"Matt Callahan," I said, clearing my throat. "I give you the mountains."

All that separated us and the mountainscape was a knee-high stone wall. Beyond that, the trees rolled in layers, spreading out into the horizon. Again, I had the fleeting wish that it was October so Matt could see the dress of autumn colors bleed into distant, subdued blues as the mountains continued their endless stretch. Instead, it was quiet between us as the wind whispered through tendrils of twigs and barren limbs. I walked forward to sit on the edge of the wall, like I had always done since I was a kid.

"Is that safe? Sitting there like that?" Matt's voice carried a waver behind me and I turned, tucking another wayward curl back behind my ear that the wind had tried to carry away. His fist was clenched on Jaws's leash.

I had to laugh a little at the irony that I was the adventurous one here. "Come on," I said. "I've got you."

"I'm putting my faith in the girl hanging off a literal cliff," Matt grumbled and he perched on the very edge of the rock beside me, his head turned over his shoulder.

I looked down at the stone we sat on. Weather and time had aged the wall. The edges were starting to splinter into tinier rock pieces, no bigger than the size of one fingernail.

I brushed away part of the debris that was close to where Matt's hand clutched the rim. His pinky twitched once from the whisper of movement where my fingers had almost touched his.

The tiny rock cascaded down the mountain, so quietly almost no one could hear.

Matt's breath was warm, close to my ear when he spoke. "It's beautiful up here."

"It is." I nudged another piece of the wall away, watching as it fell into the silence.

**

We got back to the house, and Matt set Jaws free from his leash. He immediately trotted off to the kitchen, demanding that more food be put in his bowl with several squeaky barks, even though I knew my dad and Ethan had fed him before they left this morning.

After giving him another small handful of his dog food, I took Matt on a quick tour of the house. We went down the steps first to see the basement where I used to spend most of my time with the expansive walls of bookshelves and oversize beanbags.

I skipped the main floor and took the steps two at a time to show him the upstairs next. The two doors on the right side of the hall led to my bedroom and my brother's. Across the hall was the double bathroom we used to share. Straight ahead was the window seat area that my dad renovated to make the ultimate reading nook. It overlooked the replica tree house my dad tried to reconstruct from our old house in an effort to normalize the move, as if a tree house had that kind of power.

"Show me your room," Matt said, smiling.

"Why?" I asked, suddenly tense. I hadn't thought about him seeing my room. I prayed there wasn't anything too terribly embarrassing in there.

"I'm looking for clues," he said, pushing past me toward the two doors. "Still trying to figure you out, remember?" He put his hand out, palm facing the door on the left. "This one?"

My lips thinned. "Other one."

"That was my second guess."

I rolled my eyes and walked to open the door. "There's nothing that exciting in here." I hoped.

I stepped aside to let him enter.

It was great living with Brynn on campus, and since starting college I had found internships as a reason to stay in Charlotte over the summers—but I did miss this room. It had a huge window on the side facing the mountainscape that let in the setting sun. That was my favorite part about it all; the warmth that spread through the hardwoods and bathed the space in light during the golden afternoon hours. That used to make homework almost enjoyable. I especially loved when I could write during that light. I also had a huge walk-in closet with enough space to organize all of my clothes first by season, then by color.

I tried to ignore the queen size bed and duvet, teal and orange like the quilt in my dorm, while Matt wandered around the room picking up odd pictures and trinkets as he went. I leaned against the door frame while he surveyed.

He stopped suddenly, a smile on his face as he turned to me. "I like it."

I chuckled. "Glad you approve."

"It's so organized."

"Much like I pretend to keep my life," I said, pushing off of the wall. "Come on. You've got to see the deck."

We went back down the stairs, Matt skipping behind me.

"I can totally see you growing up here. It's so you."

"What do you mean?" I hit the bottom step with a thump and padded back toward the kitchen where the hallway spilled out onto the back deck.

"It feels like a writer should live here," he said. "You were right. Very inspiring."

"Well, my dad does live here." I stopped at the sliding glass doors, unlocking them.

He elbowed my side. "I was talking about you, genius."

I flushed and addressed his first comment instead of the latest. "I didn't actually grow up here. Dad, Ethan, and I moved here when I was ten, right after the divorce."

He was quiet a beat as the door clicked open. "Still. It's pretty cool."

I slid open the doors and stepped outside, Matt Callahan in tow. The view was similar to the one we had just seen from the walking trail, but now it was framed by the old cedar timbers of the deck, complete with outdoor couches and a coffee table to the left, and two high-top seats around a taller circular table to the right.

I sat down in one of the chairs and just breathed. Matt followed suit, leaning back silently, gazing out at the rolling hills.

"It is pretty cool," I said, finally.

He rolled his head toward me. "I think this deck deserves to be in the story somewhere."

***

We stayed out there watching the wispy clouds thread through the mountains several minutes longer.

We ended up working on the giant U-shaped couch in the living room that faced the television. Opposite sides of the U.

I was going to start drafting the next scene I was supposed to write, where Lena spends the night in the mountains after visiting the hospital, but Matt wanted me to read over the hand-holding flashback he just finished. I finally got him to agree to email it to me instead of switching computers so he could keep writing. My legs were stretched out in front of me on the ottoman, my laptop balanced carefully on my thighs. I quickly adjusted my glasses that I pulled out of my bag.

Matt noticed my fidgeting and looked up from his screen. "Ember?"

"Yes."

He threw me a smile. "I like your glasses."

I snorted. They were just thick, black frames on big lenses. "Uh, thanks. You've seen them before." I wore them every time I worked on my computer.

"I know. I hadn't told you yet, though." He went back to typing.

I shook my head at him and started reading his scene. As Lena and Wesley made it out of the grocery store and practically trampled the man revealed to be her father, my body seemed to grow heavier, and I ached from inside. I didn't like where this was heading.

Slowly, Matt revealed through dialogue and description the weight of this encounter. From the implied affair and Lena's reaction, I felt as if I were reliving memories I would have preferred remain untouched.

My chest was tight. "So to clarify," I said when I finished the scene, "Lena's father is cheating on Lena's mother. And then later in the story, you want Wesley to cheat on Lena?"

"Makes his betrayal dig a little deeper," he replied without looking up from his screen. "Don't you think?"

"That's cruel," I said.

"That's life."

"Are your parents still together?"

He took a deep breath and looked up, raking a hand through his short hair. "Yeah, they are. I'm pretty lucky."

"How did you write this, then?" I hated how quiet my voice had gotten.

He looked confused. "What do you mean?"

"This part with her father. It's so … real." And sharp. His words were slicing thin ribbons through my heart with every sentence on the page.

"Ah," he said, looking a little amused and a lot cautious. I didn't think he realized he was hitting so close to home. "So there is a little loophole in Van Dam's philosophy. I have not lived this, but I listen to those who have experienced something similar. And I have lived heartbreak. Put those two together and based on your reaction, I nailed a pretty good re-creation."

I nodded at the screen. He was right. This wasn't an experience uniquely mine. Just because it hurt me, too, I wasn't any more special than the next kid of divorced parents.

"Yeah, you got it right," I finally said. "You got it exactly right."

Chapter Fifteen

We worked until hunger drove us to break for lunch. I sent Matt out with Jaws again, since the fluffy rat seemed to like him better anyway. They returned twenty minutes later when I had turkey and cheese sitting on top of bread and an array of condiments on the kitchen counter. My sandwich was already dressed with lettuce and mayonnaise, and I was munching on an open bag of chips.

"What took you so long?" I called when the scuttling of claws and the tap of Matt's shoes crossed the hardwood of the foyer.

Matt unclipped Jaws from his leash and came into the kitchen. "He wanted another walk." He paused in the doorway. "Did you make me a sandwich?"

"No. I only made you half a sandwich. You are more than capable of finishing it." I bit my lip. "Plus, I didn't know what you wanted on it."

"So if you knew, you would have made me a sandwich?" He was smirking as he spoke.

"Only because I didn't want to walk the dog."

"Of course."

The smirk was still on his face, but I let it slide as he decorated his sandwich with *literally everything* I put out on the table. Potato chips included.

"What's the plan for the afternoon?" he eventually asked in between bites.

"I think the next big thing we have to do is plan out the fight Lena and Wes are supposed to have."

"Right," he said and took another bite. "But after that?"

"What do you mean?"

He finished chewing and swallowed before responding. "Like, dinner? Or the town? I have barely seen any of the town yet."

"I guess we could go out for dinner," I said, biting my lip. I really hadn't given this adventure any forethought whatsoever. It was so unlike me.

"What's your favorite restaurant?" Matt asked.

"Besides the diner?" I joked. "There's actually a cute British pub down on Main Street we used to go to every weekend."

"Well look at that," Matt said. "It's Saturday. Perfect excuse to go."

My phone started buzzing in the back pocket of my jeans. I set down my half-eaten sandwich to fish it out. It was my dad.

My nerves jumped as I answered the phone. He obviously thought I was here alone and didn't know anything about the man currently munching on a potato-chip-laden sandwich in front of me.

Said man was looking very interested in his plate as I said in a voice maybe an ounce too chipper, "Hey, Dad!"

"Hey, Emmy. Did you make it to the house okay?"

"Sure did!" My exuberance earned a lifted eyebrow from Matt. I turned my volume down a notch. "Are you guys in Raleigh?"

"Been here about an hour already." My dad sounded tired on the phone. There was a pause and the muffled sound of a door closing before he continued. "It's hard to see your brother like this. He really loved that girl."

"I know he did." I lowered my voice. "I'm sorry." And I meant it.

"You should tell him that," my dad said. "I think he needs all the support he can get right now."

I bit back the sharp retort that threatened to fly out of my mouth—*he seems just fine with Mom in his corner instead.*

But my dad didn't need that spite. I could only imagine how this was triggering his own memories, even though he always encouraged me and Ethan to keep a relationship with our mother and seemed genuinely disappointed when we fought against it. Ethan would just get quiet and say nothing when my dad handed us the phone. I got really good at extravagant lies and excuses not to have to even touch the phone. My dad's later suggestion of visitation hadn't gone over well, with her being so far away and launching her acting career.

I dropped contact other than opening her occasional greeting cards a few years ago.

"I can try to call Ethan later," I lied.

"That's good," my dad said, and he cleared his throat on the line. "How's Jaws?"

I looked down at the tyrant in question. He was laying at Matt's feet, looking like he was sleeping.

Matt's socks today were rainbow checkered.

"He's fine," I said. "Don't worry about us."

"I appreciate you going up there."

Matt finished the last bite of his sandwich and started cleaning up the kitchen island, putting his plate in the sink and the condiments back in the fridge.

"Not a problem," I said, stepping away from Matt's noise, cutting him a hard stare.

Matt gave me a toothy grin then grabbed the potato chip bag and crinkled it. Loudly.

"So, um, I've got to go," I said a little louder over Matt's laughter. "I've got more writing to do."

"That's right. How is that story for the contest going?"

Matt stepped around the island toward me.

"Um, great! Really great. I'll let you read the draft when it's done, but I have to go work on it right now."

"Send it my way whenever," my dad said.

Matt slowly lifted the chip bag closer to my head, threatening to crinkle it again with a devious grin on his face.

"Greatloveyoubye!" I said quickly and ended the call.

I turned my attention to Matt. "Are you twelve or something? That was my dad!"

"And based on your reaction, he has no idea I'm here, does he?"

"Obviously not. And best to keep it that way, dumbass. They've got enough going on."

Matt cocked his head. "What? Are you embarrassed by me or something?"

I groaned. "I'm not embarrassed by you, Matt."

"So what's the big deal? Are you not allowed to have friends over or something?"

Friends. He was right. It wasn't a problem for him to be here. We were friends. Right?

"I guess it's fine," I muttered.

"Great," Matt said. "So why are you death glaring me still?"

"This is my happy face."

He chuckled. "Whatever you say, grumpy."

It turned out Matt already had a pretty good plan for his next few scenes. I finished putting the last few things away from our lunch break, and we moved to sit back on the couch. Matt waved me off when I threw out flashback suggestions, saying he had it under control.

"Just focus on the present," he said. "Let me dwell in the past."

"That doesn't sound healthy."

"Probably not, but then you can at least go back and make it sound pretty."

Matt seemed to get more focused the closer we got to the tension in our characters' past, and I wondered how much of this plot was left to imagination. He got shorter in his responses to me, his fingers moving faster with each passing hour.

***

We worked for several hours without speaking, closing the gap on the climax of the story. We had to get through at least the flashback that originally drove our characters apart before workshop on Monday. I figured we could put the rest of our notes at the end of the scene so the class had an idea of where we were heading for resolution. It might even save time in the long run if they ended up hating what we wrote, and we had to change it anyway.

I didn't want to think about that. I hated revision. William Faulkner once said, "In writing, you must kill your darlings." It was always painful for me to hit the delete button on a chunk of text that wasn't quite working in a scene, even if I did love those darling words.

The afternoon sun had long since passed behind the curtain of tree bark in the distance, and whatever light remaining was dimming. Matt closed his laptop and set it on the coffee table. I was still hunched over mine, eyes narrowed through my glasses, typing away. I felt him stand and watched as he stretched his arms high above his head, letting out a small groan. The hem of his sweater rose up just an inch, exposing a small sliver of skin. I looked away.

His hands came to rest on either side of my laptop, closing it.

"Hi," he said.

I titled my chin, and my eyes latched onto his deep, brown ones. Our noses were close. Probably only another nose width away.

The corner of his mouth pulled up into a smile. "Are you hungry yet?"

I managed a nod. I opened my mouth to speak, but the words caught in my dry throat from not speaking the majority of the afternoon. I licked my lips once and cleared my throat. "Yes."

Matt took the laptop off of my lap and set it next to his, careful to touch only the computer as he did so.

"Great. I'm starving."

He moved away from the couches and with his back to me, said, "I'll take Jaws out again if you want to go get ready."

He really was being rather considerate. In a clumsy sort of fashion, I wiggled out of the cross-legged position I had been favoring and stood, tripping only slightly. "Okay," I said, once righted. "Thank you."

I dashed up the steps, two at a time toward my bathroom. I set my glasses on the sink before peeing quickly, washing my hands, and dabbing water under my eyes to wake them up, careful to not smudge my mascara. I set my hands on either side of the sink and leaned closer to the mirror. My reflection stared back at me, the expression on her face solemn and serious. The face could almost be pretty, I thought, if the edges were less harsh. I felt the muscles holding my taut expression flicker as I tried to soften my own expression. The result was pretty much a frown, and I shook my head.

I ran my fingers through my curls, trying to stroke some life back into them. I thought about opening the drawer beside the sink where I knew I had a small stash of makeup, then immediately erased the thought, horrified that it had even crossed my mind. Besides my normal mascara, lip balm, and the occasional sweep of eyeshadow, I had never been great at the whole face painting deal. Besides, Matt had seen me looking like a hot, studious mess all day. Changing that aesthetic now would be ridiculous.

I tugged my hair into a ponytail at the top of my head and almost walked out. I looked back at the counter where my glasses were currently resting. I didn't *really* need them.

I tugged my sweater over one of my hands, staring at the black frames. I bit my lip, then grabbed them, slipping them back on and went downstairs to meet Matt for dinner.

**

I drove us down the mountain, which meant I got to show off my subpar parallel parking skills in front of the restaurant. Matt was a total gentleman and didn't acknowledge the fact that my bumper was still pretty much dipping into Main Street.

Dinner was excellent, as always. I ordered the ploughman's lunch, per usual, and Matt had the shepherd's pie.

"Ember? Is that you?"

I looked up, a nice hunk of bread halfway in my mouth, to see a friend of mine from high school. I forgot he worked as a waiter part time. "Keegan," I said, nearly spitting out the loaf. I dusted my hands together. "Hey, how are you?"

"Great!" His face beamed as he walked over to our table. He had messy brown hair, and freckles adorned every inch of his face and hands visible beneath his uniform. "I didn't see you at all this holiday. Did you come back to visit?"

I nodded. "I did, but I didn't stay long."

Keegan and I weren't exactly what I would call *best* friends. That title still belonged to Spencer. But the town was small, so the school was small, and Keegan and I ended up sharing a bunch of classes together over the years. He always saved a seat for me in pre-calculus, but I assumed that was for convenience's sake when we had a pop quiz. He was kind, although the friends he used to hang out with were known to be less than.

"How long are you here this time?" Keegan asked.

"Just the weekend."

"Always on the move." Keegan turned his attention across the table. "This your man?"

I blushed. "Oops, sorry. Matt, this is Keegan. We went to high school together."

"Nice to meet you," Keegan said. He extended his arm, and Matt shook it firmly.

"Likewise," Matt said. I thought I felt a butterfly in my stomach at seeing him flash his broad smile in greeting. Or maybe it was the start of food poisoning, who knew.

"Take care of this one," Keegan told him, gently squeezing my shoulder and giving me a soft smile.

The muscle underneath Matt's jawline tightened, and it was in that moment that I realized how in tune I had gotten to Matt's body and the way it moved, the way he reacted. It was hard to notice the change behind his easygoing demeanor if you didn't know him.

"That's the plan," Matt said, but the smile slipped from his eyes.

After Keegan walked away, there was a sudden thickness in the air around our table. I didn't know how to break it.

"Sorry," I said. "It's always weird running into people from school. It feels like it was a different life or something."

Matt shrugged. "He seemed nice enough, I guess."

I lifted a brow. "Um, yeah. He's all right."

"Were you guys close? In high school?"

I decided to tease Matt and maybe ease the tension. "Why? Are you jealous?"

"Terribly," he said, but there was laughter in his eyes. For a moment, I didn't think I wanted to laugh.

"I would've loved to know what you were like in high school," Matt added.

"Probably not much different than I am now," I said.

"Did you have a boyfriend?"

"Not really."

"That's not a no," Matt said, then jutted his chin back toward the kitchen. "Did you date that guy?"

"That would be a definite no," I said, probably a touch too sharply. "I had a crush on a friend of his at one point."

Matt went back to his meal, and the surrounding tension dissipated. "I'm waiting for the story …"

I stabbed my fork into the side salad on my plate. "His name was Jake, and he was a jerk. That's about all there is to know."

"But you got hurt," Matt said between bites. It wasn't a question. It was an observation.

I let my shoulders fall. "I did."

"Why?" Matt pressed. I knew I could have deflected, kept him out and let the memory remain dormant. I took a deep breath instead.

"Jake was on the basketball team," I said. "He was cool in our school, but then again I think *cool* is a relative term when the student body is the size of a pea."

Matt smiled, but he didn't interrupt.

"Everyone liked him. We had English together, and we were paired to work on a project. I remember we were reading *Pride and Prejudice* of all things." I rolled my eyes at the irony. "I thought I liked him. I really did. He was really nice to me and, I don't know, he made me feel … special."

I bit my lip. "Then, one day, Spencer told me that he had overheard Jake bragging to the other boys on the basketball team about having the movie star's daughter wrapped around his finger."

"Shit," Matt said.

I nodded. "Yeah. That sucked to find out. Also made me feel like an idiot when I heard he was still dating the cheerleader that dramatically broke up with him a few months prior. Guess they got back together."

"Was she a bitch?" he asked, sympathetic.

I gave him half a smile. "Kind of. But she was pretty."

"You're pretty."

I shook my head, trying to wash away the blush that colored my cheeks. "Not like that. I don't know, I always hate when people treat me different after they find out about my family."

"Don't worry," Matt said with a small smile. "You still are and always will be Ember first. Not just Owens."

***

After dinner, we walked the few doors down to Kilwins, as promised. Despite the chill in the evening air, we both wanted ice cream. We opted to eat on a bench in the sitting area of the shop next to the fireplace, instead of heading to the warmth of my car. That way, no ice cream would drip onto Bugsy's seats. I also didn't feel like heading home and ending our night on the town yet.

Matt sat next to me, casually leaned back against the wooden frame. I sat angled toward him, my feet tucked underneath me again as I held my ice cream with sweater-clad hands. I watched the edge of Matt's profile catch the firelight glow, framing his face in a silhouette. Without looking at me, Matt said, "You know, you didn't deny it."

I furrowed my brow, bewildered. "Deny what?"

He took a lick from his ice cream, birthday cake-flavored. "At the restaurant. Your waiter friend probably thinks we're dating."

"We aren't," I said quickly, realizing he was right. I hadn't corrected Keegan's assumption.

"I know that." Matt rolled his eyes. "But it's not for my lack of asking you out. Because I did. And you turned me down."

I blushed and looked away. "I'm sorry."

Matt shook his head. "Don't be. It's good character building to have to face rejection every once in a while." He turned to me and dropped a wink. "I'm just not going to ask you again."

Ouch. That stung a bit more than I would've liked, but I refused to let any disappointment show. "Okay," I said and took a slow bite of ice cream to numb the feelings.

Matt was still looking smug when he said, "I think the deal should be that you're going to have to ask me out when you're ready."

I coughed. "Excuse me?"

"You heard me. I'm not going to put any pressure on you by asking again because I have a feeling," he raised an eyebrow as he took another lick of his ice cream, "that you might just cave in and say yes."

My jaw was on the floor.

"I'm still not really seeing anyone right now," he continued as he put his full attention back on his dessert. "Just in case you were wondering."

"I wasn't." (I really was.)

"If you say so." He grinned. "In all seriousness, it could just be one date you ask me on. If you decide I'm actually the asshole you've branded me to be in your head, then you don't have to ask for another."

"I don't think you're an asshole," I said without thinking. My eyes shot open at the confession, and Matt burst out laughing.

"She finally admits she was wrong!"

"Hey, don't get that carried away! I still think you have jerk-like tendencies." I bit my lip. "But wouldn't this sort of already count as a date? Dinner, dessert, that whole thing?"

Matt shook his head fervently. "This is absolutely not a date."

"Why not?"

"Well first off," he said and licked his cone, "I would have driven us to dinner. Second, if we were on a date right now (lick), you would not be that far away from me, that's for sure. You're obviously cold despite this nice cozy fire (lick) since you're holding your ice cream with your sweater instead of your bare hands. If this were a date, I would have you so close to me that you couldn't possibly be cold from all of our body heat."

If I was cold before, I definitely wasn't anymore. Matt's words sent blood rushing to the tips of my nose, ears, and down to my belly.

"But this isn't a date (lick), so you're going to have to freeze a little bit longer."

I didn't know how to respond to such a statement. I panicked. "Why do you date so much anyway?"

Matt gave me a pained expression and looked around the nearly empty room. "Damn, Owens. Way to kill a mood."

"I'm sorry."

"Stop apologizing." He finished his ice cream and started crunching on the cone. "So, I've actually got a theory about dating."

"Oh? Do tell." I tried to regain some composure. "Curious minds are dying to know."

Matt paused. "My theory is that there are really only two reasons that people date. The first is for companionship. While you are getting to know the person, you go on dates, and if you decide you like their company, you keep the dates up. It's easy, it's fun, you have a great time together, so why would you stop it?"

"I don't know," I said. "You tell me. Why do you stop them?"

Matt gestured with wide hands. "Because of the second reason. Some people date to explore the chance of a possible future."

"Like, getting married?"

"Not necessarily marriage. It could be, but a future could just be something where you could see yourself as a partner for that person beyond just enjoying each other's company."

"So *you* date to find a partner?"

"No."

"Then what is it?

Matt's voice fell into a serious tone, and he got very interested in his ice cream cone. "I date because I want to figure out what I need in a partner and what I can give as a partner. I'd like to learn as much as I can about creating a better partnership that might last one day." He regained the confident charade with an impish smile. "Once I find out what doesn't work, I find a way to get out. Nicely of course."

"Leaving a string of girls in your wake," I reasoned.

"It's a vicious cycle."

It was surprising, truly, Matt's dating history and how much thought he put into the process. Just when I thought there wasn't much more that could be refuted about Matt, he does it again.

But his viewpoint was ... mature. So much more so than I had heard from anyone else I've talked to about relationships. I wondered how he developed such an outlook.

"Okay," I said. "Tell me about what you've learned then about partnerships. Start at the beginning. What did you learn from your first relationship?"

Matt's mood immediately darkened, and it was like a movie scene in slow motion as I watched him physically withdraw, shrinking into himself. It was like my question had delivered an effective sucker punch.

But he regained his composure in miracle time and cleared his throat. "Anna is a long story."

Anna. That name held so much power in Matt's pained eyes. My shoulders wilted with guilt. I had no idea I was pushing on a sensitive subject. Curiosity tore its vicious claws across my tongue, begging to ask the million questions burning in my mind. But I couldn't. I didn't know how long ago *Anna* was, but the hurt was something he clearly still carried.

"Maybe you can tell it to me one day," I said quietly.

He gave me a soft smile. "I might." But there was infinite gratitude in his eyes for not having to bare it just yet.

We sat in silence until Matt's cone was gone, and I couldn't eat anymore. I stood and tossed the remainder of mine in the trash. "Are you ready to go back?"

Matt looked at me, horrified. "You did not just throw away a perfectly good half of an ice cream cone?"

I chuckled. "Yes, yes I did. I'm very sorry."

"I'm ashamed of you." He stood, and he surprised me by threading his fingers through mine as we walked toward the door.

I jolted at the contact, as did he.

"Jeez, Ember! Your hands are freezing." He didn't let go, though, and opened the shop door with his opposite shoulder.

"Um, yeah. Cold like my soul," I said and mentally slapped myself. Real smooth.

"That sounds like a dangerous condition."

We got to the car, and I unlocked it with my free hand. Like the gentleman he was proving himself to be, Matt opened my door for me before scampering into the passenger side. I cranked the engine and blew on my hands while Bugsy warmed up.

Matt buckled his seat belt, laughed, then asked, "Have you always had a cold soul?"

I choked back a chuckle and clicked my own seat belt into place. "I couldn't tell you for sure, but I bet it probably got colder when my mom left." I pulled out of the parking spot and started the drive back up the mountains.

"You know," I continued, cautiously. "There is actually a lot more to that story. I've really only given you the short version." I'm not sure why I said it, but Matt had obviously shared a little of something he usually kept secret, and I felt like spilling more of my own truths in response.

He reached across the console for my hand again, and rubbed his thumb over my knuckles, repeatedly.

I should have pulled away. Rationally, I knew I should have. But I didn't want to. I liked the feel of my hand in his.

Matt was slow to respond, but when he did, he said, "You don't have to share if you don't want to, but I'm all ears if you do."

I drew a shaky breath. I didn't have anything to lose by telling him the details.

Chapter Sixteen

Ethan had been the first to find my dad lying on the floor of his study. It was a small room, nothing compared to the sunroom he currently used as an office. It was actually the dining room of our old house that he had taken over and converted into his personal workshop, much to my mother's dismay. Sticky notes were scattered on every wall; many others were crumpled into tiny balls on the carpet.

My mom left us prior to the heart attack. She said it was time for a change. This wasn't working for her anymore. And my personal favorite, "It's not all your fault, Sam. I've just always felt that I was meant for more."

She packed her things and walked away. It was funny how much she chose to leave behind. Almost all of the pictures and memories remained in their frames for my dad to gently stow away later that year when we moved.

No one knew it—not Ethan, not my dad—but I kept a family candid from years ago. Ethan was probably seven, and I was four. We were having a picnic, a real-life picnic, up on the iconic Blowing Rock trail. My dad took the selfie of all of us with his flip phone and had it printed at the drug store. The result was a grainy close-up on my dad's receding hairline with the trio of us in the background.

Ethan was hanging off of my mom's shoulders as she sat, and I was bouncing in her lap.

Although I hadn't looked at it in years, I knew the photo remained tucked in the bottom drawer of my dresser in this house.

It wasn't until an envelope arrived in our mailbox, two weeks after my mom's departure, that we found out the depth of her reasoning for leaving all those photos.

Dear Sam ... the husband is always the last to know ... your wife has been having an affair with Joshua Reynolds for the past six months ...

There had been no return address and no name on the letter. To this day, my dad never found out who sent the note.

Ethan and I only found the letter because it was on my dad's desk, on top of the mess of manuscript pages he was editing when he opened it. That was when the heart attack that had been building in his system finally hit.

During the short interval between my mom walking out the door and the arrival of the letter, my dad had been all consumed with finishing the book.

"I've got to know that I can do it," he said to me late one night, not entirely coherent. "I've got to know that I didn't lose her for nothing."

He rarely slept and when he did, it was an hour here or an hour there for those two weeks. It was summer, so there wasn't school to worry about. Ethan and I were mildly concerned about our dad's erratic behavior, but Jack kept us well fed at the diner and the walk there was good exercise anyway. He always sent plates back with us for my dad. They would remain untouched. All he ate was popcorn and chips from the pantry, downing energy drinks and coffee as if they were ambrosia.

The poor diet and lack of sleep aside, the doctors in the hospital knew our dad and our dad's dad, and his dad's dad before that, and they said it was genetic.

But we didn't know that.

Ethan and I didn't know much at thirteen and ten.

All we knew was that Dad was on the floor, not moving, no matter how many times we called his name or pushed his arm.

"Call 9-1-1!" Ethan yelled at me.

"I can't!" I cried, and to this day, I don't know why. Physically, it was about three steps to the desk and a few buttons on my dad's phone. It should have been easy.

But I stood, paralyzed as the icy fear of losing not one, but two parents wrapped around my gut like barbed wire.

Ethan snapped at me once more, but I couldn't budge. He groaned and leaped up from Dad's not moving side to grab the phone.

"Hi, 9-1-1? I need an ambulance. My dad isn't moving, and we need him ..."

We needed both of them.

The eight minutes we waited for the ambulance to leave its station and climb our mountain were probably the worst eight minutes of my life. I sank to my knees by my dad's head, palms spread on the floor by his side. I rocked back and forth to the beat of my own snuffling cries. Ethan had gone eerily quiet.

He and I both rode in the back of the ambulance next to my dad's limp form and the paramedics. They asked if they needed to call anyone, but Grandpa and Grandma didn't live in town anymore.

"What about your mom?" the lady paramedic asked.

"Don't have one," I said, and that shut her up.

My brother and I stayed in the hospital waiting room overnight. Jack had heard the news and tried to get us to go home, saying that he would wait up for Dad.

We refused and ended up all waiting together.

We were able to go back into the room and see him the next morning. Jack had to go and open the diner, but he said he would be back as soon as he could.

That wasn't soon enough because if Jack had been with us, he would have been able to stop the tornado that was Ava Owens.

"A heart attack!" Her voice was as flustered and disheveled as her hair as she raced through the door. She looked like she had just stepped off a plane where she was strapped to its wings. "The hospital called me as soon as they checked you in, Sam."

We later learned that she was spending time in California, on the opposite side of the country. She must have jumped on the first flight out.

Dad was sitting up in his bed. Ethan and I sat protectively on either side of him. I was closest to the door, blocking my mom's view of his body.

I crossed my arms. "What are you doing here?" My voice was bitter. Hard.

"I ..." Ava started, but trailed off. She looked a lot like the person that used to be my mom, but dressed in finer clothes and more lipstick. "I couldn't not come."

"You could have not left," I spat, then turned my back to her. "Go away."

"Emmy," my dad chastised, then fell into a fit of violent coughing. The monitor beside him made louder noises.

A flurry of nurses stationed nearby rushed into the room and fussed around him. Ethan and I stepped away to let them work, but only a few steps.

My dad's voice was frail when he spoke again, hollow and raspy. His eyes fluttered back and forth between me and Ethan. "I love you."

I choked at those words and fled, pushing past the nurses and my mom, who was lodged in the doorway wearing a bewildered expression. I shrank my body, sucking in my stomach so that our shirts wouldn't touch as I slid past her, and then padded away from the commotion in the room.

Tears were burning in the back of my eyes as I made my way through the endless turns in the halls, my legs shaking and breath hitching. I ended up sitting down in a corner somewhere with my knees tucked up to my chin, forehead pressed to the denim.

Eventually, it was my mom that sat down next to me, a good hands distance apart. I felt the movement beside me and rotated my chin just enough to confirm it was her before hanging my head back down, quieting my tears. She had her hand raised as if she was going to set it on my shoulder or back, but then thought better of the gesture.

We sat quietly for a minute or two before she finally broke the silence. "He's doing fine. They got his heart rate back under control."

I hiccupped, but other than the childish noise, I said nothing.

"Why did you run?" Her voice was soft.

I lifted my head and leaned against the wall, staring at nothing. "Because. Isn't that what people say?"

"What do you mean?"

I took a deep breath. "He said, 'I love you.' Isn't that what people say right before they die?" My voice cracked on the last word and tumbled into an uncontrollable sob.

"Oh, honey."

It grew into one of those awful cries. The wailing, screaming, can't-breathe-through-the-ugly-face sort of cry. It was as if every emotion that had been running through my body was filling me up since she left, and I reached a boiling point, the contents spewing over. I couldn't lose him too.

She gathered me into her arms, pulling my head close to her chest while she rocked, saying nonsense words that I couldn't make out over my noise. I let my arms go freely around her, clutching at her blazer stretched taut around her shoulders.

I cried for my dad. I cried for me and Ethan. I cried for my mom too. It shook my whole body.

Eventually, the tears subsided, and I pushed away from her.

There were tears brimming in her eyes too. "He's going to be okay."

"I know."

She looked me straight in the eye. "You are going to be okay, Ember."

"I know," I said again, this time with less conviction.

That was the last time I let myself touch her.

**

We pulled into the driveway, and I cut the engine, but we sat inside Bugsy a few moments longer.

"What happened after that?" Matt asked.

I shrugged. "She went back to California. She only stayed with that Joshua guy long enough to launch her career. He was a movie producer and got her a few auditions. As soon as she got that movie role, he became really overprotective and bossy, so she ditched him. At least that's what the tabloids said."

"You kept up with her?"

"News traveled fast around here. Everyone supported my dad, but that didn't mean they didn't keep up with her. She was the new star from small-town America, after all."

"But then your dad got famous too."

"More so, I guess. His first book was a big enough hit to buy this place."

"And he's been writing ever since." Matt's voice was laced with awe.

"Yeah. He never looked back at his manager job at the golf course."

Matt nodded to himself, looking away. "I can't believe your mom left you guys like that. Right in the middle of a heart attack recovery of all things."

"You weren't the only one. The whole town ached for him." I sighed. "And don't forget she cheated."

Matt shook his head. "I'm sorry, Ember."

"Don't be." My voice was terse as I got out of the car, Matt following my lead. "It's not your fault."

"But still. That kind of hurt isn't something to be brushed off."

I fumbled with my keys in the door latch.

"Hey," he said softly. He touched my shoulder. "Are you okay?"

"Yeah." I got the door to unlock, and Jaws was before us, teeth bared again. I stepped inside quickly to grab his leash.

Matt took it from me wordlessly and clipped it to his collar. Jaws padded outside and stayed there just long enough to free his pee off the edge of our porch before rushing back inside out of the cold.

I locked both Bugsy and the door behind us as we followed the dog to the kitchen.

"Do you want anything to drink?" I asked, rummaging through the fridge.

Matt came to lean against the kitchen island behind me. "Something is bothering you."

I sighed and settled on pulling out the milk jug. "It's nothing."

"Is it more than just telling me that story?" Matt asked. He opened the fridge back up and looked through the shelves in the door until he found a bottle of chocolate syrup.

"No," I whispered and watched as he found two glasses from the cabinetry and poured milk into both. One at a time, he set each glass in the microwave.

"What are you doing?" I asked.

He turned back to me. "Hot chocolate. Duh."

Of course. I watched him finish heating both glasses and stir the chocolate syrup into them. He set one of them in front of me, and I mumbled my thanks. Tentatively taking a sip, I had to admit it wasn't half bad.

I put my glass down on the counter and jumped up on the island to sit beside it. I swung my legs a few times. "She's getting married."

Matt peered up at me over the rim of his glass. He waited a few beats to respond. "Is she now?"

I was grateful he was smart enough not to have to ask who. I don't think I could have gotten her title past the rock lodged in my throat. "I am invited to the wedding," I said, even quieter.

"Oh, so like ... soon?"

"Beginning of April."

He moved to lean on the counter beside my hip, facing the same direction so that he wasn't looking at me. He was looking at the stove across from us, instead. "I'm assuming you're not going?" he finally asked.

"I haven't spoken to her in years," I said by way of answering. I bit my lip. "Ethan is, though."

"Does he talk to her?"

"Apparently."

"Do you and he not get along?"

"Not always."

He was quiet a bit longer, processing. "I know it doesn't make it better, and I know it's not my fault, but I am still sorry, Ember."

I swirled my drink in its glass. After a few moments, I nudged his knee with my shoe.

"Thank you."

* * *

I showed Matt to his room, then jumped in the shower first. I was quick to wash my hair and body, but slower to pull on my pajama shorts and shirt. I was studying myself in the mirror again, trying to imagine how I might look in someone else's eyes and wondering what they would see first or what they would notice. Or what walls they would see through.

In just a few short weeks, Matt had managed to locate almost every one and had me disassembling them without request. It was unsettling.

I gathered my clothes and towel, then tiptoed to his room, knocking on the door. "Shower is all yours."

He was laying against the headboard of the bed, scrolling through his phone. He looked up and nearly did a double take. "Oh. Okay."

I held my bundle tighter to my chest. "You good?"

"Of course. It's just … your hair is wet."

I gave him a confused smile. "Yes, that tends to happen when I wash it."

He shook his head. "I just wasn't expecting it, that's all. I've never seen you ready for bed."

I flushed. "Well, that's where I'm heading."

"I figured." He smirked and stood up, gathering his things.

Man, I was awkward. This was awkward. "Okay, well, goodnight."

"Ember?"

I was halfway out the door already. I turned back. "Yes?"

The smile on his face wasn't wide, but it was deep and sincere. "Thank you for inviting me this weekend."

"Of course, partner. See you tomorrow." I cringed and scampered off to my room next door. *Partner?* That was lame.

As I was tucking myself into the covers, I heard the bathroom door close and the water start.

I sank into my bed and listened until the water cut off, secretly hoping that Matt would stop by my door once more before heading to bed. Not that I thought I was going to get an ounce of sleep with him so close.

Yet, still a wall between us.

The door to my brother's room opened and closed again.

I groaned and buried my head in my pillow. Damn. I had never felt so lonely in my own bed. Part of me could still feel Matt's body weight at my back from the night on his couch; I wanted to feel his arm wrapped around my waist again. For once, probably the first time in my life since my family broke, I didn't want to be alone.

And that thought was terrifying.

Chapter Seventeen

Based on the noises clamoring up the stairs to my bedroom, either Matt's a morning person or a family of starving rhinos was pillaging my kitchen.

I had always been Team Anti-Morning, but with a loud groan, I opened my eyes. The soft morning light of the sun had not yet stretched its full arm's length across the sky. I was tempted to burrow my head underneath my pillow to block out the loud sounds, but I figured it probably wasn't a family of rhinoceroses in my kitchen and that I should go check on my guest.

I got up, tucked my feet into slippers, pulled a hoodie on to hide my bed head, and shuffled down the steps.

"Why are you alive at this hour?" I grumbled, my eyes still halfway shut.

"Good morning, sleepy." Matt smiled. "We've got work to do."

"At 7:30 in the morning?" I moved toward the cupboard by sliding my feet across the hardwoods instead of taking actual steps to complete the zombie aesthetic I was currently sporting.

"Got to start at some point. Deadline is tomorrow. French toast?"

I reached for my favorite mug. It was handmade by a trader in town and had a line from a T. S. Eliot poem inscribed along the handle. *I have measured out my life with coffee spoons.*

"Since when do people have the time to make French toast? And I wouldn't have thought there would be ingredients in the fridge."

"You make the time," Matt said. He plated a few slices. "And you'd be surprised how easy it is."

"Hmm," I mumbled. "Coffee?"

"I've had two already."

I plopped a coffee pod into the slot and pressed the button to start the machine. "That explains so much."

Matt shrugged. "It's habit. Our gym sessions are always early in the morning for lacrosse."

I topped my cup with cream from the fridge, and by the time I replaced the carton, Matt had both plates ready.

"Syrup?" he asked.

"Yes, I'm not a heathen."

He chuckled, and we both reached for the handle of the container at the same time, bumping our hands together. I dropped my hand, letting him go first. He did cook, after all.

He didn't grab the handle. Instead, he paused and looked at my face through the gray hood that shrouded my features. The smile that played on his expression was relaxed. Comfortable. I had a brief flash of the smug façade he once wore when we were first partnered together, and I realized maybe I wasn't the only one that had let down my guard.

"Can I tell you something?" Matt asked.

I nervously grabbed for my coffee mug, just to have something to hold onto while I waited. I hated that I had no idea what was going to fall out of his mouth next. I cleared my throat. "Uh, Sure."

The smile on his lips traveled to his eyes, bright and genuine. "I had a really good time with you last night. It was fun getting to know you a little better."

I relaxed my grip on the handle and decided to be honest with him. "I did too. Really."

Matt finally broke the eye contact he had been holding and reached for my hand that had been touching my mug. He picked it up and placed it on the syrup. With a suave wink, he said, "Ladies first."

But he didn't immediately remove his hand from mine. And once again, I didn't mind. Rather, I savored the warm contact.

I let out my breath when he finally let go. I poured a generous amount of syrup, then picked up my plate in one hand, coffee mug in the other. "Where do you want to eat?" I asked.

"Table. I'm not a heathen." There was a glint in his eye as he joked, and I couldn't help the overpowering impulse that demanded action.

As I walked around his tall body toward the kitchen table, I stood tall on my tiptoes to press my lips to his cheek.

"Thanks for breakfast." I kept moving before I could doubt what I had done.

***

"Tell me something, kitten."

I looked over at Matt. After a long day of off-and-on screen time, we were back on the couch after dinner trying to crank out the remainder of our story. The darkness outside served as a reminder that our time up here was waning, and our deadline was looming.

"What would you like to hear?" I asked and stilled my fingers, letting them fall from the keyboard.

"Have you ever written a make out scene?"

"Excuse me?" My voice squeaked.

Matt sighed and dragged both hands across his face. Pressing his cheeks together, he said through the gap in his fingers, "I'm reading what we've got so far for the scene where Lena and Wesley finally get together—and don't take this the wrong way—but I'm just not feeling it."

I prickled. "What do you mean, 'not feeling it'?"

Matt let his hands fall to his sides. "When you read a romance, you should feel something. I don't know, this just feels mechanical. Like, there's no passion."

My fists balled in the space between my sweatshirt and the couch cushions. "Don't forget, you wrote half of it too!"

"Relax, I'm not saying that it's all your fault," Matt said calmly. "I'm just saying that I think this part needs a little bit of work before we turn it in."

"We are running out of time," I clipped.

"Just take a breath and humor me. Have you written a make out scene before?" he asked again.

My voice was small and sour. "No. Have you?"

"No, but I've made out a lot." Matt's grin was cheeky.

I scowled. "Great. Good for you."

He chuckled. "I'm just playing. I hoped you would laugh."

I didn't laugh, but I unclenched my fists.

"Reread the scene for me. Tell me what you think is missing." He handed his laptop over to me.

I gently set mine aside and cradled his, our fingers touching in the exchange. "I've already read it," I said. "I'm not sure how much good this is going to do."

"It's like you're trying to test my patience or something." Matt rolled his eyes. "I asked you to humor me. Read it again and think about it as if this were a movie scene; visualize it in your head. Tell me what is missing."

"Theme music," I muttered and pushed my glasses tighter to the bridge of my nose.

"There's always my jam playlist," Matt said.

"Wrong vibe." I crossed my arms and began reading.

One of my least favorite things to do in the world was admit when I am wrong. And, unfortunately, Matt won this round. My eyes trailed across the page until the scene ended and the characters finished their kiss.

I closed the laptop. "You're right. It feels rusty. Feel free to fix it." I all but thrust it back into Matt's hands.

He took it back with a kind smile. "We can fix it together."

"I'd rather not," I said. My lack of experience in anything passionate was embarrassing.

Matt stood up and walked toward the wall behind us and flicked off the lights, plunging us into darkness.

"What are you doing?"

The overhead light from the kitchen was the only glow in the room. I could hear Matt's footsteps padding back toward the couch as he spoke. "I think the problem is, there's not enough feeling in the story right now. And I mean literal feeling. This is in Lena's head, but when I read it, I feel like I'm watching instead of experiencing, which is creepy, voyeuristic, and not my thing."

Even though he couldn't see my face, I glared at the wall.

"So my idea is that we should practice relying on other senses a little bit more." There was a weight that pressed at the back of the couch behind me, and Matt's breath brushed close to the back of my neck. "Because you cannot write it unless you live it, right?"

The hair at the base of my neck rose at his proximity. "I hate you," I whispered. He had an unfair advantage when he used Van Dam's words against me.

Matt made the daring move to touch me; his fingers slowly lifted my hair from my back and set it over my shoulder. "But do you agree?"

Agree with Oliver Van Dam's philosophy of writing? "Probably." But agree with whatever master plan was running through Matt's head right now causing the nerves underneath his touch to be going haywire? That one was a little scarier.

"So anything that's about to happen is for the good of the contest. Research. To make the story better." He spoke clearly, but I didn't know which one of us he was convincing.

"What exactly is going to happen?" I asked, cursing the hitch in my breath. I turned to look back at him. I could barely make out his silhouette, but the soft light behind him illuminated his golden hair like a dark halo.

His eyes were locked steady on mine. "Ember, I'd really like to kiss you right now. But you've got to tell me: Do you want me to stop?"

No man. *No one* had ever looked at me the way Matt bore into my soul in that moment.

Everything broke, cracked, fissured. The decision was easy. "No," I breathed.

The corner of his mouth turned up. He leaned forward and touched his forehead to mine. "Close those beautiful green eyes."

I could feel my pulse racing, but I did as he said. My eyelids fell closed, and I shifted to face forward once more. The couch cushions swallowed the edges of my body, and I took a breath. "Okay."

I could almost feel Matt's amusement behind me. "It was missing theme music, you said?" His voice was low, husky.

"That was more of a joke." My voice was soft in comparison. Less sure of the words I spoke.

The pressure at the back of the couch shifted, bringing Matt closer to me. I felt his elbows on either side of my shoulders. "Listen. What do you hear?"

He took one finger and trailed it along the collar of my sweatshirt. He made a slow circle at the base of my throat, moving around the back of my neck. My chin jerked. Part of me hated my vulnerability in the moment and my body's response to him that I couldn't control. The other part never wanted the pad of his finger to stop moving.

"Um, there's the ceiling fan."

"Very romantic," Matt quipped. His finger paused, and he leaned forward, bringing his cheek close to mine. "Keep going."

I took a slow breath and whispered, "The wind in the trees outside."

"What's it doing?" he asked, and then his mouth brushed my neck.

I shuddered under the warmth of his kiss and let my head fall to the side. He started just above my sweatshirt and moved his lips toward my ear, pressing kisses as he went. My chest rose and fell faster. I kept my mouth pressed closed, but the sound of exhalation through my nose was deafening.

Matt's bottom lip dragged against my ear then nipped the bottom of it playfully. "What is the wind doing, kitten?"

My jaw fell slack at his voice, his breath caressing my ear. Goosebumps ran down my spine. "Whistling."

Matt curled his mouth into a small O shape and gently whistled. The narrow stream of air he blew hit behind my ear, and the sound he made rang high and steady, almost eerie. I shivered, despite the comfort of my living room.

"What about you?" I dared the question and opened my eyes. "What do you hear?"

Matt stood up, and I immediately felt the loss of his warmth at my back. His footsteps echoed as he walked to sit beside me on the couch, much closer than we had been all weekend. His thigh pressed against mine, and he lifted his hand to my chin, tugging it toward him.

Matt was beautiful. His eyes were dark, unsettling, captivating.

His other arm wound around the small of my back, pulling my waist toward him. I let my body soften and follow.

"I hear your heart," he said. "It's loud." He kissed my cheek. "And steady." He kissed my temple. "And fragile."

My eyelids fluttered when his lips moved over them.

"I hear your breathing, when it hitches." His hand at my cheek dipped lower, and his thumb grazed my throat. "I hear the depth of your sigh when it leaves your lips."

Matt moved his face closer to mine until there was just a breath of space between our mouths.

It was so unlike me, but the question was right there, begging to be asked. "What about taste?" My lips ghosted over his as I asked the question. "For educational purposes, what would this scene taste like?"

Matt waited a beat, then gave me my answer. In a slow sweep of his tongue, Matt glided a kiss across my lips, and I opened my mouth for him. We kissed for what felt like forever but also not nearly enough time.

With a gentle command of his palms and body weight against mine, Matt lowered me onto my back against the couch cushions. I sank under his weight into a comfort I had never quite known.

The kiss deepened. Grew. Became all encompassing. His mouth sought mine in ways none had ever ventured before. His hands ran the length of my body, up, down, up to settle at my hip again.

And mine followed his pattern, across the broad stretch of his back, down his chest to his waistband.

His fingertips found the skin between my pants and my sweatshirt, and I stilled.

Matt felt it instantly. "Are you okay?"

"Yeah," I managed and flushed. "But, um, we probably shouldn't write about much more than this. You know, Pollard is still going to read this, after all."

Matt didn't move for a moment. "Right," he finally said and sat up, off of me.

I righted myself too and tugged at my top.

Matt cleared his throat and then awkwardly reached out to pat the top of my head. "Good job, grasshopper. I think you're educated."

I clasped my hands together in front of me, running one thumb along the top of the other. "Thanks, I guess. I'm a, uh, quick study," I said with a weird chuckle. "And you're not a bad research partner."

He laughed and looked back over at me. The smile he wore made me feel bare as he saw right through me. There was genuine care in that smile, and for the vulnerability that washed over me with it, I might as well have had my shirt all the way off.

I opened my mouth without really knowing what I was going to say. Matt granted me a reprieve when he leaned forward once more, covering my mouth with his. He kissed me again, and I thought about melting right in between the couch cushions.

He removed his lips, but left his forehead pressing against mine. In a soft whisper he said, "Research aside, you're not a bad partner, Ember."

Chapter Eighteen

We got up Monday morning and submitted our *very* rough draft online before driving back to campus. I was grateful that the moment on the couch had seemed to seep into a blissful memory without hanging around us in a cloud of awkwardness. We drove back home similar to how we had gotten to the mountains, listening to music and able to be just Matt and just Ember. I was grateful for the normalcy.

What I wasn't expecting when I got to Advanced Prose Monday night, however, was to see him already seated, comfortable in his new spot in the back of the classroom. My eyes bulged at his open laptop and lean frame draped casually across a seat and a half at our table.

"Am I seeing this right, or is this an apparition? Is Matt Callahan," I paused as I walked toward him, "*the* Matt Callahan, early enough to beat me to class tonight?"

The smirk that I had grown comfortable around stretched itself further toward the crinkled corners of his eyes. "Very funny, Ember." He had what I assumed was his own infamous copy of Van Dam's *To Write* spreading onto my side of the table. He swiped it closer to him, but he left his arm settled across the back of the chair next to him.

I eyed both his arm and the book as I slid in beside him. "What's the special occasion? Did hell freeze over? Or did it rain in the Sahara?"

"First metaphor, cliché. Second one, just plain lame." The cheesy grin was still plastered on his face as he looked at me, our faces approximately a foot away from each other. "I can't believe I know about something happening tonight that you don't."

I straightened my back, hiding my confusion. "How do you know that I don't know what you seem to think you know?"

He quirked an eyebrow, and I replayed that line in my head, praying that it made a whiff of sense. "You're cute when you're flustered."

"Am not!" I cried, then backtracked. "Flustered, I mean. I … I'm totally cute." Real smooth.

"Mhmm. I know." The smile was back.

I gave in. "Should I know about something special happening tonight?"

I glanced around. The seats in the classroom had slowly started to fill with students as Matt and I bantered from our corner. Brynn and Spencer still weren't here yet. I hadn't seen either of them since we got back this morning. My stomach turned, praying that neither one asked about my trip home. They were both unaware that Matt had accompanied me; thus, they had no inkling of the kiss he and I shared. And I intended to keep it that way.

Matt finally turned toward the front of the classroom, retracting his arm from my shoulder and folding his hands neatly in front of him. "Supposedly we are being graced with the presence of a highly esteemed guest speaker tonight."

"J. K. Rowling?"

He flicked a playful eye toward me. "Close."

Brynn and Spencer walked in together. Brynn offered a friendly wave, which Matt exuberantly returned of course. Spencer smiled, too, but I could see the strain in it at seeing Matt sitting next to me again. I felt bad.

Just as they sat down and Brynn turned to say something to us, the door to the classroom thudded to a close. Two men walked in: Professor Pollard, clad in a pinstripe coat and khakis, and a smaller, wiry gentleman, dressed in jeans, an unbuttoned, collared, white shirt over a graphic T-shirt that seemed to have a portrait of Shakespeare on it and read, *I put the Lit in Literature.*

"Oh my god," Matt whispered beside me. "This night just got even better. I need to ask him where he got his shirt."

"Matt," I hissed. It felt like my heart was in my throat, and I couldn't get anything past the lump besides my partner's name. I knew that second man. There was no way that he was actually here, in our class, in the flesh, right now. Pollard withdrew his notes from his briefcase, and the man sat down on top of the table at the front of the room, legs crossed at the ankles and swinging.

"Good evening, everyone," Pollard said as he shuffled his papers from behind the computer on the podium. "You guys are in for a surprise. We have a guest lecturer who has come tonight to gift us with some sage words of wisdom."

"Ha!" the man chortled. "I'm glad you think me wise, Caine. Hate to disappoint the audience with false affirmations of insight, though. I got started on the same teachings you are spitting out here, probably."

Pollard shook his head. "All the same. Class, please join me in welcoming Mr. Oliver Van Dam to talk with us today about some tips and tricks useful to us aspiring writers."

I robotically jerked my head toward Matt's sly grin. I sputtered in a hushed rush. "You knew about this? How did you know about this?"

Oliver Van Dam. Van Dam was actually here in our class. Right now. Going to *lecture*.

Matt shrugged. "I thought it was pretty funny that we both enjoyed him. I did a little extra sleuthing and found out he and Pollard actually went to the same undergrad school. I stopped by his office hours to see if there was a chance that they knew each

other. Turns out, they had a lot of classes together. Pollard agreed
that it would be worth a shot trying to get him in to class here."

I was stunned speechless.

"Now, for those of you who don't know Mr. Van Dam—"
Pollard continued, but my idol interrupted him.

"Puleez," Van Dam said, rolling his head around his shoulders.
"Call me Ollie. Being back on a campus makes me feel young again.
Reminds me of my own wild and crazy college days."

Pollard started again, obviously immune to the genius that
radiated off his friend's being. "Oliver has had several short stories
published, as well as a lengthy series of science fiction novels called
the *Moon Spark Chronicles.*"

"Perhaps you've heard of it," Van Dam said.

"How could we not?" Matt said. His toe nudged my ankle as he
spoke. "The last movie was totally sold out when I tried to go see
it opening night."

Oliver Van Dam pointed at him, shaking his finger. "Right on,
boy. I knew this would be a worthwhile visit."

I was impressed that Matt had tried to attend the premier of the
last *Moon Spark* movie, but I was too transfixed to move. Oliver
Van Dam was looking right at us.

"Aside from his success with the series," Pollard went on,
"Oliver also has a nonfiction book titled, *To Write or to Dream
About Writing,* which he will be pulling from to speak with you
all about tonight. And as a special treat, he has also agreed to read
over your drafts for your stories and offer feedback. Let's give him
a warm welcome."

I clapped along with the class, but Pollard's last bit made my
arms heavy. Van Dam was going to be reading our story? No. He
couldn't be. That wasn't possible. It was almost like Van Dam had
been a figment of my imagination all these years I thought I had
known him through his books. And here he was, finally in front
of me.

Van Dam leaped off his perch on the table and strolled around
to the backside, flourishing a black marker from the tray at the

whiteboard. "Thank you for your kind introduction. In case you all did not know, Caine and I happened to study together back in the olden days, thirty some odd years ago now? Crazy how time flies and people develop. Now he's teaching my writings." He chuckled, flicking open the marker's cap and holding it like a delicate wand. "But enough about the past. I'm here today to hopefully impose some advice on you young things that you can take forward into your own future of writing. As per stereotype, writers can be a narcissistic bunch of assholes, so I'm here to talk about myself and my own process for putting together a story. Take it for what it's worth."

I couldn't believe this was happening. I nearly turned to Matt to ask him to pinch me to make sure I wasn't dreaming, but thought better of it. I couldn't afford distraction. I wanted to drink every word that dripped from Van Dam's lips, hoping that some of his gift of storytelling could somehow seep into my own words. I reached into my bag to pull out my own notebook and pen.

"Caine tells me this is an Advanced Prose class, correct?" Van Dam asked.

The class buzzed a chorus of yeses. I didn't trust myself not to shout the word, so I stayed still, giddy with excitement, not noticing that Matt was eyeing me more than the famous author in front of us.

"Caine told me about your little contest and partnerships. I've had a few of my stories published in *Noted and Quoted*. Therefore, I feel fairly qualified to impart my opinion that the requirement to force you to write together is absolute crap."

I couldn't help my chuckle that bubbled alongside the rest of my classmates. Pollard rolled his eyes and took a seat at one of the student desks before saying, "Don't forget, we had to do the same thing at one point. And were we not better for it in the long run?"

Van Dam pointed his opened marker at his friend, pinkie slightly raised. "Speak for yourself; it was torturous." He paused, then whispered. "Unfortunately, he's right. Collaboration is for your own good, regardless of the inconvenience that another mind and opinion impose on one's own creative being. But back to the lecture at hand."

He turned to write a large number one on the whiteboard behind him. "The first step that I follow in drafting any story is to write an extraordinarily terrible first draft."

The class sucked in a breath at the absurdity of the accomplished novelist writing *SHITTY FIRST TRY* across the entirety of the board's length when his own books were filled with the words of a mastermind. I finally relaxed a bit in my chair. I understood this philosophy. I had heard this advice time and time before, in Van Dam's own voice that spoke inside my head as I read the opening chapter of *To Write* multiple times. Though, I hadn't thought his tone to be as nasally as it was in actuality.

Van Dam turned back toward us, capping his marker. "When I sit down to write a short story, I usually have a spark of an idea, a picture of a beginning, and maybe if I'm lucky, a few things that could happen in the middle. Then there is only an empty void of an ending. There have been several times that I have tried to block out every scene and plan every step that I wanted my stories to take, but every time I do this, I fail and end up having wasted several hours of my precious and invaluable time."

As a planner myself, I couldn't fathom his write-by-the-seat-of-your-pants method, but it obviously seemed to work for him.

"You see," he continued. "For me, stories have a way of shaping themselves as they go. It's a bit like archeology. After I write a few awful pages of prose and go back and start to sift through the wreckage, I can usually find a sentence here or there that has potential, and those treasures may lead the story in an entirely new direction than I had once thought. Perhaps the bones of the story are actually supposed to resemble a velociraptor rather than a crocodile."

Van Dam quickly uncapped his marker again to sketch out what I'm sure was supposed to be some fantastical prehistoric beast to help develop his metaphor but resembled more of a cow. He continued to speak as he drew. "The words you write will collaborate in order to tell the tale that needs to be told." Cow doodle complete, he turned back to us, shaking his marker again in our direction. "Believe in that."

He then wrote out in swirling cursive a large number two. "The second piece of advice I can give you hatchlings is a series of tips regarding revisions." *MAJOR REVISIONS* adorned the whiteboard in a similar script. "The first revision that I cannot stress enough importance on is that Character. Drives. Plot." He wrote out the phrase and underlined it, twice, then resumed his perch on the front table, legs recrossed at the ankles. "Plot does NOT drive character. If you find your main character starting to be taken for a ride by the events that you want to happen in the plot, you are writing wrong.

"Let me tell you a story." Van Dam capped his marker and leaned back with his arms stretched behind him, suddenly wistful. "I sat in on a college creative writing class in Texas once. It was their workshop day, and the story that was up for speculation was written by a bright young man. Before the critiques came flowing in, the man read the first page of his story to the class to orient them in the world before diving in. And you know what?" He paused, a moment and a half, leaving us all on the edge of our seats, me probably more literally than the rest of the crowd. "I was hooked."

Matt laughed beside me along with the rest of the class.

Van Dam continued with his own baffled chuckle. "It was truly beautiful. I mean, this man had painted a fantasy landscape that was hot, dirty, smoldering, inhabited by the strangest half-men half-mechanical creatures, and in just a few paragraphs, I was living in this world alongside his hero. And then he let me down." His tone sobered up. "This student had the audacity to take a strong, determined, ambitious character and literally put him into the antagonist's flying car. The bad guy then drove the hero to the neighboring town where the evil lair was located. There, he proceeded to kick the hero out of the car and tell him, 'Take care of yourself ... find your own way home ... you're not my problem, kid.' "

Van Dam ran a hand through his gray hair. "The point is, things shouldn't ever just happen to your characters. Characters are not interesting if they never make any choices. The good news is, this can be an easy revision. Go back through your draft and find places where your story can present your character with a choice. Even actively choosing not to do something is still making a choice. I repeat: your character drives the plot forward by the choices he or she makes. In the aforementioned example, the student went back and put a little more fight into the kidnapping and later had his hero choose to take over the hovercraft, ultimately wrecking it to try to escape."

My mind immediately shot to the story we spent the entire weekend drafting, mentally going through each plot point and trying to think if there were any holes we had fallen into where Lena had become passive. I jotted down a few notes.

"The other favorite tidbit of advice for revision that I have is regarding pacing." Without rising from his seat, Van Dam tucked his knees to his chest and swung back around to the whiteboard to write the word out before swiveling forward again. "In prose, you are granted the freedom of time. Jump it. Live in it. Wallow in it, even. The difference between a story and an article is that the writer of a story uses this timely freedom to slow down the most important scenes he has to tell. By carefully picking out which scenes are important enough to be developed slowly and methodically, the pacing shifts, and the writer can basically call out to the reader, Here Is My Point! You Should Pay Attention! Thematic Significance Up Ahead!" Van Dam emphasized his increase in tone with a double jazz hand. "The result is that these slower scenes carry more weight, and the reader garners a deeper understanding for the actions, thoughts, reactions in these parts of the story, rather than if the writer were to just steamroll on through without making the reader pause to consider the worth nestled between the words. And how might one slow down these scenes?"

Oliver Van Dam looked around at the sea of students, none of them willing to raise their hand for a guess at the answer. I plucked up some courage from the dream I seemed to be living in and raised my own hand, tentatively.

Van Dam fixed his wild eyes on me and beamed. "Yes, dear? Go on."

My voice was a single squeak. "Details?"

He clapped twice, a thunderous noise to the hushed classroom. "Right on. Details, friends. But not just any details. Significant details. Take this room, for instance." Van Dam looked around. "If I were to describe this room, wanting to convey the mood of the environment, I would not choose to tell my reader about the faded, ugly, mustard-colored walls nor the wheezing old projector that sputtered a protest every time it was called upon to do its job. No, I would choose to describe the fervent scratching of pens across paper, or the furious tapping of keys on a keyboard as the throng of students were inspired to grasp at the words the artist before them recited, eager to become their own version of creative writers."

I wrote down another line of notes in my book and glanced over at Matt's laptop. He had a blank word document pulled up. I nudged his ankle, wiggling my pen between my fingers when he turned toward me. He tapped his pointer finger to his temple, then pressed it to his lips, silencing me. I rolled my eyes.

"And how to describe these significant details? Metaphors. Fresh metaphors. Another common pitfall for developing writers is to try on existing metaphors for size, thinking themselves accomplished because they didn't use like or as. I berate you all: stay away from the cliché."

It was Matt's turn to deliver the pointed look speared in my direction laced with an arrogant gleam in his eye as if to say *I told you so*. That, deserved a kick to his ankle. He jerked it back, careful to not let his expression give way to the commotion going on under our table, then rested his foot next to mine, turning back to Van Dam.

"I do not want to read," Van Dam continued, "about a lovely lady who has ocean blue eyes. I have read about so many ladies, and gentlemen alike, with eyes as deep and mysterious as the ocean blue, and quite frankly I am bored of those eyes. I want to read about blue eyes that are kiddie swimming pools, bleached pale as if by too much chlorine and stripped of innocence that used to laugh there. Or blue eyes that are hard and crystalized like a blue raspberry candy, that look too sickly sweet to digest so you smile and nod and promise yourself to spit out the lies they fed you later, when you are alone."

I let my pen roll off my fingertips, thumping against my notes. This man was a literary god.

"And lastly," Van Dam reached back once again to write on the board, pulling the cap off his marker with his teeth. "You've got to make the story true. Make it visceral. Make it real," he spoke around the cap in his mouth, distorting the speech, but the message was clear as he wrote number three on the board, *Human Experience Is Truth*. He turned to face us. "Now, if your character is slaying a dragon in your story, I'm not saying you have to have literal experience slaying said dragons. But you need to consider the emotional charge of a scene like that. What might your character be feeling?"

The crowd was quiet.

"That was not a rhetorical question, children." Van Dam rolled his eyes. "Come on, think about it. Give me some feelings you might have if you are faced with the prospect of having to slay a dragon? Yes, you in the back? Black sweatshirt."

I turned to see Holly plopping her hand back down on her desk. "Fear."

"Yes of course, fear. What else?"

Bravery, courage, and the force of adrenaline were tossed around the class, each met with glowing approval from Oliver Van Dam. "Yes, yes, all of these yes. Here's the trick: in order for a story to be successful, it needs a human element of truth if it is to be read and loved and felt by humans. You as the writer need to be able to stitch as many layers of truth to your words as you can. If a character is slaying a dragon, when I am reading that scene, I want to be afraid not for that character just because this dragon is terrifying. No, I want to be afraid *with* that character because I am seeing the beast through their eyes and feeling their fear down to my own bones. And to be able to write and convey that feeling, you have to at least have felt deeply once in your life, or else you are writing blind and lying to both yourself and your reader.

"So the last advice I can leave you with is to live. Live a full life, tasting as many experiences that your path has to offer, or better yet, deviate from your life's path a step or two and taste another exotic treasure. Build your repertoire of experiences so that your toolbox is stocked full when you need application for a story." Van Dam paused, a finger to his lip. "Actually, I lied. There's one more piece of advice I can give, and that's grammar." He reached back to scratch the word sloppily at the bottom of the whiteboard. "But really," he said as he capped the pen, finally placing it back on the tray, "that is the editor's job after all—hell that's what they are paid to do anyway. You could even slip in a few verb tense switches just to try to trick them up."

Pollard cleared his throat as he rose to return to the front of the classroom.

"Just kidding," said Van Dam. "Don't do that, or at least try not to."

My pen continued across my page while Van Dam spoke, adding several lines of notes from the lecture as well as things to check back on in our story.

When the clock tower struck 7:30, signaling our usual halfway point through night class. Oliver Van Dam had finished with impressive punctuality, earning a standing ovation from the class. Literally.

Professor Pollard took over the podium as the applause subsided. "Thank you all for giving Mr. Van Dam your attention tonight, and thank you, Oliver, for sharing both your time and your wisdom."

He earned an encore of applause again as he gave a dramatic bow and thanked us all.

"As a reminder," Pollard continued. "You all should have uploaded your rough drafts prior to coming to class. For next week, you will need to print and annotate the other five stories from the class, as well as write a letter for each story with critiques. We will have a formal workshop in class to discuss each story, but it would be beneficial to you all to have a hard copy of the other students' suggestions. I will also make sure you get copies of Mr. Van Dam's feedback with this workshop. After this final revision, I will grade the stories, and they will be sent to the magazine for judging. Now, we are going to go ahead and take a short break. When we come back, we can do a Q and A with Mr. Van Dam for the remainder of the evening."

"Yes," Van Dam said. "Please pick my brains ... after I go get more coffee."

The prospect of my idol's eyes on my words was overwhelming as Pollard and Oliver Van Dam stepped out of the classroom for their break.

As soon as the door clicked behind them, Brynn turned to me. "How was home, Ember?"

"Good," I said quickly, packing up my bag to avoid meeting her eye. "Quiet. It was nice. How was your weekend?"

Matt was silent beside me as he slid his computer into his bag.

"It was good. I spent most of it in the library finishing up the draft." Her eyes cut to Holly and narrowed before focusing back on me with a soft smile. "Missed you, though."

Brynn code for *I'm sorry.* It was rare that I got a sentiment like that from her. It wasn't often that she sought my company on purpose. I was just always *there.* In class, in the room, the gym, the library. We happened to share so many spaces, she didn't need to reach out beyond them. Saying she missed me this weekend could have only meant she still felt bad about belittling my lack of extracurriculars on Friday.

I mean, my inferiority was obvious. She didn't have to point it out.

"Missed you too," I said, but the words were flat.

Chapter Nineteen

My phone buzzed with a text from Matt when Spencer, Brynn, and I were at The House that night after class.

brynn doesnt know I was with you when you went home does she

I grimaced, then responded.

No.

My fingers hovered above the keyboard before adding:

I'm sorry.

dont be, was his response.

I set my phone down on the table and sipped my coffee. Spencer was rambling about something, the details escaped me. According to his waving hands and general exuberance, he was happy.

I couldn't muster the energy to match his euphoria. I hadn't technically been lying. Brynn didn't ask if I had gone home alone, or if anyone accompanied me. If she had, I'm sure I would have told her Matt went with me. I would've had to at that point. But still, I felt bad about the subterfuge.

Because this weekend had been ... nice.

Beyond nice, actually. Almost perfect.

"Ember," Spencer whined. "You're not paying attention to me at all."

"Sorry," I mumbled. I set my coffee cup down and crossed my arms. "You were saying?"

"I was trying to tell you about my latest girlfriend. I'm coming out again. This time as straight."

"Really?" I blinked twice. "I'm happy for you."

He rolled his eyes. "No, of course not Ember. Have you been listening at all? I'm trying to tell you guys the story of my latest online date and it's epic failure that ended in the hospital."

"Are you okay?" He had my full attention now.

"Oh yeah." He waved me off. "Poor Jason, or Mason, or whatever his name was, I'm not so sure about. I left after the ambulance came to pick him up. He ate a pepper that was too hot for him at the Mexican restaurant. Wimp."

I shook my head.

"Hey." Brynn reached out to touch my hand once. "Is there something on your mind?"

"Not really," I said, folding my hands in my lap. "Maybe I'm just tired."

It wasn't something.

It was someone.

∗

On the top ten list of things being on my mind, I had gotten much better at making my mom a background thought. Maybe a solid number eleven in the hierarchy list. That had changed when her wedding invitation arrived, but she definitely crossed the top of the list when she called Wednesday afternoon.

I had stopped answering her calls years ago, and she stopped calling shortly after that. She had no right to be calling now.

I gritted my teeth as I sat on the edge of my bed, holding my phone with both hands, staring at the caller ID that buzzed beneath my touch.

Ava Owens: Mobile. Slide to Answer.

I blew out a breath before I slid the button on the screen to accept the call. "Ava." Her name was sharp on my tongue.

There was a pause on the other end of the line. My mom must have been shocked that I actually answered. She drew a slow breath before saying, "Ember. It's good to hear your voice."

Not likely, I thought. "What do you need?"

"I was just … calling to see how things are going. What's new?"

This was so weird. "Nothing, really."

A heavy pause filled the static hum.

"How about boys? Do you have a boyfriend now?"

"Seriously?" Of course boys would be the first thing she would go to. A supposed mother – daughter bonding strategy. Something a normal college girl might have had a well-equipped answer for. "No," I said. "I don't."

"Surely there's got to be someone you have an eye on. Any crushes around campus?"

I bit back the retort about her obvious wandering eyes. "Nope," I lied.

"You know," she continued. "If you like a boy, your best bet is to just come clean and tell him how you feel. It's so twentieth century for the boy to have to make the first move."

This conversation was getting stranger by the second. "I don't need boy advice …" I stopped myself short before I said *Mom.* "Why are you really calling? Surely it's not just to pester your estranged daughter about her love life."

"I can't call just to catch up?" Her voice was cheery, almost with a singsong lilt to it.

"Not without a motive."

Her voice dropped an octave. "You haven't RSVP'd to my wedding yet."

My eyes flickered to the top of my desk.

"Your brother is coming," she added when I didn't say anything.

"So I've heard." My voice was flat.

"I would love for you to be there."

"Ava," I said, sitting up a little straighter in bed. "What is today?"

"Today is Wednesday, honey."

"Interesting. And what is tomorrow?"

"Well," she started, the confusion evident in her voice, "tomorrow is Thursday."

"Wrong answer," I snapped. "Tomorrow is my birthday. My twenty-*first* birthday."

"Ember, I—"

"Goodbye, Ava." I hung up the phone before tossing it on the comforter beside me.

It was always the same. Always all about her. I wrung my hands together over and over and over again before leaning over my knees and pinching the bridge of my nose, keeping the prickling tears at bay. I was done shedding them for her.

The door opened as Brynn came in, but I remained hunched over.

She set her bag and keys down at her desk then plopped beside me on my bed. "What's wrong?"

I let out a deep sigh and righted myself. "Nothing."

"Yes, that's why you're sitting here all mopey. Because nothing is wrong."

"I'm not mopey."

"You're totally mopey."

I turned to look at her. Her hair was pulled up into its trademark bun, pencils sticking out in crazy directions with loose lavender ends framing her narrow face. Her slanted eyes were perfectly lined in a black cat eye, and her deep brown, almost black, irises were filled with kindness.

I got up and grabbed the pink envelope, handing it to her as I sat back down.

Brynn was one of the only people who knew about my parents—anything about them—here at school. Spencer did, too, by default, but only because he had been around town when everything happened. I accidentally told Brynn during our freshman year, on one of the nights Spencer came over to our dorm with his secret stash of Tito's vodka. *The good stuff,* he told us. *Only the good stuff for my ladies.*

Well, that good stuff led to a night alternating between sleeping with my cheek pressed against the cool bathroom floor and puking, followed by a wicked hangover in the morning. I never drank that much again.

Prior to those events was the involuntary slip of my own cursed tongue. *My dad writes, and my mom is an actress. Well, a failed one, but that serves her right for cheating and leaving us all in the first place. Funny how karma works, right?* And then I promptly ran to the bathroom to hurl my guts up.

I never brought my parents up again, and neither did Brynn.

Her long fingers delicately pulled the card out, and her eyes narrowed as she scanned it. Once finished, she gently placed it back into the envelope and put an arm around my shoulders, saying nothing.

I leaned my head against her sweater, the cashmere was soft against my cheek.

"You know you can talk to me, right?" Brynn said.

The weird urge to confide in her about everything, and I mean *everything*, was almost unbearable. From the anger at my mom and her Hollywood wedding, the confusion and unease at my brother's divorce and not knowing how to help without just getting in the way and starting a fight, to above all, my own conflicting feelings surrounding the enigma that was Matt Callahan. I felt like I was going to explode from all the churning.

"I know," I finally said, but nothing more.

***

I came out of American Literature the next day to find Matt Callahan leaning one shoulder against the yellow drywall in the hallway. It was almost unfair how good he could look in a sweater and jeans. He had a paper coffee cup in one hand and was scrolling absently through his phone with the other.

He lifted his gaze as the students ahead of me filed out of the room. He smiled at me in time with the little flip my chest performed as our eyes met.

"Hey," he said.

"What's up?" I asked, gripping the straps of my backpack by my hips.

"Word on the street is that today is going to be a great day."

"Why's that?"

He pushed off the wall and gestured for me to go first down the staircase. I obliged, and he followed, his shoes clicking on the laminate as he skipped behind me. "Because. We have plans tonight."

Something squeezed my gut at his words. The door closed behind us, and I turned to face him. "Do we now?"

"Indeed."

"What are you doing here?" I asked. It pained me to admit I had been keeping half an eye out for him, but I hadn't seen him pass by since the first day he came to ask to meet up.

He held out the coffee cup he had been toting. "I had to give you your birthday coffee. Happy birthday, kitten."

I couldn't stop the small smile that crept along my mouth as I reached to take it from his outstretched hand. "I ..." I started, then shook my head. "You didn't have to do that." I popped the lid off to check the contents. The dark roast aroma steamed up to tickle my face. The color was a nice amber.

"I think I got the formula right. About seven-eighths coffee, one-eighth cream, no sugar." He shrugged. "I've watched you make it a time or two."

The corners of my eyes crinkled. "That was really nice of you. Thank you." I took a sip. It was pretty much perfect. "Now what about these plans we supposedly have?"

"Ah, yes. Those. I ran into Brynn this morning, and she said you had a bit of a rough night."

I immediately stiffened. What did she tell him? Not that Matt didn't know about my crazy family, but the thought of the two of them talking about me without me there to steer the conversation made me nervous.

"Not to worry," Matt said, noticing my tension. "She guarded your affliction with tight lips. She just said you were feeling down, so I thought we all could have a little get together tonight at my place to celebrate you."

Usually, Brynn, Spencer, and I would go down the street to the Mexican restaurant and eat our body weight in tacos, chips, and salsa for our birthdays. It was sort of a tradition between the three of us, but the gleam in Matt's eye had my chest softening to the idea of changing tradition. "Who is 'all of us'?"

"Whoever you want."

This was going to be embarrassing. I didn't have a whole slew of friends to choose from when it came to a house party. I didn't even really know what constituted a house party. Did a "little get together" at Matt's apartment count?

"I usually like smaller groups," I ended up saying.

"Perfect. You, me, Brynn, Bash, and Spencer it is."

I tried to hide my sigh of relief. "You've put some thought into this, haven't you?"

His grin was sly. "Don't give me too much credit," he said as he stepped away from me to move toward the Business School building. "Facebook reminded me it was your birthday this morning."

I smiled at the back of his head, then paused. "Wait!" I cried. "We aren't even friends on Facebook!"

He made it almost halfway across the green. He turned his head back over his shoulder and winked a chocolate eye at me.

Chapter Twenty

"**Y**ou can't wear that," Brynn said as she burst through our door.

"Why not?" I asked, immediately defensive of the outfit I just spent an embarrassingly long time pulling together for the party. My hair was up in a ponytail, and I had my glasses on over mascara, lip gloss, and a neutral bronze eye shadow. I was wearing a pair of dark skinny jeans with one of my nicer blouses. It had flowers on it. An online search engine informed me this was acceptable for a "small party with friends."

"Because, Ember," Brynn sounded exasperated as she threw her bag to her bed and started rummaging through her closet, "it's your freaking birthday! You have to dress up."

"I am dressed up! These are my nice jeans."

She rolled her head toward me. "You're not wearing jeans tonight."

I sat down on my bed in a defeated heap. "I like jeans."

Brynn came over and plopped an armful of clothes onto the comforter. She put her hands on my shoulders and leaned down to match my eye level. "And I like you. Therefore, I am not letting you go to a nice little party for your TWENTY-FIRST BIRTHDAY—"

Her voice was loud in my face. I squinted my eyes at her while she continued.

"—looking like a librarian."

"What's wrong with librarians?"

She sighed. "Nothing is wrong with librarians, honey. They just don't go wild for a birthday party."

"I don't think I do that either."

"Well, tonight you do!" She rummaged through her stack. "Is Spencer coming?"

"No," I said. "He's not."

I had skipped up to Spencer's room immediately after Matt brought me birthday coffee to ask if he would come with us. The smile on his lips was thin and sad compared to my wide one.

"Damn, I wish I could, but I have to go home this afternoon and get my wisdom teeth out tomorrow, of all things."

"You scheduled surgery over my birthday weekend?"

"In fairness, my mom did. And I can never remember your birthday anyway."

"That's a total failure of best-friendmanship."

"That's not a thing."

"Is now."

"Ember, you know I love you," Spencer said. "And I know you like to think that Matt isn't in love with you. But in addition to having my teeth forcibly ripped out of my skull, it would be pretty hard to play pretend all night long. It still sort of hurts to see him and know he could never be mine."

My heart sank. I should have thought of that. "It's okay, I understand."

"I'm sorry. Have fun tonight for me."

"Bash should be there," I said to Brynn's back as she continued to make piles of her clothes, holding up odd garments for inspection that all shared the commonality of being very tiny.

"I know," she said. "He texted me to make sure I was coming."

"Are you two, like, a *thing*?" I asked, unsure of how to phrase the question.

"Bash?" She turned around. A black, leather mini skirt was in one hand and a dark green sleeveless turtleneck that looked way too short to be a shirt was in the other. "Of course not. You know me, I don't like to be tied down. Don't get me wrong, I like him a lot. But we are casual, you know? Chill."

Chill. I mulled over the idea of finding something casually chill in my life. I just didn't know how. I think it took a certain kind of confidence I absolutely did not possess. "What does 'chill' entail, exactly?"

A grin cracked along her face. "Exactly?"

"Don't answer that. Your face says it all. As far as I know, he has only ever kissed your cheek, nice and innocent."

"Yeah, all four of them."

"STOP!"

Brynn giggled then looked back down at the clothes she picked once more before thrusting them into my hands. "These are good. You just need some eyeliner and a dark red lipstick, then you should be good to go."

I looked at the small, foreign objects in my hands. "Brynn, you are a good four inches taller than me with about half of my ass and chest. There is no way that I am going to fit into these."

She waved me off, already back in her closet looking for something to wear. "You're going to look hot. And besides," she smiled back at me, "green brings out your eyes."

***

Due to my extremely short torso, the skirt I was currently dressed up in sat just on top of my hips, cinching at my waist, and the hemline of the green shirt landed just at the bottom of my rib cage, practically lining up perfectly with the skirt.

As long as I didn't raise my arms above my head, Brynn's clothes seemed to fit.

"Raise the roof!" she chanted as she came back from the bathroom, her own hands pumping in the air. She wore a similar cut top to the one I was currently tugging at, and skintight, black leather pants with strappy heels.

"Oh, would you stop fussing." She swatted my hands away from the shirt. "Have you looked in the mirror? You look ah-maz-ing."

I had looked in the mirror. I *stared* at the version of me that apparently wore eyeliner and lipstick. Brynn left my hair in the high ponytail, but she made me ditch the glasses. I did, however, stick firm in my choice of footwear: flats.

At least the skirt had pockets. I slipped my phone into one of them after checking the time.

"Come on," she sang out, grabbing her keys. "We are going to be late."

"We are already late."

"No, this is *fashionably* late. Which means we are on time. But no later than this." She took one final glance in the mirror and seemed to be pleased, then she grabbed two jackets out of her closet and chucked one at me. "Let's go."

***

Their apartment door opened, and we were met with a booming bass and a cheery smile.

"Ladies," Bash said, but he only had eyes for Brynn. "You two made it!"

"Thanks for hosting," Brynn said and stepped into his arms for a real cute side hug.

"Of course," Bash said, letting her go and stepping aside to let us through. "No Spencer?"

I shook my head. "No Spencer."

"That's a shame. Well, come on in. Bar is open." Bash stopped me with a gentle touch on my arm after Brynn passed through. "Happy birthday, Ember."

His smile was genuine, and I decided then and there that I approved of Bash. Brynn should get off the "chill" kick she was on. He obviously liked her.

I offered a smile back. "Thank you."

"Callahan!" I heard Brynn's voice call out. The music was louder inside and seemed to be coming from a speaker in the kitchen. Brynn had moved closer to the source of the noise and was embracing Matt as he set the bottles he was holding down on the counter.

"Hey!" he hugged Brynn back. "Good to see you." His gaze settled beyond her and found me. Call me crazy, but I think his eyes widened in surprise as I shrugged out of my coat. And I am pretty sure there was a stutter in his usual swift countenance at seeing me dressed up.

"Ember," he said and released Brynn. "Hi."

"Hey."

There was a beat of silence, quickly covered up by Bash saying, "Let's get this party started!"

⁂

It didn't take long for Bash's playlist and the alcohol served to get a gentle buzz humming in the apartment's air. But that also could have been the faulty air conditioning that kept the temperature tundra-like.

Once they got their drinks in hand, Bash and Brynn immediately started setting up a foldable table for beer pong. Bash's head continually bobbed to the rhythm of the music, unashamed, while the two of them bantered and worked.

I propped myself on top of the kitchen table, crossing my legs at the ankles and letting them swing. "I didn't know they made pop-up pong tables," I said to Matt while I held the glass he had gifted me with both hands. It was some sort of white wine, bubbly and fruity. It almost tasted like juice.

Matt finished putting all of the bottles back in the refrigerator and pulled out a twelve pack of beer. Cracking one open, he said, "It comes in handy from time to time."

"Do you have people over often?" *In other words, do you host parties often? Do you host parties with girls at your apartment often? Do you give girls nice-tasting fruity wine at your parties often?*

"Every now and then," he replied simply and came toward my perch. Matt disregarded my personal space when he sat his drink down. He lowered the heels of his hands to the edge of the table, his thumbs grazing the hem of my skirt.

I held my breath.

His face was so close to mine. He smiled when I flicked my eyes toward our company, hoping they weren't watching the kitchen too closely.

Matt dropped his voice to a much lower, slower octave when he said, "You're my favorite person that's been over here though."

I tried to snort, but the sound came out strangled.

Matt pressed forward, bringing his cheek to my ear. His knees knocked lightly against mine when he said, "You look lovely tonight, Ember."

My voice was small. "Thank you." I wiggled in my seat, and Matt leaned away, looking rather proud of himself.

"Hey, Owens!" Bash called, and Matt stepped away from the table with a sly smirk.

I cleared my throat. "Yeah?"

"Do you have any plans for this Saturday yet? One of my mates is hosting a party. You and Brynn are both more than welcome to come."

"What kind of party?" Brynn asked, leaning against the table on her forearms. The neckline of her top drooped as she did so.

Bash rolled his eyes. "A frat party, what else would it be? You guys in?"

Brynn looked over at me. "I'm in if you are, Ember."

My heart swelled a little at her inclusion. Even though she always asked if I'd like to join her when she went out, something about this time felt more real. "I'm down."

"Great," Brynn said, looking down at the table. "Now, are you guys ready to play or what?"

At least the red cup trope I had seen in all the movies was true. They had plastic cups arranged in identical triangles on either side of the table.

"Only if you're ready to have your ass royally whoped by yours truly," Matt called back with a grin. He turned to me to ask in a softer voice. "Have you ever played?"

I shook my head, not trusting my tongue to hold back the thoughts about how close his lips were to mine just then. I was still thinking about our kiss in the mountains.

I wondered if he was too.

Matt nudged my shoulder with his and stood up. "Come on. It's pretty easy."

I took two big sips of my drink to finish it off and followed Matt into the living room.

"I'm thinking," Bash said, "that this should be a good old-fashioned game played boys against girls."

"Oh, it is so on." Brynn smirked and took her position opposite Bash and Matt. She elbowed my side, but continued staring down the pair. "We are taking you two down."

I leaned closer to her to whisper, "Debatable."

"Shush."

"Ladies first," Bash said and tossed Brynn a small, white ball.

She caught it deftly with one outstretched hand. "Our pleasure." She said to me, "I've got this first one."

She closed one eye and squinted the other, her hand making odd pendulum movements back and forth by her ear, practicing her trajectory. When she launched the tiny sphere, it landed in the right cup of the second row of the pyramid with a celebratory *plop*.

"Yes!" she cried. "Drink up, friend."

Bash looked a little sour as he fished the ball out of the cup and chugged it. "Lucky shot," he muttered, then clapped Matt's shoulder. "You're up, man."

Matt took the ball from Bash. Eyeing his track similarly to the way Brynn had, Matt sunk his shot in a cup right in front of me.

His smile was wide. "Score."

"You have to drink that one now," Brynn said to me.

"Yeah, I gathered that." I picked up the cup. Narrowing my eyes, I wiggled my fingers to pull the ball out. The beer wasn't as good as the wine already in my stomach, but I kept it down.

As awesome as it would have been to sink my first shot in my first-ever game of beer pong, I missed the cups gloriously. Like, didn't even touch them.

But Bash missed, too, so all was fair.

The ambiance alternated between a few choice words and exuberant cheering, but by the time all of the boys' cups were gone, we were the clear winners—thanks to Brynn's spectacular aim.

And Bash was a little tipsy.

"I don't like this game anymore," he said, swiping up the cups and stacking them.

"Do we have a sore loser on our hands, little Bashy?" Brynn teased.

He glared at her and went to put the cups in the trash.

"I guess that means no round two?" Matt asked with a laugh.

"No round two." Bash closed the lid with a bit more force than necessary. "How about we get out of here?"

"Bar Code?" Brynn's eyes lit up.

Bash shrugged. "I'm in. What do you think, birthday girl? Have you had enough of a pregame to head out yet?"

"Out?" I asked, dumbly. I was already out.

Matt chuckled. "Yes. Out. Do you want to go to the club?"

"I've never been."

"Well, no time like the present!" Bash said, a little loud as he swung his arm over my shoulders. "I'll call a cab. Let me get my phone off the charger."

Brynn cheered and followed him to fetch his phone from his room.

Matt appeared at my side. "We don't have to go, if you don't want to," he said, concern tracing the edges of his careful words.

"No, it's okay," I said, hugging my arms to my side. "I … I think I want to go." I realized the truth of the words as I spoke them. I felt the effects of our pregaming starting to loosen my head. Between Bash, Brynn, and Matt, I had the perfect experienced group to go out with. I presumed Brynn and I were already dressed the part.

Matt was looking at me. No, not me, my body.

I pulled at the hem of my shirt.

"Are you sure?" he asked, lifting his gaze to meet mine again.

For someone who was supposed to be the life of the party, he certainly was being quite the party pooper.

I nodded and crossed my arms in front of my chest. "Yes, I'm sure."

Bash came back out of his room, Brynn clinging to his arm, giddy.

The smile on Bash's face was wide. "Cab is five minutes out!"

Chapter Twenty-One

Music assaulted not only my ears, but my entire body. I could feel the bass reverberating between each of my ribs, pounding with my heart.

I had never felt more alive.

But that could've been the Fireball whiskey speaking that was currently burning my throat.

"You okay?" Matt leaned in closer to me to ask, his lips practically on my neck to make sure I heard him over the club noise.

I nodded and coughed, only once, before setting the shot glass back on the bar. "I'm good!" I shouted back over the music.

"You sure?" He touched my wrist lightly as he spoke.

I nodded again.

The cab ride to the center of the city hadn't taken more than ten minutes. Bash sat in the front and chatted up our middle-aged single mother of a driver. (Don't ask how we know this about Anne. We also know that she was never married. She had a sperm donor.) Brynn sat in the middle of the back seat between Matt and me, her shoulders touching both of ours in the small vehicle. I wished I had been in her seat, brushing shoulders with Matt instead of the cold window.

When we piled out at the edge of the entrance to the club, Bash stayed seated a few seconds longer to wish our driver luck with her hellion of a teenage daughter. (She snuck out of the house six times this week. And it was only Thursday.) Matt spilled out first and waited by the car door until I clambered out last. Brynn didn't wait for any of us, but rather hightailed it to cut off another group of people. After Bash finally waved goodbye to Anne, we joined Brynn in line.

When we got to the front of the crowd, I fished out my ID from the back of my phone, earning a *happy birthday* and a wink from the bouncer.

"Ember!" Brynn cried from further down the bar beside Bash. "Did you take the shot?"

I gave her a thumbs-up, and she squealed before pushing off the metal counter and shimmying her way toward me. "Dance with me!"

She grabbed my hands and tugged me after her, weaving through the crowd. My skin felt hot as we pressed forward.

Darkness lined the walls and floor of the club, breaking only for neon strobes of light that pierced the air, flashing greens and reds and blues on an arm here, or a leg there, or a smile painted on a dreamy expression.

Brynn stopped when she found a space, big enough for just us two among the other club-goers, and started swinging her hips and hair to the rhythm of the song. I tried to mimic her movements because I had to admit she looked good doing them, and I wasn't sure if I was dancing right. The more I moved, though, the easier it got to surrender myself to the environment, sinking a little deeper into blissful oblivion of those around me with every beat drop.

I think I had the alcohol to thank for that.

That was until a pair of large hands came to rest on my hips.

No, rest was the wrong word. The hands were holding me. And they were heavy.

My eyes flew wide, and I locked onto Brynn's sly expression.

He's cute, she mouthed and closed her eyes again, swaying to the music.

"Do you want to dance with me?" The voice belonging to the stranger gripping me from behind was rough, just like the heels of his hands on the bare skin of my exposed midriff.

"I don't think I'm a very good dancer," I said, loud enough to be heard. I turned my head to look at the man.

He was tall, much taller than me, but not quite as tall as Matt. He was much broader than Matt, though. His chest filled out his black T-shirt well enough. And his teeth were a startlingly bright shade of white, in sharp contrast with his dark hair and tanned skin.

"Oh, come on." He was smiling as he spoke, but his hands were still on my waist. "I can show you how."

I cut a glance over to Brynn, but she was already occupied with another guy. She was in the front. He was in the back. Their hips were moving together as one. There was a soft smile on her face and her eyes were closed.

"Okay, I guess," I said.

The man behind me tugged my waist until I felt his body against my backside. I let him lead, for I certainly didn't have any experience, and that was all the encouragement he needed as he ground his hips against me.

Holy shit. This was dancing? This was what Brynn was out doing every Thursday night?

I looked up at her, but she and her partner had already been swallowed by the crowd, letting the ebb and flow of the club-goers take them away from me.

I let the guy continue showing me the ropes for approximately three seconds longer. At that point, I decided that for as much as he seemed to be enjoying it, I didn't like dancing very much.

I turned around to tell him so. Instead of listening to what my open mouth was about to say, he pulled my waist with a sharp tug so that I was flush against him and then crushed his mouth against mine.

I think I squealed at the jolt and tried to jump away from him, but his grip was strong. I wrenched my face away from his and sputtered, "I ... I'm sorry, but I don't ... I'm not—"

"Come on." The glint in his eye held frustration behind the tease. "You said you wanted to dance." He leaned closer to my ear, and I turned away from him, trying to push his chest away. "Just one dance," he hissed.

"I—"

"She said no." The voice that snapped beside us appeared out of nowhere. I shook my head and wriggled free to find Matt glaring at my dance partner. The tone of his voice had a much sharper bite than I had ever heard come from his mouth. And his shoulders were drawn and square, echoing the same tension edging his jaw.

I took a step back from both of them.

"Easy, man," the guy said over the music with his hands up in mock surrender. "We were just dancing."

"You better back off and leave her alone," Matt's voice was low, hard, and the look in his eye was downright murderous. I had never seen it before.

The guy cut me one last hard glance before muttering something like *no bitch is worth this shit* and walked off.

I let out a breath and shuddered. I could still feel his hands.

"Are you okay?" Matt asked, leaning close but not touching me. His gaze was still furious, but I didn't think it was me he wanted to kill.

I looked down at his hands, still balled into fists, clenched at his side. I took one of them in mine and uncurled his fingers as I nodded. "Thank you."

He closed his eyes and let out a sigh before wrapping his arms around me and pulling me into a hug. I let my cheek press against his chest. His heart was hammering underneath his button-down. The people around us continued moving.

"I think I need another drink," he said and eventually peeled himself away from me. His hand remained clasping mine as he led the two of us toward the bar.

***

It took two more shots for the shake in Matt's hands to settle. I sipped the edge of a very sweet pink drink he ordered for me in the meantime.

I mean, sure, the dancing guy *had* been a little forward. But nothing bad happened, right?

Matt had to have been watching the whole time.

And knew exactly when to step in.

I put my hand back over Matt's. "Are you okay?"

He turned his head to me and scoffed, shaking his head and removing his hand from underneath mine. "I should be asking you that."

"I'm fine."

He took my drink from my hands and took a sip for himself. He had to be hammered at this point. Or he just had a very efficient liver. Maybe both.

"I'm sorry," he said. "I'm really sorry, Ember."

I was bewildered. "You don't have anything to be sorry for."

He shook his head again. "If you only knew," he muttered.

I took my drink back from him and chugged the remainder. Setting the empty glass back down on the counter, I grabbed his hand. "Dance with me."

He was stunned. "You can't be serious."

I stood up and tried to yank him up with me; he didn't budge. "I am totally serious." I needed to get back out there. I didn't want that experience to be my only memory.

And I wanted this new one to be with Matt. Because, well ... I trusted him. And if I was being entirely honest, I wanted to feel *his* hands on my body again.

"Please," I said.

He was looking at me as if I had another head attached to my neck. I pleaded with my eyes until he finally relented.

"Fine," he said and stood up. "But I'm putting it on record. I would be happy to leave this place right now instead."

"Not happening." I grasped his palm more surely in mine, this time taking the lead back into the crowd. I weaved in and out of strangers and their bodies, keeping one eye out for Brynn, and the other focused on finding a space for the two of us.

Matt followed willingly, his lithe body angling between the others like the regular he was.

He tugged me to stop, meaning that this would do. I didn't know if it was that *he* didn't want to be in the thick of the crowd or he didn't want me to be.

Either way, this was fine. I didn't really know what I was doing, but I started sort of bouncing up and down to the bass of whatever terrible song was playing. Pretty soon, my hands were in the air with the rest of the crowd.

Matt's moves were about on par with mine, but I couldn't help but think how much cooler he probably looked than me. He moved with confidence and a sort of grace. As graceful as you could get in a club, I suppose.

There was a shift in the people around us. Someone was stepping closer to me, again. Matt closed the distance between us and put a hand on the small my back. His fingers grazed the space between my shirt and the waistband of my skirt.

The guy that tried to get behind me backed off, turning the other way.

I looked up at Matt. His expression was cold again, but softened when he met my gaze.

Without words, our movements started to match one another until we were swaying on the same beats. We were facing each other, so I took both of his hands in mine and started swinging our arms, back and forth. He shook his head and laughed, letting me continue to lead our "dancing" for a few more strokes. He finally gave one of my arms a tug that pulled me closer to him, long enough for him to say, "You know, that's not how I usually dance when I'm here."

I felt brave. Or tipsy. Maybe both, but I put a hand behind his neck and stood on my tiptoes to reach his ear. "How about you show me then?"

His usual sly grin finally erupted back on his face for the first time the entire night. "You want me to show you my smooth moves?" He drawled the question.

I grinned in response. "Unless you're afraid you can't keep up with my moves?" I started doing the robot for good measure.

"Oh God!" he cried. "Make it stop!"

I giggled, and Matt settled his hands on my waist, tugging me closer to him once more. Continuing to sway to the music, he leaned down and pressed his lips against my ear as he said, "Turn around."

I did.

We were close as he rocked his hips to the rhythm of the music. Close enough to be touching, but not too close to be pressed. Close enough to feel his knees against the back of mine, but not close enough.

I reached one hand up and behind me, and I found his hair.

His grip against my skirt tightened.

I closed my eyes and settled my other hand over top of his.

Here, dancing in the club, it was easy, so easy to pretend that the physical space that diminished between us somehow meant something. That as our bodies melted, so could every rational thought that wanted to tell me to stop and step away.

But I didn't step away. I was tired of pretending that I wanted to. I danced with Matt as if no one else could see. As if no one else was there. It didn't feel like anyone else was there. It felt like it was just the two of us and the pounding bass in every beat that dropped.

Until my phone buzzed in the pocket of my skirt, at the most inopportune moment.

I cursed lightly under my breath, but apparently not quiet enough for Matt not to hear. He chuckled softly, then slipped *his own hand* into my pocket to pull out my phone. Our dancing slowed down as he handed me my phone, but we kept moving.

The screen lit up at my face. It was Brynn. Just one emoji followed by Bash's name and a plethora of question marks: the purple smiley with the devil horns. They had to be off together, somewhere on the dance floor since I hadn't seen either of them in a while.

I groaned. It was my birthday, of all nights.

"Everything okay?" Matt's voice was low in my ear.

I turned my cheek to press it alongside Matt's. "Sounds like you'll be lacking a roommate tonight."

"Oh," he said.

"I think I've been evicted."

He paused. "You need a place to crash?"

"That couch of yours seemed to like me last time."

My phone buzzed again.

> I know im the worst but maybe youll thank me later??? With a winking face.

Maybe this was Brynn's backwards way of a birthday present.

I slid my phone back into my pocket. "I'm ready to leave when you are."

***

The cab ride back seemed even faster than the first one. The living room was charged when Matt's keys finally gave in the lock and we stepped through the threshold. And it wasn't just the buzzing in my ears. I felt as though if I were to reach out and touch Matt's arm as he stepped behind me to close the door, my fingertips would have sparked from the tension burning between us. That had been burning since we sat in the back seat of the ride together, not touching each other, not saying anything.

"Well, we've got the place to ourselves," he said, stepping back around me and slipping his shoes off. I followed suit while Matt teetered on the balls of his feet and put his hands awkwardly into his pockets. "What do you want to do?"

My heart jumped, suddenly nervous. "Snacks," I said.

"Your wish is my command, birthday girl." He turned and strode into the kitchen. I followed close behind.

"You know, it's not really my birthday yet. Technically, I'm still underage."

He paused in front of the refrigerator. "Is that so?"

"11:52 p.m."

He flicked his wrist out to check his watch. "It's past midnight now. You're officially in the twenty-fun club."

I closed the distance between us to take his wrist in mine, checking the time for my own fuzzy edged eyesight. "Huh, would you look at that? I'm old."

Matt's chuckle moved the curls against the bottom of my ear, and I didn't let go of his hand. I squeezed it when I looked up into his dark eyes and deadpanned, "I need cheese."

"Cheese?"

"Yes. It's my go-to snack. White cheddar."

Matt opened the fridge with his free hand, still holding mine with the other. "I have a few slices of American."

I audibly gagged and dropped his hand. "That's not real cheese. I'm ashamed to call you a friend for keeping that shit stocked in your fridge."

His eyebrow quirked up. "Friend? Is that official now? Should I add you on Facebook?"

I rolled my eyes and walked to the couch. "Yeah, yeah, yeah. I guess we would have to be friends for you to throw me a birthday party. Or else that would just be weird."

He laughed again from the kitchen, and something tightened in my chest. I picked up one of the pillows and started tugging on the corner.

After he shuffled around the apartment a bit more, Matt came in and sat down beside me, far enough away that I could fit a whole hand in between our legs. If I had a hand free to measure the distance. Mine was still wrapped around the pillow, hugging it to my chest. He handed me a full glass and a pair of sweatpants. "Drink this, then put these on if you want to be more comfortable."

I scrunched my face. "No more drinks."

"It's water. You'll thank me later."

I waited a beat then reached with both palms to take the items from him.

I gulped the entire glass and set it down on the table. Twining my fingers through the soft fabric of the sweats, I said softly, "Hey."

Matt turned his chest toward me. He wore a small smile equal parts sleepy, happy, and peaceful. "Hey," he said. His hand rested on the couch between us.

"You want to know what the best birthday present I have ever gotten is?"

"This cute little party."

"Close," I said. "My dad built us a tree house once."

"Ah," he said, looking around the room. "I don't have any trees in here."

"No," I said as an idea sparked in my mind. "But you have pillows. And blankets. And couches. And everything needed to build a kick-ass pillow fort."

His grin spread across his face. "Yes, we are so building a fort."

He leaped up from his seat and tugged me after him. "Go change in my room and get all my pillows and blankets. We can raid Bash's bed, too, if we need to."

He ripped the cushions from their place on the couch and placed them at the foot of the couch instead. I moved toward his room, feeling funny about stepping through that doorway as I thought about the other girls who might have been in there before me. I pushed the thought aside and quickly changed into his sweatpants, then set to work stripping the bed. I doubted anyone else had built a fort in the middle of Matt Callahan's living room before.

I came back with a bundle larger than my own frame to find Matt had pushed the standing lamp against the back of the couch and was positioning the ottomans along either side of the couch's arms so that he created a horseshoe shape. The sheets were draped from the lamp's shade, across the back of the couch, and secured along the ottomans with several heavy books he found from their library. Together, we layered the duvet cover on the floor inside of the tent, lining the perimeter with more pillows and stuffing more blankets into the cavernous hole. Matt emerged from the fort after clicking on the standing lamp and jogged to the front door to turn off the overhead light.

The edges of the room went dark; the only light was glowing pale yellow from within the fort, beckoning.

"You going to try it out?" Matt asked as he walked up behind me.

I hugged my arms around my center, looking at the most exquisite pillow fort I could have ever imagined before turning back to Matt's cheeky grin. "Obviously."

I got down on my elbows and knees, army crawling my way into the heart of the fort, thankful for the pants. Matt followed close behind in similar fashion as I was propping myself up against the couch cushions. He lay next to me on his side, holding himself up by his right elbow.

I surveyed our territory. "I have to admit, this isn't half bad." And it wasn't. It had decent height to it thanks to the lamp that Matt thought to install.

He was looking out at our toes; his were hidden behind his black socks and mine were already tucking themselves in between the folds of the blankets.

We were quiet. The only audible sounds were our breaths and the slow whir of the ceiling fan above us. I would've thought Matt could hear my heartbeat rattling within my rib cage, but if he did, he didn't mention it. Maybe his was racing too.

"You getting sleepy over there?" Matt's whisper was gravelly.

"Mhmm," I replied and let my eyelids touch one another.

It was silent again. I let my eyes stay closed as I counted the beats between my slowing breaths.

"Do you want me to let you get to bed?" Matt's question was barely audible. I blinked slowly and saw the question in his eyes. Did I want him to leave?

I scooted lower in the fort so I was lying down, closer to where he lounged on his side. I reached over and threaded my fingers through his before gently tugging his arm toward me. "Don't go," I whispered. My voice didn't sound like me. It sounded vulnerable. "Stay."

His fingers tightened against mine. "Okay."

He sunk into the blankets beside me. I tugged his arm across my side and held his hand close to my chest. He used that grip to pull my body flush against his as he held me even closer than he had that night on the couch. His breath was warm against my ear, and I marveled at how comfortable, how natural it seemed, how easy it was lying here under our pillow fort, feeling Matt's heartbeat against my back.

"Ember," he started, and the word stirred against my neck.

I tilted my chin, leaning back into his chest. "Yeah?"

He was quiet, and I could almost picture words inside of his head, pinballing within their confinement, trying to find a way out as we lay in silence several beats too long.

"Are we friends?" he finally asked.

"I said we were."

"I know," he said, his voice a hoarse whisper. "I mean, I guess what I'm asking is, do you want to be friends? Just friends?"

He was thinking about our kiss. He had to be. I know I was. I just didn't know how to answer his question with words.

Without dwelling too much on it, I lifted the hand I had entwined with Matt's up to my lips, pressing them slowly into the back of Matt's palm. His breathing rattled.

"Ember," he said again.

"Yes?" I whispered. I still held his hand tucked underneath my chin.

"Look at me a second." The command was weak in his voice.

I rolled over and found myself curled in his embrace, leaning against his chest. He moved his arm from my waist, bringing it to my face, cupping my cheek. His dark eyes were full of emotion.

I didn't think. I just moved.

I leaned in and closed the space between us, bringing my mouth up to his. Our lips fell together in a kiss that made me feel as if I were floating. Dreaming. I had to be dreaming. This wasn't real.

But it felt real. It felt real as Matt moved his lips against mine, pulling me closer to him until it wasn't humanly possible to get any closer. Every part of my body was touching his.

It felt real as his hands shifted from my cheek to thread through my hair. His fingers tightened through my loose curls.

There was nothing in this kiss that was under the guise of a project, or a story that belonged to anyone other than us this time. This was Matt, and this was me.

I broke my mouth away from his, trying to catch the breath that he had so easily taken. That I had so easily given him. His mouth continued a trail of kisses down my neck, leading back up to my jaw when he met the neckline of my shirt.

It felt real when his hand slipped from my hair, trailed along my rib cage, and gripped my hip.

I found his mouth again with my own.

His hands grew braver, slipping underneath the fabric of my shirt, palms splayed along either side of my rib cage. Matt gripped my sides, crushing my body to him. I responded with equal pressure against his open lips.

At some point, I didn't know when, the kiss slowed until it stopped altogether. The last thing I remembered was the kiss he dropped on my forehead and the way he smoothed my hair back from my face. I fell asleep listening to both of our hearts, beating in succession.

Chapter Twenty-Two

I woke to sunrays filtering through the canopy of the fort and the weight of Matt's chest at my back. Neither of us had moved for several hours.

When I finally did stir, I opened my eyes just barely to register his hand still wrapped around me. I squeezed it once and burrowed closer.

Matt was awake, too, and his voice was groggy when he croaked, "Good morning."

I was expecting at least a little headache after last night, but nothing hurt. I cleared my throat once, my voice cracking. "You know why I like the expression *good morning*?"

He chuckled lightly in my ear. "Because then you know I'm the first thing you're thinking about."

He absolutely was.

Matt told me to keep the sweatpants and found me a spare T-shirt so I didn't have to arrive at the parking deck in my birthday outfit. After I scrubbed my face clean, he kissed me once more before I drove back.

We left the pillow fort intact.

It was a little after nine thirty in the morning when I parked, just after Brynn's class was supposed to start. I walked myself down to the coffee shop and ordered a dark roast and muffin, just in case she and her company were slower to start moving than I was.

I didn't know what to think about last night. It was starting to be too much to process, so I focused on the facts and the details. It was my birthday. We had a small party that ended up transporting to the club. (I went to a club!) I danced with Brynn. I danced with strangers. I danced with Matt. I kissed Matt. Again. This time, I slept beside Matt all night long.

I kept these recaps on repeat because I knew that if I didn't latch and hold onto those, I would spiral into more unanswered, abstract questions. Like the big one I kept gently shutting the lid on: Could Matt really have feelings for me? And its even bigger friend: Did I have feelings for Matt?

The answer to the latter one had been confirmed in last night's actions. Yes, I had feelings for Matt. I had feelings in every touch and glance and kiss. I wouldn't deny it anymore, and while part of that left me uneasy, a larger part felt like floating.

I finished my muffin and sipped the last of my coffee. I didn't know where else to go after throwing away my crumbs. I briefly considered sending Spencer a picture to tell him good luck with his surgery, but then decided a faceless text was better. After all, I was wearing Matt's clothes.

The clock tower chimed ten. I picked up my keys and phone, heading toward my room.

The library floor was sparse, with just a few students milling about. I skipped the elevator, opting for the stairs, taking them two at a time.

I took my time wiggling my keys around in the lock, announcing my arrival with as much noise as I could manage. The room was empty when the door swung open. Maybe Brynn actually went to class.

I set to work rummaging through my clothes, pulling out leggings and a shirt of my own. I figured I might as well make use of the morning and hit the gym while it was quiet.

The door swung open as I was slipping off Matt's shirt and shimmying into mine. It was Brynn, dressed in her shower robe and flip-flops with her hair wrapped in a towel. Her face still had water droplets on her cheeks.

"Oh, hey," she said, doing a double take in the doorway before finally stepping through the threshold and closing the door behind her.

"Hi," I said, tucking Matt's shirt into the corner of my closet.

She didn't say anything else as she started pulling out her clothes for the day.

"Did Bash go home?" I asked, stupidly. Of course he went home if he wasn't here.

She nodded. Still quiet.

"Is everything okay?"

"Yeah," she said. "Did you have fun last night?"

"I did," I said. I set the clothes I borrowed from Brynn in my own laundry hamper to wash later. "Thank you."

Brynn said nothing as she carried her clothes to her bed, the fluffy pink robe still wrapped tightly around her body. Her silence was unnerving.

"Are you sure everything is okay?"

Her back was still to me when she asked, "Where did you stay last night?"

I paused, my leggings halfway on. I thought about lying, but she probably already knew the truth. I mean, she had to have assumed as much when she asked to have the room last night. "I was with Matt."

The back of her head nodded as she stepped into pants. I pulled my own up and sat down on my bed.

"Nothing happened," I said, defensively. "If that's why you're asking." Besides kissing. Besides the best kiss I have ever had.

"It would be fine if something did," she said flatly. "But that wasn't the first time you've stayed, was it?" Her voice was barely audible.

Shit. I fidgeted with my socks. Bash told her.

Brynn turned to me now, fully dressed. Her eyes were sad. "And when you went home last weekend? You took him with you?"

My chest tightened, and I felt like heaving at the glaring exposure she had just thrown on me and my lies. "Brynn, I—"

"You know, I get that you don't have to tell me everything you do, but I just want to know why you felt like you couldn't talk to me about Matt," she said. "I mean, isn't that what friends do for each other?"

"Of course," I said, but the affirmation stuck in my throat. Were we friends? She was mine, for sure. Besides Spencer, who had been like a brother as long as I have known him, who else did I really have? She had so many other people in her circle. She didn't really need me.

"I just ..." I tried again, but the words wouldn't come. "I'm sorry, I just wasn't ready ..."

"Ready for what?" she pressed. "What did you think I would say? Or do?"

"I don't know!" My voice climbed. "It's just, for once it was ... me."

Her almond eyes narrowed in confusion. I took a sharp breath and continued in almost a whine. "It's always you. You are always the one that all the guys want, that everyone wants to be friends with, that everything seems so easy for. And with Matt, I didn't even know how I felt or what he feels or what is going on really, but for once, it was me. And it didn't feel real because it's never me." *And I wanted it to be real. So badly.*

It killed me to admit it to her, the jealousy I had harbored inside me throughout our entire friendship. Maybe that relationship had been a lie, too, then.

I felt sick. I felt angry.

"That's not true," Brynn said.

"It is!" I cried, the previously unspoken admission finally ringing clear between both of us. "Every time I do something, it's always as your tagalong friend."

"Stop—"

"Don't deny it! Our whole friendship is based on convenience. Same major, same classes, even the same dorm room."

"Ember! You know that's not true." Her eyes were hard now. "And I'm not going to let you turn this into a pity party when you are the one who has been lying to me!"

"It's not a pity party if it's the truth!"

"The truth?" she cried. "Now you want to talk about truth? Ember, if you weren't so goddamn insecure and just told me that you were hanging out with Matt, I would have been happy for you! But you didn't even give me that chance. You just kept secrets instead."

The bite in her voice shredded me, but I didn't back down. "How are you so sure about that? You said it yourself, you didn't think that he was my type of guy. You didn't think that he would ever go for me."

"Don't you dare put words in my mouth," she snapped. "I never said that he wouldn't go for you. All I said was to be careful—"

"Why? Because I'm not you?"

"You've got to be kidding me right now," she grumbled and pinched the bridge of her nose. I was seething, and she was trying to calm herself down like I wished I knew how to.

When she finally opened her eyes, her expression was built to freeze. "You're being petty and lashing out at me right now, but that isn't going to change the fact that you've been lying. And it's certainly not going to fix the problem in the mirror."

"What are you talking about?"

She threw her hands in the air. "Ember, you can't ever get out of your own way and think about anyone else! When is the last time you asked me about my friends, or my classes, or anything else important to me?"

Her words hit me in the gut as I realized she was right. I couldn't tell her when I had put myself in her shoes or thought about what was going on in her life other than to notice the parts where I didn't fit in.

It reminded me of my mother. How she only ever fended for herself. It was something I hated in her, and I was behaving the same way. I wanted to fade into nothing right then.

Brynn kept hammering. "You're the one who creates the problem by alienating yourself from everyone and everything. It's not my fault that you can't see that or that you can't let anyone in. And believe me, I have tried to get close to you but if this is how you truly feel, then I'm the idiot here and should just give up."

She turned on her heels and pulled a drawstring bag out of her closet.

"What are you doing?" I whispered.

"I need some space right now." She was a blur, flitting around the room throwing clothes and toiletries into the bag and slinging her backpack over her shoulder.

My chest deflated. "Brynn—"

"Stop," she said curtly and then opened the door. "Just ... stop."

She closed the door behind her with a soft click, but I wish she had slammed it.

My legs were shaking as I sank onto my bed. Brynn was right. I didn't know how to let anyone in. And here I was. By myself. Because I picked a fight and pushed away one of the only people who always stuck by me.

Because I didn't know how not to.

**

I went to the gym and ran longer than I probably ever have, but my heart still hurt when I got back to the empty room.

I showered quickly, then took myself down to the cafeteria for lunch. I plugged in headphones and sat at a table by myself, pretending to skim over a book while I ate.

By late afternoon, Brynn had yet to return, and I doubted she would come back at all tonight.

Spencer texted me once in his post-anesthesia stupor. Some meme he thought was funny.

I didn't respond.

***

Late afternoon (college dinner time, by Brynn's standards), Matt called me.

I was lying in bed without a good enough excuse not to answer the phone.

"Hi," I said.

"Hey, gorgeous." I didn't know how it was possible, but I was pretty sure I could hear the smile on his face through the phone.

Any other day, I probably would have smiled at the compliment from him. But not today. "Hey," I said flatly.

"Just calling to check in," he said. "See how your day was going."

"Not great."

He didn't miss a beat. "Would you like to talk about it?"

"No."

Now he paused, the confusion evident in his sigh. "Well, what else would you like to talk about then?"

"Nothing."

"Ember, if you're upset about last night—"

"I'm not."

"Okay." I could hear his deep breath rattling through the phone. "Could we talk about last night though?"

Oh God. Did he regret kissing me? The first kiss would have been easy to chalk up to the moment and the stress of the contest getting to us, if that's what the both of us had really wanted to do. But now after last night? I couldn't take that rejection, especially not right now, and especially not after I had come to terms with my Pandora box of feelings, aching from breaking open. It felt like my lungs were collapsing, and it was a miracle I managed the single syllable. "Yeah?"

"I just ..." he sighed. "If anything about last night has to do with why you sound like you do right now—"

His hands, his mouth, his body.

"It doesn't." The whisper was hoarse against my throat. Was he trying to find a way to justify his regret? Would it be easier to say it shouldn't have happened if he thought that's how I felt too?

"Are you sure?"

I hardened my voice, steeling myself taller on the bed. "Matt, if you have something to say, just say it."

He paused. "What are you talking about?"

"Are you trying to find a way out?"

"A way out of what?"

"This?" I sighed, exasperated and frustrated that I had to spell it out for him. "Me? Last night?"

"What? No," he stammered. "Absolutely not."

"Why do you keep asking about it then?"

"Because," he said. "You sound like something has completely obliterated your day, and I'm hoping that whatever we have going on isn't the cause of it."

"Why do you care?" I snapped, because I couldn't help it. "We aren't even really dating. It's not your job."

He was quiet a beat. "You don't want me to care?"

"You shouldn't."

"But what if I do?"

What if he does? I bit my lip and recoiled my sharp tongue. Cradling my phone with two hands, I said, "I don't think you actually do. You may think you do ..." I squeezed my eyes shut as I forced out my biggest fear in this whole Matt Callahan venture, "but you're probably just lonely."

The silence on Matt's end of the line rang loud in my ear. His voice plummeted several octaves when he finally said, "That's not fair, Ember."

"I'm sorry," I whispered. Then before I could talk myself out of it, I hung up the phone.

***

I took a few melatonin pills to help sleep that night, and I didn't set an alarm. I tossed and turned for several hours, and when I finally got to sleep, it was well past three in the morning. I slept with a hoodie pulled over my head and the covers mounted around me, and didn't get up until early afternoon.

When I finally did wake up, it was due to a very large pillow being thrown against my head.

"You've got to get up." It was Brynn, and her voice was sharp.

"Why?" The pillow on top of me was actually helping to block the overhead light that she rudely threw on.

"You need to eat."

I turned my face into my own pillow, squeezing my eyes shut. "I repeat. Why?"

Her sigh was heavy and dramatic. "Because then we need to start getting ready."

"For what?"

"Seriously?" she said and ripped her pillow back away from me. "Bash's party. We have to go. We said we were going."

"I don't want to," I said and finally opened my eyes. "And why are you here? I thought you were mad."

She was tearing through her closet and didn't bother looking at me. "I'm still mad."

"Okay."

She turned to me. "I'm still really mad. Especially after I heard the way you treated Matt on the phone too."

Her words rang on repeat in my head. "I guess you were with them last night?"

"Yep."

It hurt knowing they were all at the apartment without me. I wondered if the pillow fort was still there.

No. There was no way it was. It had probably long since been torn down, easily rolled up, discarded, *forgotten*.

"It's one thing to shut me out," she said and plopped down on her bed, scrolling through her phone. "I'm like a boomerang. Maybe I'm stupid, but I just keep coming back. But Matt? I thought that was a pretty shitty thing to do. He seems to care a lot about you."

There it was again. That caring thing. I rolled over in bed so I was facing the wall when I said, "He shouldn't."

"I doubt that will stop him though."

"What do you mean? What did he say?"

"I am not going to tell you anything. If you want to know what's on his mind, then you need to own up and apologize for acting like a brat. Hence, why you are going to this party," she paused. "And while you're there, you might as well tell him you care too."

"You don't know that."

"You wouldn't have shut down on him like that if you didn't. I know you, Ember." She leaned out of her bed and tugged open one of the drawers from underneath. "It's a defense mechanism thing of yours."

Fishing through the drawer a few times, Brynn pulled out what looked like a dress and tossed it at me without aiming. It landed across my midsection, draping over my legs.

"I'm still mad," she said. "For the record."

I was, too, but I wasn't really the one with the reason. Being mad was just easier than falling apart. But being mad wasn't going to fix anything. Against the fire still rolling inside of me, I decided to take the first step in dousing it.

"I'm sorry, Brynn," I said. "Really. I feel like all I did last night was just project my feelings onto you, and that wasn't fair." I paused. "I've spent so much time watching and finding ways to prove that I don't fit in your life, I never realized how much of that was on me."

"Wow," Brynn said, but she wore a surprised smile on her face. "I didn't think you were capable of stringing words together like that."

I rolled over and hugged a pillow close to my chest and smiled halfway. "How's the sorority? Your other classes? Other important things?"

"Too far." Brynn gave a sympathetic smile. "But thanks."

I squeezed the pillow tighter and asked in a smaller voice. "Do I have to go tonight?"

Brynn sat down opposite of me. "No, but if you're asking me what I think you should do, I think it's worth trying to talk to him."

"I am trying to talk to you," I said. "Apparently, I need the practice."

"Well, consider step one done," Brynn said with a smile that I didn't deserve. "Come on. Let's go to the cafeteria together."

Chapter Twenty-Three

B rynn and I slowly got the banter rolling between us again while we ate and then got ready for Bash's party. The dress she loaned me was cotton, plain black with long sleeves. It looked like funeral attire—until I put it on and fussed at the fabric for clinging to my curves the way no funeral dress ever should.

"Keep it," Brynn said as I tugged on it. "It fits you better than me."

She offered to do my eyeliner again, but I politely declined. I didn't want to hide behind too much face paint tonight.

Brynn had on her trademark black skirt, this time paired with a cropped sweater with a broken heart printed across her chest. She looked edgy, and I told her so.

"Thanks," she said while she slipped on a pair of boots.

Traditionally, there were no sorority or fraternity houses on campus. It was too small. One of the alums, who coincidentally was in a fraternity during his time on campus, purchased a house adjacent to the campus grounds and donated it to Greek Life as a sort of home base for their gatherings. The billionaire donor had paid handsomely to soundproof the walls of the Party House, and as long as the fraternities and sororities kept it presentable, they were free to use it whenever.

I had heard about it, but had never been, so Brynn led the way. We had both thrown on jackets to make the trek, but even with the down wrapped around my chest, the air still had a bite to it. When we got to the front door, I could feel the heat from the flush rising from my cheeks at trying to keep up with Brynn's efficient pace in the brisk chill.

Brynn knocked three times in a row. The first of many someones that I didn't know opened the door.

"Brynn! You made it." The stranger's smile was wide; then he turned to me. "Who is this?"

"My roommate," Brynn made the introduction for me. "Ember, this is Jared."

"Nice to meet you," I said quietly, looking beyond his dark hair. There were so many people in the house already.

"Likewise," he said, his eyes roaming back to Brynn. "You two are welcome to keep your jackets here in the closet with the others."

"Thanks!" She shrugged out of her coat, exposing the bare skin of her back when her sweater rode up as she reached for a hanger. She handed a spare hanger to me, and I slipped out of mine as well.

"Bar is open and in the kitchen. I assume you remember where that is?" Jared quirked a smile at Brynn, seeming to imply some sort of inside information I lacked.

She laughed and playfully swatted his arm as she walked by. "You know I do. See you later."

I scurried after her. "What's so special about the kitchen?"

"Jared held my hair once freshman year while I puked in the trash. He has never let me forget it."

"Oh."

"Brynn!" We were stopped again by another someone who apparently knew Brynn, barely having made it to the foyer. Intercepting our path was a tall lanky guy I vaguely recognized, dressed in a polo shirt and belted khakis, the shirt looking rumpled in a half tucked, half untucked sort of fashion. Maybe it was trendy. I wouldn't know.

"Oh, hi Kyle! Good to see you," was Brynn's response, and she let him go in for a casual hug.

Kyle. Brynn's friend from the lacrosse game that felt like ages ago.

He squeezed Brynn tightly and dropped a kiss on her cheek, slow, and not so casual.

I tried not to let my expression change.

"How have you been?" he asked as he withdrew from the embrace, letting his hands run down her arms before dropping the contact.

Brynn shrugged. "Good. Busy. Already wishing for spring break."

He chuckled. "I understand. The worst part about being in school is having to do the actual school part." He seemed to have realized that I was hanging in the shadows of their conversation. He looked over at me and seemed taken aback. "Sorry, didn't see you there. I'm Kyle Redding. You are?"

Someone you have already introduced yourself to, but obviously forgotten. "Going to the bar," I smiled with what I hoped was enough charm that he would think the comment sarcastic instead of evasive, but if not, I didn't feel too badly.

Brynn laughed. "I'm heading there too. I'll see you later, Kyle!"

"Brynn," Kyle called again as we were walking away. We both turned, and I saw his smile deepen. "You look good."

I'm pretty sure I saw Brynn wink. "Back at ya."

"Wait, have you two dated or something?" I hissed once she turned back and started to lead the way. "Why did he kiss your cheek?"

"Ember. Again. I don't date." She sighed. "And it was just a kiss. It doesn't mean anything."

"So you're telling me that there's never been anything between the two of you."

"Well, we've hooked up a few times."

"Recently?!"

"Define 'recently.' "

I contemplated this and settled with, "Bash recently."

"I've told you. Bash and I aren't together."

I noticed she didn't really answer my question.

"But," she continued, "in terms of Bash recently?" She got this small sort of smile on her face. "Since meeting him, I wouldn't really want to go any farther than kissing with anyone else."

"You two made it!"

Speak of the devil. Bash entered the kitchen through the opposite door as we strode in as well.

"Hey!" Brynn's entire face lit up as she walked into his arms for a hug.

"Good to see you," he said when she let go before hugging me as well. "Glad you could come too, Ember."

He seemed sincere, and I was surprised. I mean, I guess Bash was always friendly, but I would have thought that after that phone call with his roommate, he wouldn't have been so thrilled to see me either.

I pulled away, but Bash was still smiling.

I needed to find Matt. Brynn was right. I had overreacted, and I needed to apologize. I offered a small smile back. "I'm glad I'm here."

"Drinks?" he offered.

"Yes, puh-lease," Brynn said, already reaching for the plastic cups.

Yes. Drinks first. Then I might have the courage to go find Matt.

Bash took the cups and did the honors of filling both of them before his. Once full, he led the way out of the kitchen into the living room where groups of people were clustered in almost every spare inch of the place. There were speakers throughout the house; the music had grown loud enough you almost had to shout to be heard. Some people were shamelessly swaying and bouncing to the beat, but many were just talking.

We didn't make it too far before Bash met a few guys I recognized from the swim team championship posters throughout campus.

After the necessary thumping guy hugs, Bash introduced us all. I sipped my lukewarm beer and nodded a greeting, but couldn't get their names to stick in my head.

The evening progressed in a fashion much like this. More wandering (more following), more names forgotten, more sips taken from my cup.

At one point, one of the people in our little cluster noticed me beyond Brynn.

"It's Amber, right?"

My eyes flitted to the guy looking at me. I checked over my shoulder first to make sure he wasn't talking to someone else. No one. "My name is Ember," I said, pointing to myself. "With an E."

He looked sheepish. "Sorry about that. I'm Will." He held his hand out.

I looked at it a moment before switching my now empty cup to the other hand and shaking his. I swear, I never knew there were this many guys I didn't know on campus. But I guess it wasn't a secret that the English Department favored the female campus population.

"Nice to meet you," I said and withdrew my hand again, keeping my elbows close to my side.

Will gestured to my cup. "Do you want a refill?"

I looked down into my empty cup and considered it. "Yes, I do actually."

He beamed. "Right this way."

I glanced over at Brynn and Bash, but they seemed engrossed in some story some other girl was telling, and Will was already making his way back to the kitchen through the crowd, so I followed.

It was less crowded in the kitchen and a little quieter. He got a new cup from the stash under the sink and started filling it. "How come I have never seen you around before?"

His smile was cute. Will was cute. In a messy sort of boyish cute. But he wasn't Matt.

I shrugged, playing it cool and tossing my old cup into the stack overflowing in the trash. "I get bogged down with a lot of papers and reading. English major problems."

He handed me the cup, filled to the brim, and filled one for himself too. I sipped at the rim so that it wouldn't spill all over me.

"I'm impressed. I can't write worth shit." He took a deep chug from his cup.

"What are you studying?"

"Finance." He grimaced. "Figured it'll help pay the bills."

"But you don't love it." It was an observation, not a question.

Will shook his head. "Can't say that I do."

"What do you love?"

He quirked an eyebrow up at me, peering at my figure over the rim of his raised cup. He took another swallow before saying, "You know, I think you're one of the only people to ask me that in a place like this."

I blushed furiously. "I'm sorry."

"No, no," he said. "It's just that, I don't talk about it much. But I love art."

My expression perked. "What's your medium?"

Will and I delved into a conversation of visual arts versus sculpture. He liked oils and clay, getting his hands dirty in the process, and could dabble in photography. I told him I tried photography once in high school, but could never get the image exactly how I pictured it in my head, so I stuck with words to describe things instead. He pulled out his phone at some point and started scrolling through to find pictures from his old portfolios.

"Crap, Will!" I exclaimed and took the phone from his grip. He favored landscapes and color, from the way he was able to make the paints layer and bleed into one another so effortlessly. "You're really talented!"

"You think?"

We were standing close in the kitchen, still not having made our way back to the others, but I didn't mind. He was looking at me with appreciation and wonder.

"Of course. What year are you?"

His expression turned quizzical. "Sophomore?"

"You have time," I said. "Could you double major? Or at least add on an art minor?"

He raked a hand through his long hair. "I'm not sure. I've thought about it once or twice, but nothing serious."

"You should," I pressed his phone back into his hand. "You're really good."

"Just because you think so, I'll think about it."

He was smiling at me. Maybe this was flirting.

My chest tightened, and I stepped away. I needed to find Matt. "I should probably go ... see if I can find Brynn," I said.

"I'll come with you," he said, pushing off the counter. "You might get lost out there with all those people."

Will touched the small of my back, and I held my cup with two hands, which was a blessing in itself for as we turned to walk out of the kitchen, in came none other than Matt Callahan. I stuttered in my step, Will's chest colliding with my back as I halted the both of us. The liquid sloshed in my cup, but I steadied it in my grip.

Matt's gaze widened at seeing me before narrowing on Will's form behind me. He chuckled and said, "Owens," by way of greeting, but it sounded more like a scoff.

"Hey," I said, but he had already moved past us.

"Let's go," Will's voice was soft, and he gently nudged me forward out of the kitchen.

Everything inside of me screamed to turn around, go back, tumble into Matt, but what would I say? How could I even begin? And here was this other boy at my side, not helping the picture. *It's not what you think,* I thought. *God, I'd take that whole phone call back if I could.*

"How do you and Callahan know each other?" Will asked as we wandered, aimless.

My eyes were scanning the crowd, but I didn't see Brynn or Bash anywhere.

"We are ... um ..."

His arms around my waist. His lips against my neck. His eyes bearing into mine, dark and vulnerable.

And I had singlehandedly obliterated that picture.

"We're writing partners," I finally said. "For a contest. And a class." And maybe that was it.

"Huh," Will said. "That's cool."

"I need to pee," I announced suddenly. "Do you know where the bathroom is?"

"Yeah, it's right down that hall ahead."

"Great! Thanks. I'll catch up with you later." And I darted away, leaving sweet Will's confused expression in my wake.

I didn't really need the bathroom. I just needed to get away. But the door was unlocked and the room was empty, so I shut it behind me and sat down beside the toilet, trying not to cry.

* * *

I only let myself have a five-minute pity party. After which, I stood up, redid my ponytail at the top of my head since it was drooping, and went back out to the party.

A quick scan told me Will had vanished, and Brynn and Bash were still nowhere to be seen. For a moment, I thought I saw Brynn's sorority sister Skylar, or maybe Mia, but there were so many other faces I didn't recognize.

And there was no sign of Matt.

I perused the living room, and when I determined he wasn't there, I considered what my next step was going to be. The kitchen seemed safe. I knew where that was. But it was unlikely he would be there, since we had both just come from there.

It was getting hard for me to breathe with the crowd pressing and bouncing and shaking to the music the way it was. I spotted a sliding glass door half open on the wall opposite me and began pushing through the crowd toward it. Air would be good.

But any air that I had left in my lungs shriveled and died inside of me as I got to the threshold.

Matt was out on the patio beyond the door. He was with what I assumed to be his lacrosse buddies. They all certainly looked the part, complete with open flannel shirts and backward baseball hats. They stood in a circle that could've been mistaken for some sort of cult "Ring Around the Rosie," except they looked casually cool in their huddle.

And Matt stood at the head of the pack, leaning against the railing of the balcony, red cup in one hand and his head thrown back in laughter. He was in his trademark sweater and outshone every other man in the group by a mile in my eyes.

Accompanying the group was a tiny brunette, who was dressed in an even tinier sweater and skinny jeans. They all seemed to be laughing at something she said. She had her arm wrapped around Matt's waist, and he smiled down at her with that small smirk that tugged just one side of his mouth. The sexy one he used as a weapon. The one he had all but abandoned using with me, favoring a wider, deeper one. But there it was again. The player's mask.

My stomach started roiling, my chest felt tight, and there was a slow burn forming behind my eyes. I felt like I was going to hurl my guts up. Here he was again, back in his natural habitat. Just like the man I had assumed he was before I got to know him. It hurt to watch him play the part.

I turned to dash away, but not before his gaze flitted to the screen door and found me. I saw his eyes widen, but I squeezed mine shut and bolted away from the patio. I was definitely going to puke now.

The crowd felt thick back in the house, like I was pushing through dense fog. I made my way past the rows of bodies, scanning faces as I went, ducking beneath an arm here or there. No one. I saw no one that I knew. I was alone in the crowd, and I didn't want to be found. I tried to retreat back to the hall bathroom, wanting nothing more than to shut the door once more. But apparently, this house had more than one hall, and the one I found first had a set of stairs. I climbed them quickly, not knowing where I was going. I just needed to get away from the mess of my feelings.

I fell to my hands and knees at the top of the stairs. The carpet burned my skin at first, but then felt nice and soft, and I thought about just curling up right then and there into a little ball.

But instead, I crawled to the first door.

There was a soft light peering through that tiny strip between the carpet and wood of the frame. I reached up and wrapped my hand around the handle, using it as a counterweight to hoist myself up to my feet.

The handle gave seamlessly as I turned it, shouldering the door open.

It was a bedroom. And it was occupied.

There, at the foot of the bed was a guy dressed in khakis and a polo, the hem of the shirt still rumpled and half-tucked in his pants. Kyle Redding.

He was leaning forward, pressing onto another figure on the bed. A girl. One of Kyle's hands was wrapped around the fabric of the girl's black skirt, bunched around her waist.

The other hand was at her throat.

Kyle turned to me at the sound of the door opening. The look on his face was wiped clean of the smug expression he wore when we spoke earlier. Now he just looked eerily intent.

The girl wrenched her face toward mine, the look in her bulging eyes wild.

My hand flew from the doorknob to my mouth. "Brynn—"

It was like everything slowed down. I couldn't comprehend exactly what I was seeing in my mind, and my movements were slow and jerky.

I took a step forward toward the bed, toward Brynn, not knowing what I was going to do, but it didn't matter. Kyle was faster, much faster than I could have ever been in that moment. He wheeled away from Brynn's body, and she slumped from the top of the comforter to the floor in a heap, her hand around her own neck.

Kyle strode toward me, shoving me back by my shoulders and all but tossing me out of the room. My back crashed against the hallway wall, one of the picture frames digging into my spine and following me to the carpet.

The bedroom door slammed shut in front of me and locked with a click, but I registered one very important detail before I lost sight of the scene.

Kyle Redding's belt was undone.

Brynn's words came flooding back to me. *I wouldn't really want to go any farther than kissing with anyone else.*

"Oh God," I whimpered and pushed toward the door. I balled my hands into fists and started pounding on the barrier. "LET ME IN! Dammit, open the door!"

I beat against the wood and cried with everything I had in me. The music from below was a dull hum now in my ears, replaced with the noise from my own shouting. I wondered if anyone could hear me, but my legs wouldn't leave the bedroom door to find out. I kept hitting it instead and crying out.

There were footsteps running up the stairs beside me. There was a hand on my shoulder, but my arms whacked it away. There were tears forming on the edge of my face as I choked out, "Brynn. She's in trouble."

"Get away from the door." The voice was low and urgent. It was Matt's voice, Matt's hand that had touched me, with Bash in tow right behind him. The look on Bash's face contorted into nothing short of fury.

I couldn't see Matt's face, but I did as he said and crawled to the wall. He wound up and rammed the door with his shoulder, once, twice, and it splintered and cracked by the third hit.

I couldn't see much beyond Kyle on top of Brynn on the floor. Matt wrenched Kyle away and let his fists fly. Bash curled around Brynn's form, pulling her closer to his chest and turning his back to the scene behind them.

Over and over and over again, Matt's fists pummeled into Kyle. I caught one glance of Matt's face. I expected to see rage, but it was cold and emotionless.

A crowd was gathering around the stairs, but no one knew what was happening. A few other guys scrambled into the room and pulled at Matt, trying to get him off of Kyle. It took four in total to get the punches to stop.

There was blood on the carpet when Matt stood up and Kyle rolled over, groaning.

Chatter sprang up, voices not carrying words filled my ears. Matt looked at me in the crowd, his brown eyes still unfeeling.

"We've got to get out of here," Bash said from behind Matt.

He helped Brynn to her feet and had an arm around her, ushering her out of the room and past the peering eyes. He nudged Matt's shoulder as he passed. "Come on."

Matt's eyes were still on me as he held out his hand to hoist me back to my feet. My shoulder cried from its collision with the wall; it would probably be bruised by morning.

When I was on my feet, Matt dropped my hand and walked ahead of me, clearing the way for the two of us to follow Brynn and Bash out of the house, leaving the growing scene in our wake.

Chapter Twenty-Four

No one called the cops that night, but by morning someone had told the school.

Bash and Matt had walked us both back to our room from the party. It was a solemn walk, no one saying a word between the four of us. Matt was leading the way, and I walked behind the other two and watched several times as Bash's hand twitched toward Brynn's then stopped, not knowing whether or not to take it.

She finally reached for his instead, and they remained clasped for the entirety of the distance.

I jumped ahead of them all when we hit the library stairs so I could open the door to our room. As I shrugged out of my coat, I could hear Bash's hushed whisper to Matt, "You good, man?"

Matt said something inaudible in response.

"Go take care of yourself. I'll see you later." Bash clapped Matt on the shoulder, and Matt turned and walked away, not looking back at any of us.

"Hey, Ember, will you come with me to the bathroom?" Brynn's voice was shaking, and her eyes were shining.

"Of course," I said.

Bash sat down on her bed and slipped off his shoes. I propped the dorm door open with the wedge at the bottom of the frame and followed Brynn. Her stride was long and hurried and by the time I opened the communal bathroom door, she already had the water running from one of the sinks and was leaning over it.

I didn't know what to do, so I just sort of leaned against the sink closest to the door.

"I don't know why Bash is here," she said finally, after rinsing her face. Her voice was so low I could barely hear her. "He should hate me."

I opened my mouth to negate that fact, but she shut the water off and continued. "Bash keeps saying that he wants something more. And I wouldn't give him a label. And now this ..." She turned to me, a single tear escaping down her cheek. "Kyle said he just wanted to talk. I guess he heard about Bash and just ... wanted to know what that meant. For him. I let him kiss me. I kissed him, and I wish I didn't because then maybe he wouldn't have thought—"

"Stop! It's not your fault. Come here." I pulled her into a hug, and she squeezed me tight, dropping her head on my shoulder and letting her tears flow freely.

I let her cry and didn't move away until she hiccupped once and pulled back.

"Maybe I should've taken a page out of your book and not gotten tangled up with so many guys," Brynn said as she wiped at her makeup under her eyes.

I thinned my lips. "It's not your fault."

***

The next morning, Bash was scrolling through Brynn's phone. "It's up to you whether or not you want to make a report," he said.

"What do you mean?" I asked before she could say anything. "Hasn't someone already reported it?"

We had all gotten a mass notification email, but Brynn received a secondary one that listed her options with how she wanted to proceed.

"According to this," Bash said, his eyes narrowed on the screen, "the school is required to inform the students about any Title IX discrimination activity, but it is up to you, Brynn, if you want to make an official report through the school, or law, or both. A school report would involve informal methods like mediation. Reporting to law enforcement would mean a more intensive process."

Brynn burrowed deeper under her blankets. "So many people already know it was me. I don't want any more to know."

"You have to report it," I said quietly. "You can't just let Kyle off the hook."

She bolted upright in her bed, the blankets falling around her waist and her shirt hanging off of her shoulder, a panicked look in her eyes. "Ember, I know you. Promise me you won't go behind my back and make the report yourself."

I bit my lip and dropped her eye contact, silent. I wanted to. I wanted to go after Kyle the only way I knew how, but doing so would break Brynn's trust in me. Was it worth that price to do what I thought needed to be done?

"Promise me, Ember," she pleaded again, then turned to Bash. "Both of you promise me."

His expression was pained, but he managed a curt nod. "I promise."

"Ember." She sought my gaze again.

I let out a sigh. The answer was no. For right now, it wasn't worth it. "I promise."

She slumped back into her bed and rolled over, toward the wall. "I just need some time to think about it."

***

Matt came by our room that afternoon. I had gone out to pick up lunch and when I came back, he was sitting at my desk. I almost dropped the bag.

He looked up at the sound of the door opening, his face schooled to show little surprise. "Hey," was all he said.

"Hi." I regained my hold on the bag and shut the door behind me. "Sorry, I didn't know you were coming back."

"Just checking in," he said and stood up. Bash and Brynn had not really moved from her bed all day.

Matt turned back to the two of them. "You do whatever you think is best." He was talking to Brynn, and she nodded.

Matt tipped his chin at me, then reopened the door, careful not to brush up against me in the process.

And because I couldn't leave well enough alone, I set the bag on Brynn's desk then scurried after him out into the hall.

"What did you mean by that? Doing what's 'best'?"

Matt stopped, nearly at the stairs, and turned around. I kept walking and met him in the lobby of our floor. I sat on the arm of a sofa and crossed my arms.

He looked tired, and I noticed he was still wearing the same button-down from the night before. It was wrinkled, and there was a speck of something dark around his right sleeve. He took a long pause before saying, "Whether or not to report the case."

I narrowed my eyes. "She has to at some point. She just said to give her time to figure it out."

"No," he said calmly. "She doesn't have to. It's her choice."

"Of course it's her choice, but I think she should. There needs to be a consequence."

"Oh, I will make sure there's a consequence, not to worry." There was a laugh in his voice, but no smile. It was a dry, ironic sound. "But she shouldn't be pushed to make a report if she doesn't want to. Least of all by her friends."

I shook my head. "But the school needs to do something. The police need to do something, for crying out loud."

"Not if she doesn't want them to."

My eyes flared. "Why are you being so casual about this? This is serious!" I hissed.

"Dammit, Ember. I know it's serious!" His voice climbed, sharper than I had ever heard him speak to me. He squeezed his eyes shut and softened his tone. "Just ... think about Brynn. If she doesn't want to keep reliving it, she shouldn't go through with the report."

"So you're fine with Kyle getting away with what he tried to do?" I snapped.

Matt shook his head and turned his back on me, heading for the stairs. "It's her choice."

I was left standing alone in the lobby, dumbstruck. When I finally turned to head back to the room, Bash was leaning against the wall, arms crossed, looking down.

"How long have you been there?" I asked.

He looked up. His eyes were sad. "Just caught the tail end of that." He walked over and put his arm around my shoulders as we walked back.

"Am I wrong?"

Bash sighed. "Personally, no, I don't think you are. I would like nothing more than to drag that piece of shit to a hearing in front of everyone and give them all the version of the story I saw. Then let the board have their way with his sorry ass." He slid his arm from around me to stop a few doors down from mine. "Look, I don't know everything that has gone on between you and Matt—"

I opened my mouth to say something defensive, but Bash held up a hand and continued. "I can guess and I can assume, but he's a pretty private guy when it comes to his feelings. It's none of my business anyway. But I do know one thing about Matt—and he has always been this way as long as I've known him—he takes care of people. His friends, his more-than-friends. He's the exact opposite of Kyle. To an extreme."

Exact opposite of Kyle. So, not an intended rapist. That's good.

I took a moment to process Bash's words, and I immediately thought back to my birthday night. I had asked Matt to stay with me, not the other way around. That kiss ... I initiated it; not Matt. When we were in the club, the look in his eye when he confronted that guy who got too handsy with me ... And when we were in the mountains and first crossed that friendship line, he asked me to be sure before anything happened.

"So he's big on consent," I said. "That's great. But so is any decent human being."

"Yeah, except he's got reason to be."

"What's the reason? He has a conscience?" I paused. "And shouldn't that mean that he would want to report this even more?"

Bash shook his head. "I only know pieces, and only because he was rather drunk one night and started talking. It's not my story to tell, but I will say he was caught in a bad scenario and it's something he still carries to this day."

I remembered the way his face had ghosted over when I asked about his first girlfriend. "Anna?"

Bash's eyes flickered with surprise. "He told you?"

So it *was* about her. I shook my head. "Only her name."

"I'm kind of shocked he even said that much." Bash turned to open the door to my room. "He must be quite fond of you or something."

Maybe he was, I thought, *but not anymore.*

***

The last thing I wanted to do was confront Matt Callahan after I saw him on the patio with Miss Itsy Bitsy Teenie Weenie last night *and* after he walked away from me this afternoon. But I needed answers as much as I needed to apologize. I needed to know what happened with Anna. So when Bash stepped out to get dinner later that evening, I decided to drive over to Matt's.

As I was heading out the door, Brynn sat up in her bed. "Where are you going?"

I bit my lip, debating whether or not to tell the truth, but I was done lying. "I need to go see Matt."

"Did you get to see him at all last night? Before ... everything?"

Again, I paused. "Um ... yeah ... I did."

She looked curious, so I continued. "He looked like he was about to be occupied ... with someone else."

Her face crumpled. "I'm so sorry, Ember."

I shook my head and opened the door. "You have nothing to be sorry for."

I made the drive in record time. It was getting dark outside when I cut Bugsy's engine and stepped out into the cold air. I wrapped my arms tightly around myself as I made my way to the Selwyn Dad door. I untangled my arms from my sweater just long enough to knock twice before tucking my hands back into my armpits.

The handle wiggled a little before it gave and the door opened. This time when our eyes met, there was no poker face. Matt looked shocked. "Ember ... what are you doing here?"

"Can I come in?" I asked meekly.

He didn't move for a few seconds, then recovered. "Yeah. Yeah, sure."

He stepped aside, and I ducked under his arm into the kitchen, where I stood awkwardly with my arms wound around myself.

Matt ended up leaning against the counter, arms crossed. "What's up?"

The tension was so strong, I thought it would snap. I wondered briefly which one of us would break first if, or when, it did.

"I ..." I cleared my throat to start again. "I just wanted to ... thank you, for coming and checking on Brynn. And for last night."

The image of Matt's fists flying was still seared in my brain, etched in something permanent and painful.

He nodded once.

It was quiet again for several beats too long, and I couldn't stop myself from whispering, "Who was the girl you were talking to on the patio?"

Matt dragged a hand over his face. "Keira," he said finally. "Her name's Keira."

"Pretty name." My voice sounded hoarse. My throat—my whole body—ached.

"We aren't ..." Matt stopped and sighed deeply. "Nothing happened between us, but I still feel like I should apologize for the way it looked."

I had been expecting the worst: for him to have been able to move on that quickly and replace me with another warm body.

"On the other hand," he continued. "You made your feelings very clear when you hung up on me, so I shouldn't feel sorry." He looked up at me, his dark eyes boring into mine, heavy. "But I am."

I couldn't hold his gaze. I dropped my eyes and said, "I'm sorry too. Everything about that call, what I said on the phone. I shouldn't have—"

"It's fine."

"It isn't." *It sent you straight into the company of someone else.*

"I'd rather not talk about it," Matt said.

"Okay ..." I said. "Then can you tell me why you don't think Brynn should report the case?"

He groaned, loud and exasperated. "If you were really so determined about the report, you would've done it already. What's stopping you?"

"I ..." My voice caught. "I can't. I don't think she would forgive me." *I just keep coming back to you,* she said after our fight. If I reported against her wishes, that might just be the straw to make her turn away once and for all.

"Well then, why don't you just drop it?"

"Because," I said weakly, "I just want to be able to do what a good friend would. I want her to know I have her back."

His voice lost its edge. "That's exactly why I don't want to push the report. I don't want her to relive it any more than she probably will."

"Does this have something to do with Anna?"

Matt looked at me as if I had struck him plain across his face. "What do you mean?"

"I'm really sorry for bringing her up," I said. "But I just want to understand."

He turned his back on me, striding toward the living room. "There's nothing to understand."

I scurried after him. "I don't believe that."

He wheeled on me. "What did Bash tell you?"

I took a step back from him. "He didn't have to tell me anything. It's written all over your face."

He turned again, walking aimlessly in circles, his fists clenching by his sides.

"Talk to me, Matt," I pleaded in a near whisper.

"Why should I?" he snapped. "You said it yourself, I'm probably just lonely, so why does it matter?"

Something about having my own words used against me made my skin boil. "I don't actually think your problem is being lonely, Matt. From what you've told me, you're someone that thrives on connection and an exploration of those connections. I think maybe you don't know how to be alone."

I realized the truth of the words as they escaped my lips. I believed him when he told me that he wanted to learn as much as he could about becoming a better partner, but the back-to-back relationships ... he was endlessly trying to fill a void left by someone else; no, not *someone*—Anna.

"What did she do to you?"

"Ha!" The laugh was one syllable, sharp and bitter. "It's not what *she* did." The look on his face hardened. "It's what *I* didn't do."

"What do you mean?"

"I wasn't there!" he cried loudly, before his voice fell. "When she needed someone, I wasn't there."

"What happened?" I pressed.

"The same damn thing that nearly happened to Brynn, that's what happened!" He shouted. "But far worse. Far, far worse."

My stomach sank, and Matt's voice grew.

"You want to hear how I was the jerk who wasn't there that night? How I stood by and chose to ignore every snide remark made every day by every girl in high school who wondered why I was with Anna? Because I didn't think those comments meant anything?"

I was confused, but Matt went on, his voice dropping an octave. "Anna and I were friends as kids, but we weren't super close until she transferred to my school junior year from her public school."

The story we wrote flashed in my head. "Childhood friends; like Lena and Wesley."

"Yep. Not a super original premise, but the truth of the real relationship's demise is far worse than the affair you and I wrote about instead." He shook his head before continuing. "She was everything any guy could ever want, but she didn't fit in with most of the girls. She was so much more mature. She didn't party, and she stayed out of the drama, which, to the other girls, made her a target. I never fed into it because, to me, it didn't matter. And I didn't think it mattered to her either.

"She was getting bullied, but I never saw it. They were sly, and she never let me see her struggle. One night, she had had enough of the comments. She finally went to a party—her first high school party, and one that I didn't go to—one that her bullies and the guys on the lacrosse team had ... planned. Without me."

The look on Matt's face as he met my eyes was nothing short of tortured. "It was awful, Ember. It was all a set up. One of the guys slipped something in her drink, and it didn't take much after that to get her alone."

"You don't have to continue," I whispered.

His eyes blazed. "Oh no, you wanted the story, so here it is. The guy ... he's behind bars now ... he was on my team. I thought he was a friend. Anna did too.

"If the r—" his voice wavered. "If the rape itself wasn't bad enough, it was the trial afterward that broke her. The onslaught of questions, the need to repeat the story over and over in front of family, friends, court. The speculation about the truth of her words; the doubt. It was a small school, and once those seeds of doubt were planted, the rumors grew nasty. Some said she asked for it and was trying to frame him. Others said she came onto him first. The drug screen told the truth but still, words can kill."

He sat down finally, on the edge of the couch, elbows resting on his knees, hanging his head. "She withdrew from me. I couldn't reach her. Nothing I did could bring back the girl I knew and loved. I went over to her house one afternoon and found her in the bathroom." He choked on his words.

"There were pills everywhere. I called 9-1-1. I rode with her to the hospital. I watched her stomach get pumped. She survived, but her family had had enough. They sent her to live with her grandparents in the middle-of-nowhere Indiana to finish her senior year."

Matt was wringing his hands together, and his eyes were wet. "I reached out every day. I never heard back from her. Her mom finally answered the phone one day and said her therapist suggested cutting all ties to help her heal. I stopped calling after that.

"I've gotten one letter from her, end of freshman year. It was a cheesy thank-you card of all things," he scoffed. "There was nothing else printed on the inside other than THANK YOU! Big capital letters, exclamation mark and all. She signed it, *I'm okay. Anna.*"

He was quiet, head turned away from me.

I had no idea what to say. What could I possibly do after learning of the invisible weight Matt had been shouldering all these years? I cleared my throat and said softly, "I don't think she blames you if she sent that card."

"How could she not?" Matt snapped and stood up, resuming his pacing around the room. "*I* blame me! I should have been there. I should have stood up for her before the bullying even got to that point. I should have done something."

"You can't hold yourself responsible for other people's actions," I tried to reason.

"Damn right I can! I could have stopped it. I could have fixed it. I could have saved her."

"How?"

"I don't know, but I try every day to find a way!"

Every day. Every relationship. Every friend. *He takes care of people,* Bash had said.

"You care so deeply about others," I started, cautiously, "because you believe you have to make up for what happened to Anna?" I shook my head. "Matt, no matter what you do, you can't change the past. Believe me, I know."

Before we were partners for the contest, Matt and I were nothing. The story brought us together, but it was Matt who managed to crack my shield, seeing through every defense. I was the girl who couldn't let anyone in, but Matt had found a way, because he couldn't be by himself. He needed someone else to invest in … because if he was devoted elsewhere, he wouldn't have to look inside at the damage that still racked his soul.

And it dawned on me that I had just been his latest diversion.

Dread seeped into my bones, and part of me already knew the answer to the question I asked next.

"Matt," I whispered, "do you think I need to be fixed? Is that why you care?" *Is that why you chose me? Almost. Almost chose me.*

"I think we all need to be fixed."

It wasn't a confirmation, but it wasn't a denial. I felt so foolish. I was nothing more than a project. Something for him to deconstruct and try to rebuild.

My fingers were curling and uncurling against my palms. My legs were shaky, so I sat down on the edge of the couch, defeated.

It was silent for too long.

"Am I that broken?" I asked, quietly. Helpless. Damaged. Weak. I *had* been weak every time it came to Matt.

"Ember, no." I lifted my gaze just enough to meet his. He looked lost, something so foreign on his features.

"Everything you've done for me, hasn't been about me." I felt sick, and none of the words strung together in my head could aptly explain how gutted I felt. Every moment we had, every glance, concern, touch … I was just the latest in a string of surrogates for Matt to attempt to redress the damage from the doomed relationship that had left him scarred.

And from the look in his dark eyes, that scarring had him breaking, fracturing from the inside out. I could see it so clearly now.

My biggest fear of getting close to Matt was that I would end up getting played. I never thought it would be like this, but the result was the same. He was going to move on, repeating his pattern again and again just so he could feel better about himself. Tears started leaking from my eyes, and I willed them to stop. I turned my head, wiping the back of my hand angrily across my face. "I need to go."

"Seriously?" Matt asked. "You're going to walk away?"

"I'm sorry," I said. "I'm sorry for what happened to you and Anna. Truly. And I ..." I stopped and took a shaky breath. "I admire your desire to want to change things. You are a good person. But you have to forgive yourself for Anna, or you're never going to heal. And you struggling to fix all the damaged people around you is going to turn you into a martyr. If that's what you want, fine. But I refuse to be your latest sacrifice."

I stood up and headed for the door. Everything inside me screamed to go to Matt instead, and tell him that it was going to be okay. Part of me wanted so desperately to love the man who invested himself so wholeheartedly into others. The other part ... I was ashamed of myself for falling so hard in the first place. I fell for a lie. His devotion ... his commitment ... everything had been a lie.

"Ember," Matt croaked as my hand wrapped around the doorknob.

I turned back to him.

"I'm so sorry." He dropped his gaze, holding his head in his hands.

"Me too," I said. I pressed my lips together to stop them from shaking and closed the door behind me.

Chapter Twenty-Five

B rynn received an email from Pollard saying she could have an excused absence from class Monday night, but she tailed me to the classroom at 5:45 p.m., regardless.

Spencer was already in the room, having just gotten back into town. He halfway stood out of his seat to greet us, but sat back down when Brynn pulled out the chair next to him, ignoring the gesture.

"I heard," Spencer said as I sat down in my usual seat behind them. "I'm so sorry, Brynn."

She was looking straight ahead at the board. "I appreciate it, but I really wish people would stop saying that."

Pollard came in next, followed by a small stream of other students. To his credit, Pollard offered our corner of the room a small nod but said nothing else.

The remainder of the students filed in over the next ten minutes, Matt bringing up the rear and closing the door behind him. He sat at the seat closest to the door, skateboard propped behind him.

He looked up and I turned my head quickly, refusing to meet his gaze.

It hurt to look at him.

The clock tower chimed 6:00 p.m. outside, and Pollard called the class to order. "Good evening, folks. I hope everyone had a good weekend."

There was an awkward pause in the room, and the professor rushed to cover it. "Your stories are due in a week's time. As promised, I am going to pass back Mr. Van Dam's comments on your drafts before we get into workshop tonight. I made two copies for each story, so everyone can have their own to revise from."

I breathed a sigh of relief. No sharing, thankfully.

Pollard started making his way through the rows of desks, passing out papers in a front-to-back method. I watched as Matt took his copy, and even from my spot all the way in the back of the classroom, I could see the dramatic scratch of purple ink all over the pages.

Oh God, I thought. There were so many notes as I watched him flip through the pages. So many lines crossed out, so many comments on the side. From the looks of it, my idol, my literary god, Oliver Van Dam, had torn our story apart.

"Just take a few moments to thumb through it all. I can answer any questions you may have, but I suggest taking the notes in with a special consideration. Mr. Van Dam is accomplished, no doubt, but his vision may be different than your own. My best advice to you is still to write your story."

My copy landed on my desk with a sound that resembled a cruel slap to my ears. Gently, I peeled back the cover sheet and started scanning the purple scrawl.

The inciting incident of the crash was fine, followed by the original flashbacks of Lena and Wesley together as kids. But the closer the story got to its climax, the more time that Lena spent in the present, trying to find a way to forgive and reconcile their past, the more purple the pages became.

My heart sank as I read a few of the lines.

Too predictable.

Near death experience forces reexamination of life. I've read this a thousand times.

So he cheated. Tons of people do. What makes this story special? I need a twist here.

If your prompt was to write a story where the main character falls in love, the only definition this draft provides is that you have to almost die to see it was there all along. #dramatic.

I kept reading, the weight of my anxiety growing heavier on my shoulders as I realized Van Dam was right. As the story stood now, there was nothing special in the events or the actions the characters took.

There was a note on the back of the last page.

Matthew Callahan and Ember Owens,

The writing here is eloquent, beautiful even. The pacing of your reveal of what happened between your characters in their past is perfectly timed. And the chemistry between your characters is vivid. As a reader, it feels as if we are living this alongside them. However, this is a story Hollywood has told us time and time again. Yes, it is true that the art of storytelling tends to follow a distinct pattern, (rise, climax, fall, yada yada) and it can be applied to almost any plot. It is the plot that is my main concern. If the purpose of your plot is to write about love, the job of the story needs to give me a definition of it. For revision, look inside yourselves and write the story that defined your idea of love. Love in real life is messy and much more complicated than it often appears on the page or on screen. I'm challenging the pair of you to come up with a more authentic definition and stitch it into this story in particular. I look forward to seeing your final draft in a week.

Best,

Oliver Van Dam

A more authentic definition. I couldn't help but raise my eyes to Matt's form in the front of the room. His elbows were propped on the table, and his head hung between his hands as he scanned the pages.

How were we going to pull this off? A part of me felt like chucking this whole contest out the window and giving up. A voice in my head chided me, saying that was a weak response. But sitting here now, wrapped in the aftermath of the past few days with these purple notes cutting my not-so-thick skin, I felt exhausted.

I didn't agree with how Matt had been living his life, defining love as a self-destructive habit he couldn't quit. I thought about my dad, my mom, my brother. Had I ever witnessed anything that could come close to an *authentic definition of love*? If someone were to ask me what I thought love was, what would I even say?

It doesn't exist, was what I wanted to write. The happy-ending fairy tale was just a story. And looking at the draft before me and at Matt hunched in the corner, I wanted to run away.

I did exactly that. Pollard was at the front of the room again, so I slipped the packet into my bag and went to the podium.

"Yes, Ember? Do you have a question about your comments?"

"Actually, I'm really not feeling good. I posted my workshop letters online, but I think I need to head back to my room. I'm sorry."

He patted my shoulder. "Feel better."

I didn't look back as I walked out the door.

***

I got back to my room and I already had a text from Matt's number, still no name attached.

> how do you want to do this

I pulled my phone out and flopped down on my bed. I typed:

> Separately.

I quickly deleted that retort before hitting send and wrote instead:

> Honestly, I can't think about it tonight. If you have any ideas, I'm good with whatever.

Matt didn't respond.

Spencer texted me at nine asking if I wanted to go to The House with him and Brynn or if I wanted anything brought back. I didn't.

As I was tucking myself into bed, my phone pinged with an email from Matt. There was no subject line but it had an attached document, detailing the changes he was planning on making with his scenes. *See if you can work with this* was the only note in the body of the email.

I locked my phone without opening the document and turned out the lamp.

***

I spent most of the week in my room, sitting at my desk, staring at my computer. Taking in fresh air and the late winter sunshine might have been healthier, but avoiding contact with the outside world also helped me avoid Matt.

I wish it would help me finish the damn story, though. The blank page on my screen with its unforgiving cursor coupled with the glaring purple ink on the pages sitting beside my laptop had worked together to sufficiently drain all of my creative energy, or any energy for that matter.

I had no desire to finish the love story. I couldn't. It was hard to finish any story without inspiration, and inspiration for this topic in particular had long since disappeared.

I briefly glanced over the notes Matt sent me regarding his changes. He had the idea to change the initial affair in his flashback from Wesley cheating on Lena, to Lena having her heartbroken at finding out she was the other woman.

I had to give him credit. That was a good way to subvert reader expectations. When I wrote, I always felt the need to protect my characters. I knew that in order to make the conflict believable, it was worth putting them at their lowest point possible, but something about that kind of betrayal in the past made my job of making Lena forgive Wesley in the present much harder.

I was tempted to just leave them at odds with each other for the ending that I had to rewrite on my own.

***

Thursday evening, I stepped out of the room and made my way to the lobby to call my dad, letting Brynn continue to make her revisions in peace. She didn't look up when I left; both of her earbuds were pushed in and her eyebrows were scrunched together.

The phone rang twice before he picked up.

"Ember?"

"Yes. Don't sound so surprised. That is the name you gifted me upon birth."

He chuckled on his end of the line. "You know what your mom wanted to name you?"

"No." I paused in my step, almost to the couch.

"Hannah," he said. "Do you know how many little girls were named Hannah the year you were born?"

"There's no telling." I sighed as I sat down.

"It cracked top five most popular."

"Guess that means I was never destined for popularity."

"You know why you got the name Ember?"

"Because even then, you knew I wouldn't be normal?" I guessed.

"Hmm," he mumbled. "Normal is overrated."

"Normalcy is nice now and again."

"You know what isn't normal? You calling me without being prompted to. Everything okay?"

I closed my eyes. "Not really." I didn't even know where to start explaining.

"What can I do?" my dad asked.

Brynn, Kyle ... Matt. "I don't think anything." I cleared my throat. "I just ... miss you a little."

My dad was obviously confused and probably a touch concerned based on the silence on his end of the line. "I miss you, too, kiddo." He paused. "Do you want to talk about what's on your mind?"

To my own credit, I considered for a hot second word vomiting all the tumultuous emotions swirling inside me. "Not really," I settled with. "Is ... is Ethan still home?"

"He is," my dad said. "I've got to say, I was impressed with how well he handled himself with the whole attorney meeting. Between you and I, he came home and cried a little. But he kept his cool the whole time throughout the arrangements."

I ached for him. For both of them. "Do you guys have plans this weekend?"

"Not particularly."

"I think I might come home," I blurted out the words without really thinking about them first. I took a deep breath. "You know, the final draft of my story is due Monday, and it needs a shit ton of revision and help and ..."

"I can help you," he said.

I puffed out a sigh.

"Back to your name ... I liked Ember because I liked the metaphors you could have associated with it."

I gave a strangled chortle. "Why does that not surprise me?"

"There is your fiery temper to start with," he said.

"Rude."

"But as you were growing up, there was one that stuck out in particular. You've always been so independent. But even if a fire is fading, the embers can still be brought back to life. They just need a little help." He sighed. "It's okay to need help sometimes, Emmy."

I got the feeling he wasn't talking about just my story anymore as he repeated, "It's okay to let someone help."

Chapter Twenty-Six

I left campus early Friday morning, packing light and carrying a heavy heart. I hadn't talked to my brother since he called to see if I was going to Mom's wedding.

I didn't know what I was going to say, or how I was going to say it, but I couldn't stay holed up in my room any longer. And home seemed like a safe place to retreat.

The trek back there this time was quiet and seemed lonely without a particular passenger.

I pushed the thought away and turned the volume on my playlist up a few notches as I opted out of the Blue Ridge Parkway, choosing the more direct path of the highway instead.

This time, I told Brynn exactly where I was going.

"Are you sure you're okay if I go away for the weekend?" I asked for the thousandth time.

"Ember, you're exhausting. Please go. I promise you that I'm fine."

"You could come with me if you want—"

"I appreciate it, seriously." Her smile was thin. "But I think you need to do this by yourself."

Do what, exactly, I wasn't so sure. But as the minutes ticked by, bringing me closer to the mountains, the more I wished I wasn't arriving alone.

When I finally parked my car in the driveway and stepped out into the morning light, the mountains rose to greet me, the tree limbs spreading their spindly welcome.

I had barely closed my car door behind me when the front door opened and Jaws came barreling through, yapping incessantly.

"Seriously?" I said, stooping low to pet the rabid beast. "When are you just going to accept the fact, I'm not going anywhere?"

My dad was leaning against the door frame, a cup of coffee in one hand and the newspaper in the other. He chuckled. "How was the drive?"

I looked up at him, and I felt like a little kid again, wanting nothing more than to rush straight into his arms. I kept my pace even as I strode toward him but then threw my arms around his neck.

"Uneventful," I said, my face burrowed in his sweater.

He patted my back before I drew away, reluctantly. The smile around his eyes was deep and crinkled, his salt and pepper hair echoing the same color as the stubble along his jaw. God, I had missed him.

"Coffee?" he asked, gesturing for me to go in first.

I hiked my bag a little higher on my shoulder. "Yes, please."

Dad lifted his chin to call into the house. "Ethan! Make one more cup. Emmy is home."

"Sure thing." My brother's voice was deep and seemingly unfazed by my arrival. Jaws skirted around my legs, darting after Ethan's voice. I followed, slower.

As I rounded the corner, I was taken aback by the smell of bacon frying. Sure enough, as I tentatively poked my head into the kitchen, there was Ethan, a kitchen towel thrown over one shoulder, stirring eggs over the stove.

"Since when do you make breakfast?" Having studied the English language for years, one would think that I could have conjured up a better greeting. I wanted to smack myself in the head.

Ethan set the bowl down on the counter, wiped his hands with the towel, and turned to face me.

His hair was a sandy brown, much like the color my dad's used to be before it grayed out. Ethan's was currently in need of a trim and was sticking up in all sorts of crazy directions. We had the same shade of light green in our eyes, though. His were currently twinkling, and a soft smile was playing at his mouth. "Don't get too excited," he said. "I can only scramble eggs."

He set the towel down and eased back against the counter, waiting for me to say something smart in return.

Again, I wished I had the right words to cough up so I could tell him exactly how sorry I was. For Hallie … for the way I reacted to Mom's wedding invitation … for the distance I didn't realize I had been carving between us until this moment, standing before him.

His smile turned a little sad, and he opened his arms to me. "Come here, kid."

There were tears burning the back of my eyes as I went willingly, all but throwing myself into his embrace. His arms tightened around me, and I squeezed my eyes shut.

Sometimes, there isn't a need for the right words. Sometimes, you don't have to say anything at all. Some things, you could just feel.

***

We had breakfast as a family, sitting together in the kitchen, which we rarely did anymore. When we were finished, I cleared the table and put the dishes in the dishwasher, leaving only the pan with the bacon grease to congeal on the stove top.

I did let Jaws lick the forks, in his effort to help clean up too.

Afterward, Ethan ran into town for some errands. I used that time to migrate to the living room and spread out all of my papers and critiques about my draft for my dad to peruse. He spent the next hour pouring over the notes, and I knew he wouldn't give his opinion about anything until he read them all.

I took my bags to my room, then made two more cups of coffee, mine with cream and Dad's black.

"What do you think?" I asked, setting his cup down on the only open sliver of space on the table.

He mumbled his thanks, then rubbed his hand over his jaw. "I met Oliver Van Dam once. He's ... eccentric."

"You're telling me."

"It was at some convention. The one where I picked up that ARC of the last book in that series you liked."

"Like," I said, smiling. "Present tense. I still like it." That Advanced Reader Copy was probably my most prized possession. I still don't know how my dad charmed his way into one of only twenty or so copies; being Sam Owens probably helped.

He harrumphed. "I could never get into the whole sci-fi thing."

"You're missing out."

"Maybe. Maybe not." He picked up the last page of my story. "First off, I've got to say, I'm pretty impressed, Emmy. In terms of the writing itself, this might be some of your best work."

My chest swelled. "You think?"

"Van Dam's not wrong, though, about the plot."

My chest deflated. "Yeah, I know," I mumbled. "I just don't know how to fix it."

Dad flipped the page to the back. "It seems like he wrote you some pretty good advice."

"If by good, you mean vague and cryptic, then sure."

He smiled at me, and set the paper down with the rest. "You're writing a love story, right?"

"Obviously."

He chuckled and stood up, taking his mug with him. "You know, honey, there's a reason that some stories resonate with us even after we've closed the book."

I picked up a pillow from the couch and hugged it tight, drawing my knees to my chin around it.

My dad continued. "It's because we see ourselves in them. That's why the art of the story will never die. We tell stories to find the truth about being human. And to me, you've hit the jackpot with this prompt. It's what brings us together, a universal desire to love and be loved." He took a long drink from his mug and sighed. "It's just human nature."

I sank deeper in my seat. My voice was quiet when I spoke. "So why is there so much heartbreak in the world?"

He gave me a sad smile. "Because, the flip side of being human is making mistakes. And learning how to move forward from them." He paused. "You have to rewrite the final scene for the story?"

I nodded, looking at the mess in front of me.

Dad came around the back of the couch to kiss the top of my head. "Well then, here is some more vague advice: listen to your heart, trust your gut, and write it how you want the story to end. Write what you think is true about love." He started walking toward the kitchen. "Or at least, what you want to be true."

***

When Ethan got back that afternoon, I suggested that we take Jaws on a hike together.

"Hiking?" He looked bewildered. "Since when do you hike?"

"I'll have you know, I started running when I got to school."

"Around campus?"

"No," I said. "On a treadmill. In the gym."

"Exactly! You don't like being outdoors."

"Not true!" I cried and crossed my arms. "I always liked the tree house."

Ethan paused, then laughed. "Yeah. That damn tree house. That's not the same as the hike to the Blowing Rock, though."

I ignored him and grabbed Jaws's leash off the wall. "Come on."

***

At least Ethan thought to grab water bottles before we went on our spontaneous hiking excursion. Even though the air was still crisp, my legs were starting to cry from the stairs, and my throat kept drying out.

"Are we there yet?" I whined.

Ethan was several paces ahead of me; Jaws chilled in his backpack, looking at me intently. Every once in a while, the rodent sized dog would curl his lip and show me just one tooth.

He laughed at the question I had been repeatedly asking and gave me the same answer. "Almost there." He amended, "I promise this time."

And we were. The trees opened up to a massive hunk of rock that seemed to be dangling from the thin wisps of clouds.

"The Blowing Rock itself," I huffed, and fished around Jaws's fluff to find my water.

Ethan had his arms crossed, looking out at the view. "It's been a while since I've been up here."

I nodded and put my bottle down on the ground so I could hoist Jaws out by his harness to let him go pee. I handed my brother the end of his leash. He took it wordlessly.

"I know," I said. "Probably since Mom brought us up here as kids."

Ethan turned and started fidgeting with his bag.

I had surprised myself by saying that, but it was true. And it was the perfect segue into the conversation we needed to have.

I took a deep breath. "If you want to go to her wedding, that's your call. It was wrong of me to judge and snap at you the way I did." I clambered onto the wall in front of us so that I was sitting on the stone, legs dangling on the edge of the world, but my upper body was secure behind the railing. "I'm still not going," I said into the void. "But I'm ... not upset at you for wanting to go. You've got to do what you think is best." I hated Matt's words coming out of my mouth. Different situation entirely, but their meaning was still applicable.

There was a deep sigh behind me, and then Ethan was stuffing his legs through the gap in the wall as well, sitting like we used to as kids. Jaws remained at the end of his leash, content to look out at the mountains without venturing too close.

"Can I just ask you something?"

Ethan grumbled. "If I said no, you would still ask anyway."

I fiddled with my thumbs a moment and turned to look at him. "Why are you going?"

He was refusing to meet my gaze and was instead looking out at the stretch of horizon that rolled into forever.

"I started seeing a therapist," he said quietly.

Whoa. I was caught immediately off guard. What are you supposed to say to that? Congrats? I'm proud?

I settled with, "Does it help?"

He shrugged. "I don't think it hurts. I've gotten some sage words of wisdom that have kind of stuck with me throughout these past couple of months." Ethan reached over to his bag to grab his own water. He took a long sip before continuing. "He told me that when it comes to making any kind of relationship work—be that family, friends, lovers—it takes two. A relationship can't survive with just one. And since getting that invitation, I've realized that when it comes to Mom, she's always been wired to only care so much about other people. She's not great at the it-taking-two thing. But I've also realized that different people have different capacities for love. In her own way, I think she's loving us the best she can right now by simply reaching out."

He turned to me then. I expected sadness in his eyes, or something of the like, but Ethan seemed at peace.

"And honestly, Emmy, after losing Hallie, I've really just come to the conclusion that I'm tired of being angry. I don't want to be angry anymore. If this is the best Mom can do, then I accept that. I don't think we can hold everyone to the same standard when it comes to their ability to love." He shrugged and looked back out into the mountains. "People have a weird way of showing they care sometimes."

I thought back to my last conversation with Matt. He cared, but it was a systematic, thought-out, preplanned approach to caring.

Our whole whatever-we-had-relationship was penance for Anna. Was that all he could offer?

"Yeah," I finally said, looking out at the mountains. "Weird."

***

Saturday afternoon, I got an email from Matt. No subject line, no body text, just an attachment.

It was his revised flashback, where Wesley and Lena originally cut their communication.

I minimized the final scene I was working on and downloaded his attachment. I skimmed the beginning, but couldn't help but pause to read the heartbreak that followed right after the two characters finally admitted their feelings for one another.

I woke the next morning as the sun was rising over the treetops, a soft light seeping through sheer curtains, to a high pitched, female cry. "What the hell, Wesley?"

I was curled on my side with one of Wesley's heavy arms wound tight around my waist, the other propped underneath my head, his breath stirring the hair on the back of my neck. I opened my eyes at the outburst to see Vanessa standing in the doorway, her hair sticking up in all sorts of crazy directions, her jaw slack, and her eyes bloodshot. "How could you?" she cried.

I froze, staring at the girl I assumed was out of Wesley's life based on the way he spoke to me last night. The way he had looked at me like I was the only good thing left in his universe. The way his soft lips found a way to break down my translucent armor with each tender kiss. But she wasn't gone at all. She was still there, here, standing in the doorway looking broken. She was still in his life and in some place in his heart. My whole body recoiled with slow understanding, and I began to feel what my head could no longer deny. It felt as though my own heart was breaking in time with Vanessa's ragged breath.

Wesley jerked awake from her raw sobbing. It took several blinks of his eyes and too many seconds to orient himself in the morning light. When the registration hit, his whole body went on instant alert.

"Oh my God, Vanessa. Shit. SHIT." He sprang away from me as if my skin burned him. He wrestled with the quilt, trying to untangle his limbs from underneath. One of his feet slapped the floor while the other got caught on the corner and he tripped, nearly falling out of bed as he righted himself to reach for her, wearing nothing but his boxers.

"Don't. Just ... don't," she choked and stumbled away from him down the hall.

"Vanessa!" He lurched once as if to follow her, then stopped, tilting his chin down and back toward me in his bed, as if he had just remembered that I was still there, dumbstruck.

He fisted the curls at the top of his head. "Lena, I'm so s—"

"Wesley," I said sharply, stopping his apology. I was already untangling myself from the blankets, searching for my shirt and shorts somewhere on the floor. "Yes or no. Are you still dating Vanessa?"

His shoulders sunk, his back still turned to me. I stood up beside the bedside table, tugging on the last of my clothing as he teetered between me and the open doorway. "Wesley, look at me and tell me the truth." I cursed the weakness that had my voice breaking on the last word. "If you are still dating Vanessa, why did you ask me to stay with—"

"It was a mistake."

The crack in his voice unleashed the well of salty tears that I had been forcing to stay capped behind my eyelids. A single, hot streak ran down my cheek. "A mistake." I let the word roll off my tongue. It stung like thick acid. "And the things you said to me?"

He finally turned to face me, his expression knotted in so many thoughts twining behind his darkened gray eyes. "Lena, I shouldn't have said anything, and I most certainly should not have let last night go as far as it did. I'm so sorry, but it was all a mistake. A big one."

Gone was the best friend I grew up laughing beside and in his place was someone cold, hard, and distant—all because of one reckless night and our weakly guarded feelings for each other that had just unraveled our worlds.

The shredded remains of my heart gave way to a new and horrifying thought. "Wesley, do you have any idea what you just made me into?"

Confusion flickered across his remorseful gaze. "What do you mean?"

My voice was low and drawn. "You just made me the other woman."

Shame struck his whole body into paralysis. His lips—God, those lips—opened and closed, fishing for something to fill the awful silence, but found nothing. Nothing could take back what had already been done.

"And what for? A drunken declaration of false feelings?"

"Lena, please stop—"

"No! Wesley, I can't." I choked, the tears and mucus in the back of my throat finally getting the best of my speech. "I have to go," I managed to say.

I could see it in Wesley's eyes—the fear, the knowledge that our lifelong friendship just fell, irrevocably, into the abyss.

"No, wait," he said, reaching for my hand. "Lena, don't do this to me."

"The only thing I have done was believe you," I spat. "And that, Wesley, was my mistake." I jerked my hand away from his, begging my memory to erase the feeling forever. "I don't ever want to see you again."

I closed my laptop when I got to the end of the flashback, my hands shaking. Just when things were getting too good to be true, there had to be someone else in Wesley's life.

Just like there was someone else in the back of Matt's mind. Was I a mistake to Matt, just like Lena had been to Wesley?

I dragged a hand across my face, gripping my hair in its bun, hurt and angry at the resemblance this scene bore to my own confused feelings.

It wasn't fair that I was stuck with the task now of supposedly reconciling this story. Did Matt really think that I could salvage Lena and Wesley's friendship after a betrayal like this?

I got up out of my chair and started pacing around my room. My brother's words came flitting back to me, and I halted my step.

It takes two.

"Oh my god," I whispered. Ethan might be part genius.

It wasn't up to just Lena. Lena and Wesley's relationship couldn't be rectified without the both of them wanting to make it work.

Write what you want to be true about love.

Somewhere deep down, I wanted it to be true that there were relationships worth fighting for in this world. But every one that I had known or seen—my mom, my dad, Ethan, Hallie—they all bailed when it got hard. And I learned that if both people weren't willing to put the work in that it took to succeed, heartbreak was inevitable.

You can't hold everyone to the same standard when it comes to their ability to love.

But that was the loophole. Not everyone was wired to love the same.

It didn't have to be the same, though, did it? It just had to be enough.

My mind sidestepped. What if Matt was giving me everything he had in him?

It takes two.

If we wanted to salvage whatever we were, it would take the both of us.

Holy shit.

My knees wobbled, and I sat on the edge of my bed as realization struck me like an iron fist to the gut: It was me who bailed, not Matt. I was the one who jumped to conclusions. I used his past to assume how he felt about me, and then I never gave him the chance to respond, to explain.

I was the one who walked away.

Chapter Twenty-Seven

I wrote with a ferocity I didn't entirely know I had in me to finish the story, racing toward the resolution I knew I had to try to make true. For Lena.

For me.

I got back to campus midday and was met with the barreling force that was Spencer as I got to the library threshold.

"Have you talked to Brynn?" he asked in a huff.

"No," I said. "Good to see you too."

"Yeah, yeah, hi," he said, brushing me off.

Spencer glanced over both shoulders, then leaned in close, dropping his voice. "She filed the report on Kyle."

"She ... what?"

He nodded his head. "Everyone has been talking about it all weekend. She went straight to the dean. Kyle's under suspension until further investigation. Both his merit and athletic scholarships had been stripped already, though, which was a little odd."

"Wow," I said, pride evident in my voice. I was thrilled with her decision, although I wondered what had solidified it for her.

"I know, right?" Spencer stuffed his hands in his pockets. "I still feel horrible that I wasn't there with you guys."

I looked over at him. His jaw was clenched as his head turned to the clock tower, eyes focused on nothing in particular.

"I don't think it would have mattered," I whispered. I was there. And I had been helpless.

"I know Brynn was hoping it would all just die down," he said. "But I'm glad he's been taken care of."

Oh, I'll make sure there is a consequence, not to worry.

My legs felt weak all of a sudden. Matt made it sound like he had a plan even though he didn't want the report filed. I wondered if he had something to do with snowballing the repercussion.

"Yeah," I said, absentmindedly. "Me too. I'll see you later in class, okay?"

"Okay," Spencer said. "You good?"

I was already moving past him. I paused just long enough to answer truthfully. "I'm not sure."

As the sliding doors whooshed open for me, I pulled out my phone from my back pocket.

Matt hadn't reached out all weekend, other than to email his flashback. Regardless, I sent him a text as I made my way upstairs.

Are you the one behind Kyle's suspension?

I kept glancing at my phone while I walked as the three little dots appeared, then disappeared, before reappearing again at the bottom of the screen.

probably

I wrote back immediately.

What did you do?

The dots flickered again.

i paid him a visit, which he wasn't too happy about. got the job done though and i sent Brynn the recording of his confession. told her it was up to her what she wanted to do with it after that

I reread the text several more times, both dumbfounded and impressed with his actions.

He started typing again.

i told you i would take care of it

The way he always took care of others. The way I wished he would take care of himself.

I had one foot perched on the last step as I drummed my fingers on the back of my phone, debating how to respond. I finally wrote:
        Thank you.

***

Both Brynn and Bash were in the room when I finally made it to the door.

"Oh," I said. "Hi, guys."

"Welcome back!" Brynn said as she shut her laptop. "How was home?"

"Good," I said, slinging my bags to the floor. "It was ... really good."

She smiled as she tucked her computer into her bag. She seemed lighter than she had when I left. I touched her knee lightly as I passed. "Spencer told me the news. You feeling okay?"

She took a deep breath. "Yeah. I really am. Thanks for letting me handle it."

I gave her a big hug. "I've got your back. Always."

"We were just about to head out to grab lunch," Bash announced, standing up and tucking his phone into his back pocket. "Care to join?"

I shook my head. "No. I'll grab something in a bit. Thank you, though."

I sat at my desk and reached for my bag to do one final read through of my story before printing it to turn in.

Brynn opened the door, holding it open for Bash to follow.

"I'll meet you in the car, love," he said, stalling by her desk.

Love? I tried not to wheel my head around in surprise. Brynn's cheeks were glowing in a soft blush as she nodded and slipped quietly outside.

I gave Bash a funny look when the door gently shut. "What did I miss?"

His grin was wide and cheeky. "Oh, nothing that my *girlfriend* probably won't tell you on her own time."

I couldn't help but chuckle a little.

"So, how ..." Bash cleared his throat. "How are you doing? With, you know, everything?"

"What do you mean *everything*?"

He looked at me pointedly, and I knew he could see right through the thin façade.

I sighed. "I'm okay. Matt and I ... well, I guess you could say we didn't leave on the best of terms with each other."

Bash nodded, gnawing on his bottom lip. For a split second, I could see where Brynn could be head over heels for this guy's sheer beauty. "You know," he said, "Matt is so good at putting on a show, not many people know that it isn't real."

We all wore a mask from time to time, leading others to believe the person they wanted to see. I knew Matt well enough by now to understand that his mask had almost become part of the identity he constructed for himself: the player, the jock, the everyman's best friend, the caretaker. But beneath that outgoing, charismatic charm was someone fractured inside. No mask could hide that kind of hurt forever.

"I know," I said quietly.

"There have been several of us," Bash continued, "who have tried to get close to him. I'd like to think he and I have reached a level of understanding where we don't bullshit each other, but we don't ask questions either." He paused. "I truly think he's let you in the most out of anyone. But based on his attitude this weekend, I'm not sure if that is a good or bad thing, because he was downright foul."

A small smile tugged the corner of my mouth at the absurdity that I could have that much power over Matt Callahan.

"Regardless, he's got to trust you at least a little bit," Bash said. "And that probably has him scared shitless."

I didn't say anything, because Bash was right. Because I would be scared shitless too. I *was* scared shitless.

Bash offered a small smile and touched my shoulder lightly. "Sure you don't want something to eat?"

I shook my head. "I'm sure. Thank you."

"I'll see you later." He turned to leave.

"Bash," I said. "He told me about her. He told me everything about Anna."

He paused. "I figured as much."

"I think …" I tried to wrestle the words in my head into a well-formulated thought. "I think he thinks about her. A lot."

"Wouldn't you?" He put a hand on the doorknob. "For what it's worth, though, I think he thinks about you more."

***

The few hours until class that night flew by in a monochromatic blur.

He thinks about you more.

He thinks about you more.

"Good evening, folks," Pollard said as he strode into the room, closing the door behind him at precisely six o'clock.

I refreshed my school email on my phone for the hundredth time to make sure that my submission had gone through to the professor. The email still sat at the top of my SENT list to Pollard. I had copied Matt on it as well, in case he was curious how it ended. I didn't really know if he cared; he hadn't asked to read it.

As Pollard was setting down his briefcase on the front table, the door squeaked open and Matt slipped into the room, unapologetic as usual.

I watched as Matt adjusted himself in his seat. His pants leg rode up to expose his socks. They had a face printed on the sides of them and it was hard to tell who it was exactly, but it looked vaguely like the same Shakespeare graphic that Oliver Van Dam had on his shirt when he came to lecture our class. I couldn't help the small smile on my lips.

Pollard nodded in Matt's direction then continued. "Well, it's our last class together before we are out for spring break. Did everyone get a chance to email your final copies to me before class tonight?"

There was a quiet murmur throughout the crowd, signaling that yes, after the past several tumultuous weeks of writing and worry, we were done. The contest at this point was out of our hands.

I had my phone resting on my lap underneath my desk. I touched the email one more time and looked at the attachment.

Second Chance
By Matthew Callahan and Ember Owens

I should have felt a wave of relief after sending that email, but with the culmination of these past few weeks, I simply sent it off like it was nothing. I felt empty.

I glanced over at Matt. He was watching me as I locked my phone and set it on my desk, but he refused to meet my eye.

Fine. I could play that game too. I focused all of my attention on Professor Pollard's messy gray hair that he had tamed back into a neat bun at the nape of his neck. "Thank you. I will evaluate and grade your revisions, then forward the final copies to the magazine editors. We will announce who won at the Art Salon the Wednesday after your return from Spring Break."

At one point, winning this contest was all I could think about. That dream had long since sputtered out with the comments Van Dam had left all over our draft. I'd like to think that this version of the story was much improved and we could still have a shot at the first-place prize, but, honestly, I didn't care anymore.

"Until then," Pollard said, sitting down at the table in the front of the room, "let's spend some time talking about the changes you all made during the revision process. Who would like to start?"

Pair by pair, we went around the room discussing revisions and changes our characters made as well as the growth we underwent as writers through this process. All that sort of crap.

When it was our turn, I let Matt detail the changes in his flashback. His voice held little inflection or enthusiasm, but his revisions were met with Pollard's approval, regardless.

"Ember? Anything else that was changed?" Pollard was inquisitive.

I tucked my hands in my lap, leaning my shoulders over my desk. Biting my lip, I said, "I worked on revising the ending of the story. In the original draft, Lena decides to visit Wesley in person after his crash to get the resolution to their relationship that she never had when they originally cut ties. When Wesley tells his side of the story and apologizes, Lena ultimately forgives him and the reader is led to believe that they have a shot at a happy ending."

I looked over at Matt. His face bore a blank expression, but his eyes were watching me as I spoke.

"Personally though, I've learned that love ... and life ... isn't always so cut-and-dry. It's not black or white. It's not good or bad. To make any relationship work, it takes a mutual effort and conscious choice to decide to keep loving a person, regardless of their flaws—or their past." I met Matt's eye briefly before drawing a breath and averting my gaze. "Real love isn't like the books or movies. It takes real work to agree to keep trying to do better, be better, for each other. It's not one-sided.

"So that's the philosophy I came at revision with. For our characters, they both had to reconcile their flaws and want a better outcome for each other. Without that mutual effort and partnership," I paused and gave a weak chuckle, "well it wouldn't be much of a partnership, would it? Kind of like this project. None of us could have done it without the other. I think this whole contest has sort of been a metaphor for that definition of love."

Professor Pollard was smiling when I finished. "I like that," he said. "I like that a lot."

I gave him a tight-lipped smile, then flitted my gaze to Matt at the other end of the room. "I do too," I said quietly.

Chapter Twenty-Eight

I waited for Matt in the hallway after class, letting everyone else pass by while I leaned against the drywall. "I'll catch up with you guys later," I said to Brynn and Spencer as they headed out.

"Want us to save you a seat at The House?" Spencer asked.

"Yeah. That would be great."

Brynn gave me an encouraging smile and Spencer winked. I rolled my eyes.

Matt was the last one to exit, with an arm around his skateboard and his eyes downcast.

"Hey," I said, pushing off the wall.

He startled a bit but regained his composure in record time. "Oh, hi Ember."

My chest tightened. "Are you in a hurry at all?"

He shook his head. "No, not really."

"Can we talk?" I held our eye contact with steely nerves I didn't really know I had.

He shrugged. "Sure. What do you want to talk about?"

I wanted to slap him for his feigned nonchalance, but I kept my cool and started walking ahead of him, out of the building. "That's a pretty dumb question, don't you think?"

"Huh. I was always taught that there are no dumb questions."

The air was cool outside, and the night sky was clear as we exited.

"Do me a favor," I said, stopping beside the fountain and turning to him. "Drop the bullshit."

He sighed. "I just don't know what else there is to say between us."

"Well, I have things to say," I said, mustering up all the courage I had in me. I stood square to face him. "Matt, I miss you. Okay? I said it. And I mean it."

He looked at me blankly, schooling his face to give away nothing.

I sighed. "Look, neither one of us is perfect. We both have baggage, and we have both let that affect us. But I don't want to let any of that come between our friendship." I paused and straightened my spine. "Or whatever else you might be game for. I care about you. A lot. And I want another shot, a real shot at something with you. You know, if that's what you want too."

He looked away, still saying nothing.

I pressed. "You told me once that you weren't going to ask me out again. That you were going to wait for me to come back to you. Well. This is me. Coming back."

I felt defeated in the awkward silence that followed. Not exactly the reaction I had been hoping for with my little speech.

He finally sighed deeply and turned back to me. "Look, Ember. I want, probably more than you know, to just be selfish and say yes. It's not really been a secret that I like you."

I like you. I like you. I like you. My heart swelled.

"But you were right. Everything you said to me that last time we spoke. You were absolutely right. I have been living my life for Anna and letting that taint every choice I make. And because of that, I'm the one that has been failing you by not looking in the mirror and doing something about myself."

I opened my mouth to argue, but he held up a hand.

"I can't be that selfish and untruthful anymore. I'm sorry, Ember. I really am. But I think it's best if we just don't talk for a while."

I was speechless. Crushed. Obliterated.

"After all," he said. "We are done with the contest too."

He might as well have swung his fist in my face. "Right," I managed to say. "I guess we are done." No more contest, no more story, no more Matt. I tucked my hands into my back pockets and fought back the tears I was surprised to feel prickling my eyes. "I'll see you around maybe," I choked out, but there wasn't much conviction behind it.

"You're a really great writer, Ember."

It was all I had in me not to scoff at the words. For once, that didn't matter to me.

For once, I wanted to be more.

"Thanks," I said and turned to head toward the parking deck. "But I think you're the one who really knows how to pack a punch with your words."

***

"I can't believe that asshat!" Spencer cried as we sat down in our usual seat at The House. He was met with several glares from customers around us. He ignored them. "And to think that I actually convinced myself that I was in love with that douchebag too."

"Spencer," Brynn chastised. "Quiet down. You're not helping anyone by having a tantrum."

"Sorry," he said, crossing his arms. "Just pisses me off."

Brynn ignored him and turned to me, putting a hand on the table between us. "Are you okay?"

When I got to The House, I told them everything. I mean everything. No more secrets. "Honestly," I said. "I think I am. I mean, I'm a little sad. And a little angry." I bit my lip. "That took a lot, you know? To talk about ..." I shuddered, "*feelings.*"

"I'm proud of you," Brynn said and tore apart a macaroon.

I picked one up as well. "Thanks. I'm proud of me too. I don't hate him. I really don't. I feel like I understand him finally."

"I'm glad you do," Brynn said. "Though I'm not so sure how he could choose to lose out on a catch like you."

I laughed.

"Change of subject." Spencer interrupted. "Brynn, have you finished your spring break itinerary? I know you said your family was leaving the cruise up to you this year since you're the best party planner."

"I was actually just working on it this morning. And since my brother decided that he's bringing his girlfriend, I texted them that I was bringing Bash too."

"Whoa," Spencer and I both said. Brynn's smile was coy.

"That's a big step. I'm impressed," Spencer said.

"Honestly, it feels like we've been together awhile," she said, resting her head in her hands in a dreamy state. "It's just so easy with him."

"I'm really happy for you," I said, and I meant it. It was hard to begrudge a happy ending when the two of them were clearly so perfect for each other.

"Ember, does that mean you're joining me next week?" Spencer turned to me with a joking smile. "I found a great deal on a house next to a nude beach."

"Pass." I took a deep breath and without overthinking my next line, I said, "I actually think I have plans for that week."

***

It was almost eleven o'clock that night when I was sitting on the edge of my bed, gripping my phone with two hands in my lap. I counted, again, the time difference between the East Coast and West Coast and when I was satisfied that it would be a decent hour to call California, I hit my mom's contact.

It rang once. Twice. Three times. A few more before finally going to voicemail.

I blew out a breath, both irritated and relieved. I left a brief message before I could talk myself out of it and hung up the phone. Then I sent Ethan a text.

> Save me a seat on the plane. I'm coming with you to the wedding.

His response was almost immediate.

You don't have to do that Emmy.
I wrote back, confident in my choice.
I know. I'm coming anyway.

Chapter Twenty-Nine

"You look gorgeous, Mom," I said as I fastened the last button on the back of her white dress.

She turned around to face me, tears glistening on the edge of her perfect eyeliner. "I can't thank you enough for coming."

I gave her a small smile and surprised us both by wrapping my arms around her shoulders, careful not to brush her cheek and smudge her makeup. "I blame Ethan. He's a bad influence."

She gave a choking laugh.

"Don't cry," I said as I pulled away. "The makeup artist did too good of a job."

She touched her updo and sniffed. "Hair stylist too."

I laughed. "Yeah, they deserve a good tip for making you look like a movie star or something."

Her painted red mouth lifted into a smile. Touching my cheek gently, she said, "I love you, sweet girl."

I waited a beat, choosing my next words carefully. "I'm glad I came." One day I might be able to say it back to her again. It wasn't today, but maybe sometime soon.

It was enough for her based on the gleam in her eye and the rise of her shoulders, as if a weight had just vanished from them with that one truth I spoke.

Someone with some sort of authority over this whole ceremony popped his head into the room. "Future Mrs. Ava Carson? Are you ready?"

She turned to me, her wide green eyes full of something that looked a lot like hope.

"Go on already." I waved her off. "I'll go find Ethan." I gave her hand one final squeeze, then ducked underneath the man's outstretched arm.

Ethan waved to me from one of the back pews of the church. He threw an arm around me when I slid in beside him, tousling my hair at the top of my head. I swatted him away and smoothed the flat ironed pieces back into place.

Music sprang up from the front of the room, and the entirety of the audience rose. It was a smaller crowd than I thought Ava would draw, but the intimacy of the crowd felt right.

And my mom looked like a goddess when the double doors opened to reveal her. Confident, poised, and professional, like she always schooled herself to be, she almost floated down the aisle with a dreamy smile on her face that I hadn't seen my mom wear for quite some time.

I glanced at the man at the altar, waiting patiently for my mom's hand. He was gorgeous, like her, and the tears in his eyes told me I couldn't hate him. For everyone's sake, I hoped they got it right.

The kiss at the end of the ceremony told me they just might.

***

Ethan and I kept to ourselves most of the reception, exchanging casual pleasantries with strangers who recognized us from our mother's shared resemblance.

So grown up, you've gotten. The both of you. I would say a polite thank-you and turn to ask Ethan who they were and if we should know them.

"Who knows," he would say. "Do you ever really know anyone?"

I rolled my eyes at my brother. "You're dramatic."

After the grand entrance of the wedding party and the onslaught of applause that followed as Mr. and Mrs. Carson made their way into the room, I had to admit that the newlyweds appeared to offer a pretty good definition of love. Ava's new husband looked absolutely smitten with her on his arm.

As they took to the dance floor for their first dance, Ethan and I found ourselves alone, and he finally asked me in a hushed tone, "So now that we are here, what changed your mind about coming?"

I had been waiting for this question the entire five-and-a-half-hour-long flight. But to his credit, Ethan never asked. Maybe he didn't trust me not to jump out the window and second guess my choices.

But I wasn't doubting them anymore. "I decided that I no longer want to be the person that denies exploring possible connections. And I think that you're right. If this is all Mom can do, then I can at least meet halfway."

And my definition of halfway was exactly that. I made the trip out here for the last Saturday of my spring break, but I wasn't staying longer than the night of the wedding. Ethan made plans to spend another week here exploring the West Coast. *Maybe I'll find a job. Or a lover. Or myself. I'm open to options,* he said when we talked on the phone about flights.

He did agree to drive me back to the airport before he went all Lewis and Clark. Maybe another time I would want to come back to the Golden State but, for right now, it still belonged to my mom. And I had edged out of my comfort zone enough to come visit.

* * *

It was nearly midnight when the newlyweds made their grand exit and left in a limo to go honeymoon in Bali, Indonesia.

I had long since forgone my high heels; they were currently slung around my wrist in a fashionable bracelet as I paced back and forth outside, waiting for the cab that my brother called for us.

"Are you still seeing that boy?" Ethan asked as he leaned against a lamppost, his arms folded patiently in front of him.

I tripped without anything to blame the stumble on. "What boy?"

"Your writing partner." Ethan continued to look out at the street, serene.

I was flustered. "How did you know I was seeing a boy?"

Ethan turned to me and winked. "I didn't. It was a lucky guess."

I tossed one of my shoes at him. "Jerk."

He picked it up from its tumble on the ground and threw it back at me in a gentle underhand. "I was right, though. You like him a lot, don't you?"

I stopped pacing and went to lean on the wall next to him. I dropped my shoes to the ground and crossed my arms. "Maybe. But I'm not sure if he likes me anymore."

Ethan shrugged. "So find out," he said simply. "Don't play games with the people you care about."

I thought about it. I already said my piece, and Matt basically brushed me off. I didn't know where we stood after that. Was I supposed to forget it ever happened? Give him space? Cyberstalk him?

While the latter was more of a joke, it did seem like a bit of a waiting game to let him dictate what clarity I got instead of me just reaching out for a conclusion.

I nudged Ethan with my shoulder. "You're smarter than people give you credit for."

He scoffed. "Everyone thinks I'm smart."

"Especially Jaws."

Ethan sighed. "No, you're the smart one out of us. Sometimes you're just too thick in the head to get to the brains." He turned to me and smiled. "You deserve to be happy, too, you know."

His words squeezed my heart. "You do too," I said.

And so did Matt. And that's what I knew I still had to tell him.

***

Because I have a little bit of self-control, I didn't text Matt the minute we got to the hotel. I waited until I was sitting in the airport gate, getting ready to board when I finally pulled my phone out to hit send on the text I spent the majority of the night crafting.

But there on the lock screen was a new message notification, from a number that still had no name attached to it, even though I would recognize it anywhere. My heart was pounding in its rib cage prison, trying to break free as I opened the first of several messages from Matt Callahan.

> I'm sorry it's taken me this long to say it back, but I miss you too. I wanted to find a way to tell you in person, but I asked Brynn where you were and turns out you're a little far away right now. I hope you're not mad that she told me what you were doing. I think it's pretty amazing.

> And then I debated the whole grand gesture of buying a ticket and flying out there to be with you this weekend. But I didn't want to make things more stressful for you in what might already be a stressful situation. I hope I made the right call in giving you the time you probably need with your mom and brother.

> I also debated whether or not to just call you, but I didn't want to interrupt. I realize this might have been a cowardly move, but the truth is, I wanted to make sure I said the right words and I'm so afraid of what I'm about to say that I don't trust myself not to mess it up if I were on the phone with you right now. Ember, I want you in my life somehow. I know pushing you away was the absolute worst way to go about it, but I want you to know that I've taken some time over break to sort through some things in my head.

> I called Anna. Well, I called her mom. She told me Anna is doing well. She's getting ready to graduate nursing school and she has a boyfriend. That was oddly satisfying to hear. I asked her mom to tell Anna that I cared for her still to this

day, but I'm really happy to hear she has moved on from her life here.

I probably won't know what she says in response but that part doesn't matter as much to me. More importantly right now, I'm asking you, Ember, for a chance to maybe restart things. I'd like to find a way to be more than a past or a reputation, and be yours instead. (Was that cheesy? I hope you're smiling, because it's true.) Could we get coffee before class Monday?

I reread the messages. Then the intercom called my flight to board and I had to pocket my phone. I made a mental note to thank my mom for the first-class seats that had me stepping on the plane before the crowd so I could rush to read the messages again.

I sat hunched over my phone while I tapped out several different responses, shielding anyone from my words.

I couldn't stop the smile on my face when I finally hit send:

I'm on the plane right now. You know my usual order.

I knew Matt had to be watching my three dots at the bottom of his screen as I was typing, for his next message came through almost immediately.

What time do you land? I'll pick you up.

It was messy, and far from perfect, but maybe ... maybe this could be something.

5:30 tonight your time. I'll see you soon.

Thank you, kitten. Fly safe.

I turned my phone to airplane mode, then tucked it under my leg in my chair. I ran my thumb against the edge of my bottom lip, tracing the smile still there.

A gentleman in a fancy suit boarded the plane and settled himself in the seat next to me. "Good morning," he said, politely.

"Do you believe in fate?" I asked, sitting up a little straighter. "Destiny? Higher power of influence guiding our life events?"

The poor man looked thoroughly confused. "I'm not sure. Probably not. I think a life is what you make out of it."

I leaned back in my seat and fished my earbuds from my pocket. Popping them into my ears, I said, "I think you're both wrong and right."

Some sort of power partnered Matt and me together when we both drew the same prompt from that hat. But it was going to be up to us if our partnership continued to work beyond the classroom.

I picked up my phone and found Matt's *greatest jam playlist of all time* and clicked play. Before locking my phone again, I exited the app and scrolled to find the number I knew by heart. Hitting the ADD TO CONTACTS button, I typed in *Matt*, just Matt, and hit save.

EPILOGUE

"Thanks for inviting me as your date," Matt said as he slid an arm around my back, offering me my own glass of whatever sparkling punch the English Department was serving.

I smiled up at him widely, accepted the glass, then reached an arm around his neck to pull his cheek to my lips. "Thank you for accepting. It means a lot. Even though you were required to be here anyway."

Brynn and Bash had disappeared together for not the first time this evening while we were all at the Arts Salon, waiting for the winner of our contest to be announced. In the meantime, we watched students from the Theatre Department perform skits, music students share songs they composed, and slideshows of student art that was set up for display in the city.

Matt let his arm slide to my hip. "Always a pleasure to dress up. Nice to break out the suit once in a while."

It was nice on him, I had to admit. And I hadn't missed the hot pink socks he tried to match to my outfit.

"You look hot," I said.

He smiled and took his turn pressing his lips to my cheek. "And you are stunningly beautiful. Can you wear a dress more often? You look good in pink."

"It's coral," I corrected, once again, and smoothed down the front of the dress I reserved for special occasions.

"Hey, Ember. Hey, Matt," I heard a voice call out from down the hall.

"Spencer!" I cried and disengaged myself from Matt's arms. "You're late."

He held out his hands in mock surrender. "It wasn't my fault! One of the campus squirrels stole my ticket and it took a while to chase it down."

I lifted a brow. "Seriously?"

"Nah," he admitted. "I was playing *Call of Duty*."

I laughed at my friend and gave him a welcoming hug. "Glad you could grace us all with your presence."

Spencer smiled at me, then turned to Matt. "Do you mind if I steal her a second?"

Matt shook his head. "Not at all. I'll be by the cheese table. I heard there was white cheddar." And he winked at me.

I shook my head at his ridiculousness, then followed Spencer outside to the terrace. "Is everything okay?"

Spencer leaned back against the railing and lifted his chin toward Matt. "I think you guys are going to be really good together."

I turned to follow his gaze and saw my man by the snack table.

"I know I had a hard time wrapping my head around it in the beginning, but I think you're good for him. And a little adventure isn't the worst thing for you."

I put a hand on his arm. "Spencer, thank you."

"I just wanted to tell you that I'm happy for you, friend."

My eyes crinkled, and I pulled him in for another hug. There was a tapping sound that came across the speakers, and we broke apart to see Pollard with the microphone at the front of the parlor.

"Can I have everyone's attention please?"

Spencer practically pushed me back inside as Pollard was speaking.

"We've come to the point in the evening that our English students have been anticipating. It is time to announce the winners of the short story contest that students in the Advanced Prose class participated in. The winning pair will have their story published in one of the top literary magazines in the country. Please join me in congratulating our winners." Pollard turned to the music station set up at the side of the stage area. "Drum roll, if you please."

The freshman at the drum set smilingly obliged.

"And your winning pair is," Pollard paused, "Holly Turner and Brynn Song with their story, *Tried and Twisted*!"

The room erupted in applause, and I whipped my head around to try to find Brynn. Thank goodness she was easy to find, near the front of the room, with Bash by her side. She looked shocked. Bash was beaming with pride.

Holly appeared by Brynn, and I even saw her crack a smile as they congratulated each other.

"A well-deserved honor, ladies," Pollard added. "Can I ask if one of you would like to read an excerpt from the story for us? I printed a copy in case."

Brynn willingly stepped up to take the microphone and paper from his hands.

"Wow, this is crazy." Brynn's voice was breathless. "Holly and I are so excited about this opportunity. I'll share a bit of the story that I wrote and then pass the mic over to her. I hope you enjoy!"

Brynn took a breath, composing and containing her elation, then began reading.

With everything that had happened in recent weeks, I never read the final draft she ended up turning in. It was good, *really* good, and I couldn't think of anyone more deserving to be the winner.

Matt found his way back to me at some point, like our bodies were magnetized to each other. He was close enough to me that when I felt my phone vibrate in my bag at my side, I could feel his make the same noise in his pocket.

We turned to each other, suspicious and confused. As Brynn was reading, he slowly took out his phone. On the screen was an email addressed to him and me.

From Oliver Van Dam.

I sucked in a breath and watched his eyes widen too. He opened the message.

> From: olivervandam@olivervandamwritesbooks.com
> To: owense@sc.edu, callahanm@sc.edu
> Date: April 8, 2019 6:30 p.m.
> Subject: Brilliant. Absolutely brilliant.
> Ember Owens and Matthew Callahan,
>
> If you didn't already know, Caine Pollard granted me access to all of his students' final drafts. I'm writing the pair of you to say I was most impressed with the revisions in your short story, Second Chance, because if I'm being entirely honest, you two had a lot of work to do.
>
> Regardless, the writing is good. Dangerously good. And the product you created after my opinions on the matter? Terrifyingly powerful.
>
> Attached is an application to the publishing house I work with in New York City. They are always looking for summer internships and, after all, the writing world is a small network.
>
> I may have dropped your names already.
>
> It was a pleasure to read your work. I hope you don't stop creating art for there is sheer talent in both of you.
> Best,
> OVD

There was silent screaming in my eyes, desperate to be let out. New. York. City. That was an opportunity most writers would die for.

Matt's jaw dropped, and a smile spread across his face.

Brynn must have stopped reading because when I stole a glance at the front of the room, Holly had the microphone.

Matt threaded his fingers through mine and his breath was suddenly warm at my ear. "Let's get out of here. We've got some celebrating to do."

"To the next adventure?" I raised my mostly empty glass toward him.

Matt Callahan raised his to touch mine with a soft *clink*. "And to the words that take us there."

ACKNOWLEDGMENTS

It was a dream of mine to one day write a book. It wasn't necessarily a goal, because a) I didn't have concrete steps or a clear picture on how I might get there one day, and b) while I was really good at starting stories, I was actually kind of bad at finishing them.

The idea of "a love story within a love story" was one of those gems that got a few chapters under its belt, then gathered dust for maybe six more years, give or take. But while Matt and Ember may have changed plots, settings, and descriptions over time, when I finally sat down and made a plan to finish a novel, it was their story I thought I could best tell first. However, this book would not be sitting in your hands without several key players who all had a special role, and I am forever indebted.

First and foremost, thank you to Mom and David, who didn't tell me "no" when I said I wanted to study Creative Writing in college.

And to my professors, thank you for furthering my education in ways unimaginable to my little freshman mind when I first walked through the doors of Queens University of Charlotte:

- Sarah Creech, the words "thank you" could never hold enough weight on their shoulders for the gratitude I have for you, your guidance, and your belief.

- Morri Creech, I miss your lectures and the discussions you led. And thank you for assuring me I made the right choice in Intro to Creative Writing.
- Renfroe, Pollard has your cool hair. Thanks for being an awesome leader. And for teaching me about literary magazines. And for giving me the reins on our own *Signet Literary Magazine* my senior year.
- JD and Professor McCrary, thank you for challenging me to look at language in a deeper way than just how it is used to tell stories. You both taught me words have power that must be wielded wisely.
- Israel, from freshman-year English class through senior-level Professional Writing courses, thank you for being a constant support.
- Professors Hull, Seelbinder, and Shishko thank you for the literature courses that inspired the rest of Ember's curriculum at Selwyn College.

To the team at Warren Publishing:

- Mindy Kuhn, truth be told, I cried when I got your acceptance email. Thank you for seeing potential in the manuscript to become this book.
- Amy Ashby and Melissa Long, thank you for your communication, hand-holding, and direction as we navigated the publication process.
- Karli Jackson, you are truly an angel. Thank you for taking this book to the next level when I got tired of reading it and dry on ideas for revision.
- Erika Nein, your level of attention to detail and dedication to your work is unparalleled. Thank you for your scrutiny. Once again, this book was elevated at your hand and input.

To the friends who read the early drafts—some more times than they would care to admit (sorry, Rylee)—I have so many thanks for your patience and encouragement to just keep putting words on the page and sticking by this story until the end:

- Rylee Rosenthal, Avery Morgan, and Lynn Morgan, fron early brainstorms to final revision sign-offs, thank you for being as invested in these characters as I am.
- Elisabeth King and Kendra Post, my cheerleaders and fellow book nerds. Thanks for fangirling alongside me, always.
- Erin McGuire, Christie Heuman, Liz Gore, and Priscilla Chapman, thank you for being willing participants in Matt and Ember's first real audience in their first draft.
- Carly Ziegler, my hype girl and typo-finder, thank you for the final read through and summarizing exactly what I wanted this story to portray.
- And Mike Bonerbo, thank you for not judging me and my happy tears when I got the publication contract delivered in my email inbox. (And, thanks for your knowledge in lacrosse and correcting my false assumption that a team could be leading a game by double digits come halftime.)

And finally, to my early editors, Dr. Piper Klemm and Rennie Dyball, who encouraged me to revise and keep on the publication goal—because at this point, it wasn't just a dream anymore: I hope Matt, Ember, and I made you proud.

CPSIA information can be obtained
at www.ICGtesting.com
Printed in the USA
JSHW020724010322
23447JS00002B/18

283